Midnight Sun

Rene Lyons

A SAMHAIN PUBLISHING, LTD. publication.

Samhain Publishing, Ltd.
2932 Ross Clark Circle, #384
Dothan, AL 36301
www.samhainpublishing.com

Midnight Sun
Copyright © 2006 by Rene Lyons
Print ISBN: 1-59998-273-0
Digital ISBN: 1-59998-067-3

Editing by Angela Knight
Cover by Scott Carpenter

First Samhain Publishing, Ltd. electronic publication: July 2006
First Samhain Publishing, Ltd. print publication: October 2006

Dedication

My Jesse, you are the miracle of my life.

Frankie, I still get butterflies every time I look at you.

Crissy, the bringer of dreams, thank you for letting me be part of your "family".

Angie, without you I'd still be wondering "when". I hope I never let you down.

Brother, I'm sorry through you I learned how fragile and short life is. I'll love you forever and miss you until I see you again. This one is for you.

Chapter One

Pennsylvania: Summer 2005

If vampires suffered headaches, Sebastian of Rydon was sure he'd have a blinding migraine by now. Though he loved his brother-in-arms, the idea of shoving a gag into Raphael's mouth was damn appealing. After hearing Rogue go on and on about Allison Parker, it was all he could think to do to shut him up.

Enough was enough already.

It was months since they came here to Damascus and took on the ragtag redhead. You'd think Raphael would get the hint and leave him alone when it came to her by now. Did he believe if he went on endlessly about the woman, Sebastian would change his mind about her nosing around Randall Manor?

The last thing any of them needed was that woman poking around their house. It was ludicrous to so much as entertain the idea. Yet here was Raphael, trying his hardest to convince him she was "harmless". Especially since Sebastian knew Allie was many things, but harmless was not one of them.

What surprised him the most was that Constantine happened to be as enamored with her as Raphael. Something about her having "brass balls", as he liked to put it, appealed to the Dragon.

None of what they said was going to sway Sebastian. He had no intention of allowing them to open the manor to Wayne County's notorious ghost hunter. For all he knew, she wouldn't uphold her promise to keep her findings secret, but slap Randall Manor on the front page of *The Specter*. It didn't make sense , why he was the only one to see the idea was a disaster waiting to happen.

Even Lucian didn't seem to mind the idea of Allie invading their home. No wonder Sebastian was known as The Sage. Lately, it seemed he was the only one with any brains among the bunch.

Something about the woman got under his skin. Whenever he was around her, which he made sure wasn't all that often, he found himself getting all kinds of hungry. Hungry for her body, for her blood, and for the promise of warmth found in the strength of her lifeforce. Bad enough her occasional visits to Seacrest left her scent behind, he didn't need his home tainted by the blasted scent of gardenia. Randall Manor was his only sanctuary, and he'd not have it overrun by her.

Sitting at a table in the back of McHenry's Tavern, Sebastian and Raphael waited for Constantine. He was bringing with him a human who supposedly had a lead about the Daystar. Whether or not there was any truth to the claim remained to be seen.

Sebastian was not the type to sit idly by, which was why six long months of waiting for a sign of the Daystar was slowly driving him mad. When Constantine chanced to overhear Kenny Buckman make mention of a tattoo he wanted, which sounded remarkably like the symbol of the Daystar, it put an end to the maddening waiting game.

Since the Daystar wasn't something the average human would know about, it was definitely a good place to start to track the Druid relic down and destroy it. God forbid it fall into any other vampire's hands. They could use it to gain the ability to walk in the light and become nearly indestructible.

Not that Sebastian was in a rush to return to England. He liked it here, lost in the mountains of farm-country Pennsylvania. After nearly seven hundred years it was nice to have a change of scenery. Though most of the Wayne County countryside looked much like Northumberland, the subtle changes and different feel of the place gave him a peace he hadn't known since before he went off to Crusade.

"Do you think this is a waste of our time? Do you think he knows where it is?"

The sudden change of subject caught Sebastian off-guard. Only a moment ago Raphael was still going on about Allie, which was why Sebastian tuned him out.

Shrugging carelessly, Sebastian took a sip of his beer. By now he barely flinched when the liquid slid down his throat like broken glass.

He hated times like now, when a vampire was forced to perform basic human activities. When among humans, eating and drinking were the two main pretenses, though it caused intense pain to their dead bodies.

"Does it matter at this point? Be glad we've finally heard *something*."

"I know it. It seems too easy, that's all."

"He'd be a bloody fool if he lied to Constantine."

Though Templars made an oath to God in exchange for the chance at redemption, nothing in the rules said they couldn't beat a human near to death—the key words being *near to death*. As long as they left the poor bastard alive, their oath would be upheld.

Which was why lying to them would be a foolish mistake on Kenny's part.

Constantine Draegon was not someone Kenny wanted to piss off. Hell, none of them were, but the Dragon was given more to violence than the rest of them.

One thing they learned quickly after being turned was that living beings were terribly fragile. It would take nothing for a vampire to end them. It said much about the Templars that they used restraint and respect when dealing with their victims, especially when caught in the throes of bloodlust. It would be all too easy to step over the line and take life, which once done would damn the Templars straight to Hell.

"Constantine will beat the shit out of him if he's lying," Raphael remarked, idly toying with the label of his Budweiser. When a waitress passed close to them, giving him a seductive glance, Raphael threw her a wink.

Women couldn't resist Raphael's blond good looks, and he, living up to the name of Rogue, welcomed their attention wholeheartedly.

"Hell, if he's lying I'll beat the shit out of the kid for making me come here."

Sebastian may be the more levelheaded of the bunch, but that didn't mean he wasn't up for giving a good beat down if the occasion called for it—and being forced to stomach this place definitely called for Kenny to be beaten senseless. Noting heads turning in the direction of the door, Sebastian knew Constantine finally joined the party.

Dragon had a tendency to draw notice to himself everywhere he went. His look said *don't fuck with me* at the same time it screamed for attention.

There he was, all six-foot-three of him, dressed in a classic Goth getup of baggy black pants teeming with dangling metal chains and a black tee shirt that read *Sarcasm: It beats killing people.* His long, straight black hair was a mess of black spikes, falling in wild disarray around his deathly pale face. Even from a distance Sebastian saw he was wearing the silver hoop nose ring in his left nostril. Sometimes he wore it, sometimes he didn't. With C, everything he did, he had to be in the right mood to do, and tonight he looked like he wanted to do bodily harm to someone. Along with Constantine, was a grubby kid with beady brown eyes and a slop of brown curls—clearly terrified and obviously strung out.

"Come on," Constantine order as he dragged the kid by the sleeve.

The kid, or rather, Kenny Buckman, scurried to keep up with Constantine's long strides. The surly vamp all but hurled him at one of the two empty chairs surrounding the table Sebastian and Raphael occupied.

Kenny's eyes bugged out of their sockets as he took them both in, but it was when Raphael threw Kenny a wink that the kid looked as if he would be sick.

His frantic gaze darted to Sebastian, who cocked a brow at him, waiting to see if the kid had balls or if he would try to make a run for it. God, he hoped Kenny wasn't that stupid.

With his hair buzzed down to nothing but stubble and dressed all in black, Sebastian looked like a hit man. On his right hand he wore a brand of the seal of the Knight Templars. The mark was of a circle, in the center of which were two knights on a single mount, arcing around it the Latin words *Sigillum Militum Cristi de Templo*. Translated it read, *Seal of the Soldiers of Christ from the Temple*.

All Templars bore the brand. It marked them for the warriors of Christ they were in life and the damned creatures they were now in death.

"Talk," Constantine ordered Kenny, dropping down in the empty chair next to the kid. He leaned back arrogantly, crossing his arms over his wide chest.

Kenny reached into his pants pocket. His hand shook as he passed a folded piece of paper to Raphael, the least threatening-looking of the bunch. "I found this in the attic of my grandmother's house."

The scrap of paper was in fact a torn piece of parchment, on it a drawing of what looked like an "S" with a dot above and below it.

All three Templars recognized it as the symbol of the Daystar.

Raphael gave the paper to Sebastian, who took one look at it before narrowing his gaze dangerously on Kenny. "You didn't find this in your grandmother's attic." Pushing aside the black duster that concealed the sword he wore strapped to his back, he tucked the paper into the inner pocket.

"Yes I did!" Kenny nearly shouted, his voice taking on a hysterical edge. "It's like I told him, I was up in my grandmother's attic looking for something and found it in some old trunk."

"He's not lying, Sage. He and a friend were looking for shit to sell for a fix," Constantine added harshly.

"What did you tell your friend about this?" Sebastian demanded.

"Nothing, I swear. I don't even know what the hell it is."

"Does your grandmother know you found this?" Raphael questioned.

"Are you kidding?" Kenny looked away, his shame clear. "If I told her I found it, she'd know what I was doing there."

The look on Constantine's face told Sebastian he was poking into the kid's mind again, searching for the truth.

Once Dragon discerned if Kenny was telling the truth he leaned forward in his chair and give him a threatening glare. "If you breathe a word of this to anyone, we'll hunt you down and hurt you. Do you understand, Kenny?"

Seeing the threat in Constantine's eyes, the kid turned white. "I won't. I swear it."

Constantine leaned back in his chair, a satisfied and humorless grin tugging at his lips, allowing a hint of his fangs to show. "Good. Now get the fuck out of here."

Kenny did exactly that, nearly overturning the chair when he shot off it. He ran out of the bar as if the devil himself was at his heels.

"Do you think he'll talk?" Raphael questioned once Kenny made a mad dash out of the bar.

Constantine watched the kid disappear through the grimy glass door. He gave them a curt shake of his head. "He'd never risk me coming after him."

Sebastian felt as if the parchment burnt a hole clean through the thick fabric of his duster. What a hell of a thing that even the symbol on a piece of parchment carried enough power to give off supernatural heat. It left no doubt in Sebastian's mind that they had to find the Daystar and find it fast. They couldn't risk any other creature finding it.

God help them all if a renegade got his hands on it before a Templar. To give a renegade, a vampire of the lowest order, the power to walk in the sun would be to unleash Hell on earth.

"What's our next move?" Raphael threw the question out.

A slow smile spread across Sebastian's face. "I say we pay a visit to Grandma Buckman."

Chapter Two

Whoever said drowning sorrows at the bottom of a bottle of beer was a good idea, was an idiot.

Actually, Allison Parker was the idiot for attempting it knowing full well how much she despised the stuff. Drinking, drugging, hanging out and raising hell, they were never her things. She was more the "hang out in a graveyard and wait for the spirits to rise" sort of person, which was why ghost hunting was the perfect profession for her.

It also made her the town weirdo, but by now it was a reputation she could live with.

Of course, it left her friendless and dateless most of the time, but again, those were things she could live without if it meant doing what she loved. Ghost hunting was a passion of hers, made even more so after the death of her brother two years ago. It pushed her to find any evidence of life after death. Unfortunately, she found it when three vampires thought to make a meal of her five months ago.

The only good to come of that incident was it caused her to cross paths with the Templars, who descended on the scene like two avenging warriors. With a few swipes of their swords—yes swords—they reduced the vampires to ash.

If they would have come only a few seconds earlier they might have saved her from having been bitten and fed from, something she knew Constantine and Raphael still felt guilty about.

Pushing aside her opened, but not even sipped at bottle of Budweiser, Allie felt her stomach twist as Jude's cruel words came back to her. She'd have gone straight home instead of making a pit stop at McHenry's Tavern, but the thought of returning to her empty house only added to her melancholy.

The entire day was a total disaster. Jude ending their relationship wasn't what bothered her so much,

It was his spiteful admission of cheating with Denise Tanner that pierced her pride. It reinforced her reasoning for why she made a point to steer clear of "normal" people.

Jude, as ordinary as they came—barring his multi-million dollar bank account of course—was Damascus' darling. Everyone loved the Golden Boy, who'd taken a small construction business and turned it into thriving company.

If people only knew what Allie learned about him in the ten months they were together, she wondered if they'd still adore him.

A coward and a mama's boy, there wasn't any justification for his arrogance. She had to wonder if the break-up had anything to do with the fact that she called five tremendous men, all whom looked every bit the medieval warriors they were, friends. Knowing him, it had to be a blow to his fragile pride.

Guess that's why he thought to even the score by cheating on me.

Jude picked a real winner with Denise, who was known as the town bike. Everyone got a chance to ride her, didn't matter to her if the guy was old or young, ugly or hot. All it took to have a go at her was a penis and a beer.

Sometimes, not even the beer.

It was a swift kick to Allie's pride. It made her want to give Jude a good hard kick back. Only instead of to his pride, nail it right to the balls.

Staring at the beer, she admitted defeat and hopped off the uncomfortable barstool. Slapping a ten-dollar bill on the bar, she turned to leave. All her misery was replaced with overwhelming relief when she spotted Raphael and Constantine walking in.

Thank God for those two. Her night finally took a turn for the better.

They saw her too, or rather they smelled her, since she saw them detect her scent and follow it until they spotted her at the bar. With a guarded grin, Raphael motioned her over to the table they were about to occupy. She rushed over and threw her arms around his waist. His brows shot up at her unexpected show of affection.

"Does this mean I finally have a chance at you, Red?" he teased, wrapping his arms tightly around her.

"Not a chance, pal." She laughed, knowing he wasn't serious, though even if he was, she wasn't about to hook up with him.

His being a vampire had nothing to do with her resolve to keep herself from falling victim to his surfer-boy looks. Her friendship with him was way too valuable to throw away on a night of good—okay, great—sex no matter how tempting it may be.

Oh, and she knew it would be *good*. The kind of good a woman never forgot. Good enough to knock all thoughts of Jude and Denise right out of her head. The old expression about a slippery slope came to mind.

"I needed a hug, that's all,"

When Constantine pinned her with a knowing look, Allie felt her cheeks flame hotly. She didn't appreciate the subtle pinch on her brain, knowing Constantine found a way into her thoughts.

"He's a bloody asshole. If you want, I can pull his spleen out through his nostrils."

Untangling herself from Raphael, Allie flopped down on the chair next to Constantine. "Tempting, but no thanks, C. I appreciate the offer though."

He shrugged indifferently. "Suit yourself."

Raphael sat next to Allie. "Let me guess, Jude's the asshole as usual?"

"Who else? He broke it off with me."

Constantine snorted. "Like that's what's bothering you."

She shot him a nasty look. "It's not and you know it. And I would appreciate it if you got the hell out of my head."

"Since some of us can't read minds—and I don't even want to know how

Constantine can read yours right now—how about letting me in here."

"Just to be spiteful, Jude made the wonderful announcement he's been cheating on me with Denise Tanner," she explained to Raphael.

He looked genuinely shocked. "You've got to be kidding me."

She shook her head. "I wish I was." She let out a dramatic sigh. "Denise of all people. How insulting is that?"

"Damn. That's bad, Red. *I* won't even tap that." Raphael always told it to her straight, which was only one of the many reason she adored him. "Why the hell would he cheat on you? Screw what Allie said, C. Go pull his spleen out."

Allie hit Raphael on the arm. "Oh please, don't you dare encourage him. No doubt after the crappy day I'm having, I'll get blamed for it and spend the rest of my life in jail."

"Like we wouldn't protect you," Constantine proclaimed gruffly. "Besides, Fate has other plans for you."

Even after five months, Allie still wasn't used to the cryptic bombs of information Constantine liked to drop on her every now and then.

Along with telepathy, Constantine had the sight. He was shown glimpses of the future, though he never shared the details of the visions with anyone. His reasoning was that he knew it wasn't for him to screw around with a person's life-path. As much as she hated to admit it, since she was dying to know some of the things he saw, she knew he was right. He could seriously alter the direction a person took with nothing more than a few words. Who knew what cosmic chaos it would cause? Best leave Fate to do her thing and go along for the ride. If Allie learned anything from her time with the Templars it was that Fate was a fickle bitch who didn't like being played with.

Besides, the visions he saw were mostly fragmented and made little to no sense at the time Fate showed them to him. Only once the event came to pass did he understand the vision.

Running her hand over Constantine's arm, Allie smiled. What a thing it was to have two medieval vampires watching her back. "I know you guys are only trying to help, but leave Jude alone. He's a pathetic wretch anyway and

I'm better off without him. I wish I were able to go back and start the day over. I'd do it much differently, believe me."

"I know the feeling."

Raphael's quiet agreement made Allie cringe. Here she was, going on about her miserable day to two men who burned to death seven hundred years ago. If that wasn't bad enough, at the moment of their death, the archangel Michael damned them. Before he threw them back to the realm of the living, no longer alive and not quite dead, he seized their souls by running his sword through their hearts. It was a horrible way to die and an even worse fate to have to suffer, especially for men who had once sacrificed everything they were for God.

How dare she complain about her crappy day to them? At least she was *allowed* a day. The Templars weren't even afforded that. They were prisoners of the dark, forced to know only the night and the cold that come from having no soul. It was a torturous existence, and if she ever doubted that, all she had to do was look in any Templar's eyes. Their pain and nightly struggle for redemption reflected in those silvery depths.

"So nothing happened at the Moning's?" Constantine changed the subject, trying not to seem too eager to find out how her hunt went.

Constantine loved a good ghost story, especially if it happened to be true. He liked to play his interest off as all cool and nonchalant.

"Absolutely nothing. Unfortunately. At least if I found some evidence of old man Moning, it might have made what happened with Jude worthwhile. Instead, the entire day ended up being a waste."

"Well, it's not a total waste," Raphael commented.

"What aren't you telling me?"

"Jude is going to get his comeuppance. Trust me."

Allie gasped with an excitement that came strictly from an evil place in her that had been imagining a good revenge against Jude all day. "Tell me!"

She knew that with their curse of vampirism came certain abilities she couldn't even begin to understand. The Templars knew things that had nothing to do with Constantine's power to read minds. It was more or less an innate ability to sense things humans couldn't.

"Denise has a nasty case of the clap."

Allie let out a loud hoot of laughter. "Good for him! I hope his thing falls right off. Not like he'd miss it since he doesn't know how to use it."

Raphael sputtered out a hard laugh. Constantine grunted and shook his head. "Remind me never to piss you off."

Allie smiled at that. "This coming from a man who wants to rip a spleen out through someone's nostrils. I'm flattered."

Sitting back watching Allie and Constantine, an odd sense of contentment came over Raphael. The four Templars were sent to Damascus to join Tristan for a very specific reason, one which would bring with it a war they would either win, or would end badly enough to rock creation itself. Still, he inwardly smiled as the three of them sat around the table going on as if everything was right and normal in their strange world.

Though for a bunch of misfits, this probably *was* normal, or at least as ordinary as things were going to get for any of them.

Allie, considered the town nutcase for her relentless pursuit of the supernatural, was fully aware of what he and Constantine were and accepted them despite their tendency to burst into flames at the merest hint of daylight. She treated them as she would two normal men. No hesitation or fear in her, a marvel of a woman who had a set of brass balls that would make any man proud.

The rest of her, however, was as feminine as it got.

What a shame he had no intention of settling down with a mate. If he had the inclination, he'd have claimed Allie as his own the night he and Constantine saved her life.

Hell, even Constantine adored her, which was saying much since the miserable bastard didn't like anyone, not even himself.

Constantine took her in as part of their unusual little family, which irked the hell out of Sebastian. Claimed by the Dragon, it was forever. He may be a miserable bastard on his best day, but he'd risk anything to keep those he cared for safe.

Knowing Constantine, Raphael almost pitied Jude. God help the man when Constantine ran into him, an event Raphael knew he'd make sure came to pass.

"What did you guys find out from Kenny?"

Constantine let out a frustrated grunt. "Not much. He saw the symbol on a piece of torn parchment."

"It's something at least, more than I thought you would find out from the crackhead."

"Junkie," Raphael corrected.

"Whatever," Allie threw back.

Those closest to her knew Allie detested drugs and the people who did them, though she never said why. Raphael suspected it had something to do with the death of her younger brother, but it was merely an assumption, not something he knew with a certainty. Her reasons were buried so deep not even Constantine could see why.

"Did he tell you guys where he found it?"

"In his grandmother's attic." Raphael made sure he kept his voice low when the sexy blonde waitress sauntered past him again. Her smiles told him he'd not have to look far to feed tonight.

Seeing Allie shake her head in disgust, he knew she correctly assumed Kenny had been looking for stuff to steal from the poor old woman.

"What did Grandma say when you guys showed up at her doorstep?"

Raphael grinned, recalling the look of astonishment on the woman's face when they came calling. "Thankfully we had Lucian with us or else we wouldn't have made it past the door."

"Gee, I wonder why not?" Allie's tone was thick with sarcasm.

"She didn't know a damn thing. Alzheimer's, man, glad I can't ever get hit with that one. Her mind was such a mess I couldn't even make out one thought from another."

"Don't worry, I'm sure more information will turn up."

"True," Raphael agreed. "But the longer we wait the worse the situation is going to get."

"I'd love to stay and bullshit, but nature calls."

Raphael knew exactly what Constantine meant by that remark. The hunger was nagging at him as well. He eyed the blonde taking an order a few tables away. His mouth watered at the thought of taking from her.

His mischievous streak coming to the forefront, Raphael wanted to end Allie's night better than her day began. The idea of ruffling Sebastian's feathers had him grinning with evil delight. Sage was going to be furious with him, but he couldn't care less, the brooding bastard was going to have to deal, plain and simple.

After he unlatched a key from the ring dangling from one of the loops of his black jeans, he handed it to Allie. "Here."

Accepting the key and the small black remote for the gate, she looked to him in question. "What's this?"

Constantine's wink told her he knew what Raphael was about by giving over the key to her.

"Isn't it obvious, Red? It's the remote for the gate and the key to the front door."

Her delighted gasp was music to his ears. From what Constantine told them, she hadn't smiled much in her life, so he was glad he was able to make her happy with something as small as the okay to hunt the ghosts known to reside at the manor.

"No way, Raphael! Oh my God, I love you." She threw her arms around him in a fierce hug.

Disentangling himself from her, he gave her a small push toward the door. "Go on," he urged her. "Sebastian shouldn't be home for hours, so you'll have plenty of time to poke around."

How he managed the lie without bursting into laughter was beyond him.

"Are you sure about this?" She looked first to Raphael and then to Constantine. "You know Sebastian going's to throw a pissy fit when he finds out."

"Let me worry about Sebastian."

Like a kid given a new toy, she giggled with excitement before planting quick kisses on Raphael and Constantine's cheeks. "Thanks guys. I owe you one for this."

"You owe us nothing. Now get the hell out of here," Constantine grumbled.

Not needing to be told again, she jetted out so fast Raphael wouldn't have been surprised if she left trails of fire in her wake. If she'd turned around she would have seen two very awe-struck vampires cupping their kissed cheeks as if the soft touch of her lips were the sweetest gift.

"I think I'm in love."

"Shut up, Rogue," Constantine barked, though he was thinking the exact same thing.

Too bad Allie wasn't for him, Constantine thought with his typical grouch. If she were his, he'd never tire of looking upon her beautiful face, or grow used to the silken feel of her long red hair. He'd never cease to appreciate the mischievous gleam in her brilliant green eyes.

Long before coming to the States, Constantine dreamt of Allie. The dream told him plainly she was meant for someone other than himself, and he knew enough about his visions to never doubt them or fuck with them. He rolled with what he saw, hating Fate every moment the blinding pain of his visions cut through his brain like a knife.

Good thing she was already half in love with her fated mate. Though it might not make things easier for her, it certainly was going to make it fun to sit back and watch the coming events unfold.

* * *

The first thing Allie remembered to do when she arrived at Randall Manor was close her mouth.

Who could blame her for her jaw dropping? Known to be a hot zone, supposedly all kinds of paranormal happenings went on here. For years rumors abounded of full apparitions, the sound of children's laughter, the typical lights that went on and off by themselves and banging doors. Reports of ghostly reflections in the mirrors and spirits gazing out from the leaded glass windows reached her as well. Name it and it happened here, which was why she was nearly foaming at the mouth to see what she might find.

Once the Templars took up residence all the activity suddenly stopped. From what Allie learned, ghosts steered clear of anything nastier than them. Since vampires were at the top of the nocturnal hierarchy, any ghosts haunting the place would have found a way to leave the manor if they were able. Of course, some spirits wouldn't have been able to escape. Those were the ghosts Allie hoped to find here tonight.

Parking her SUV behind a gorgeous, and insanely expensive, black BMW, Allie noticed an array of impressive Harley Davidsons. The VRSCD Night Rod, which she knew belonged to Constantine, was one hell of a hot ride.

Must be nice to have money.

Flat broke, Allie learned a long time back how to stretch the meager living she eked out as a ghost hunter. She may not always pay the bills on time, but she enjoyed what she did. If she had to go without a phone every now and then, it was worth it since she got to do what she loved. Some might call it irresponsible, but after failing at conformity, she gave up trying and decided she was going to live her life as she saw fit and enjoy every moment of it.

Seeing what was taken away from the Templars, Allie knew she'd made the right choice for her life.

After climbing out of her beat up Honda Passport, Allie crossed the short distance to the manor, stopping short at the foot of the six steps that led to a massive wrap-around porch. She felt tiny standing in the shadow of the manor, which was more a work of art than a home. It made her parent's house, impressive in its own right, look like a garage.

Constructed in gray stone, the steeped roof was topped with mean looking spires. A four level square tower jutted out from the far left corner, and at the very top of it were two windows, which gave the impression of watchful eyes staring down on her.

The rest of the many windows were decorated with delicate tracery, behind which thick drapes were drawn tightly shut, preventing her from getting a peek inside the place.

The manor was as magnificent as it was imposing.

Her excitement riding her, she bounded up the steps and fit the key in the lock with bated breath, half expecting to be greeted by a specter. She crossed the threshold without a hint of hesitation.

Given the dark and sinister outside, from what she saw, the interior was inviting and surprisingly modern.

Allie stood in the foyer, to the right was a formal parlor, to the left a dining room. Breathless with excitement at finally being inside the manor, Allie stepped deeper in as if she were walking into holy ground. Locating a light switch on the wall close to the entrance, she flicked it on, bathing the grand oval entrance in a soft glow. Looking up, she gaped at the elaborate painted ceiling depicted an archangel guiding five warriors to Heaven. Gorgeous, the representation of Michael leading the Templars back to God pulled at her heart.

Sensing nothing supernatural around her, Allie spared a quick glance in the parlor and dinning rooms, amazed at the elegance of them. Black marble and wrought iron were the dominant features, lending both rooms an undeniable sense of wealth and sophistication.

The foyer opened to a long hallway. Following it down, Allie glanced up the darkened staircase to the right. Knowing the Templars' rooms were right above her, her mischievous streak came to the forefront. She couldn't wait to go snooping around their private lairs. Heading into a large, yet cozy, family room, Allie turned on the floor lamp near the entryway. She blew out a low whistle when she caught sight of the giant plasma television dominating the black lacquer entertainment center.

Noting the wall of windows, she couldn't help but surmise it wasn't the best thing for a house where vampires lived. Nevertheless, the stained glass portraying scenes of Crusade were stunning.

Taking a moment to feel for any ghosts, she felt nothing, not even a slight shift in the energy or temperature of the room. If she didn't know better she'd swear one of the Templars were still at home. Raphael assured her Sebastian was gone for the night and with him and Constantine still at the bar, that left only Lucian. He, she knew, was out looking for the girl who went missing a few nights ago.

Stepping out of the family room, she gave a quick check in the kitchen at the end of the hallway. Nothing was to be felt there either. Barely sparing it a second thought, her mind went to those rooms upstairs. There was snooping to done and she didn't have all night to do it.

Doing her best to keep herself open to any sensations of ghosts, Allie flipped on the dim overhead and followed the steps to the second floor. Most of the doors where closed, and after giving them a check, she found them to be locked as well.

Her curious nature couldn't resist cracking open the only unlocked door. Her heart leapt into her throat when she was met by the warm glow of candlelight. Holding her breath in anticipation, she poked her head in and peeked into the masculine room. From the black furniture to the deep gray comforter on the bed, everything was just so—dark. Heavy black curtains were drawn and tied; Luis Royo works decorated dark brown walls. Everywhere she looked there were medieval themed collectables. Half the stuff looked like it came from the Nobel Collection catalogue. The other half could only be from the Franklin Mint.

Without a doubt she knew this was Sebastian's room. If she needed further proof, the back-hanging baldric he always wore was thrown on the bed. The translucent red cross pattee winking in the hilt proclaimed it as a sword of the Knight Templars.

Now, the smart thing to do would be to back her nosey self out and quietly leave whence she came, but it was a fact Allie rarely did the "smart thing".

Bold as you please, Allie pushed the door open all the way. She thought to take a quick peek around then haul ass out of there before Sebastian was the wiser.

That's what she *meant* to do, but the huge ruby ring on the dresser caught her attention. Unable to resist herself, she picked it up and saw the inside bore an inscription. It read *Ad maiorem dei gloriam.*

For the glory of God.

She looked around to make sure she was alone before slipping the ring on her finger. Too big, when she held up her finger to admire it, it slipped off and hit the floor with a dull thud.

As if Fate gave the thing a push, it rolled under the bed. Damn these old floors with their funky pitches. Or was it the ghosts working their stuff? Whatever it was, all Allie knew was she had to put the ring back and get out of there before she got caught red-handed where she didn't belong.

Chapter Three

That was one hell of a nice ass.

Sebastian appreciated the nice view of a shapely behind waving in the air. Of course, said backside happened to be attached to the woman he'd been trying to avoid like the plague. He should have known better since Allie Parker was a person not to be sidestepped. She was, in fact, a force of nature.

Right then, her storm was cutting a path through his room—or rather under his bed.

With an ass like that he much preferred her *in* his bed.

Standing in the doorway, hip leaning against the frame and arms folded over his chest, Sebastian raised one brow when Allie let out a string of some of the foulest words he'd ever heard—having existed for close to seven centuries, that was saying something.

Obviously not able to reach what she was searching for under his bed, she cursed some more. He bit back a laugh when she pounded her fist on the floor in frustration.

Oh, this was priceless. It was exactly what Sebastian needed, though he was loath to admit it since it meant Raphael was right. He needed what Rogue called spice.

Allie Parker was nothing if not spicy.

Sebastian could do the gentlemanly thing, quietly back out of the room and wait for the tiny paranormal extraordinaire to finish whatever business she had under his bed. Too bad Sebastian wasn't a gentleman, not by any stretch of the imagination.

True to his nature, Sebastian silently walked up to Allie and gave her rear a good, sound smack.

It took all of his willpower, but Sebastian managed to swallow his laugh when she jumped to her feet shrieking like a demon from Hell. Spinning around, she faced him down with the gall to look offended.

"How dare you smack my ass!"

He cocked a brow at her. "How dare you break into my house?"

The woman didn't have the good grace to look repentant. "I didn't break in. I have the key."

"Just because a certain troublemaker gave you a key, it doesn't give you the right to around in my room."

She shrugged indifferently. "I didn't know it was your room."

She was lying "Do you always take it upon yourself to invade a person's bedroom?"

"Of course not." Her chin rose a notch and a defiant gleam lit her amazing green eyes. "And again, I didn't 'invade' your room."

"Yes you did."

"No I didn't."

"That's the only way of looking at it."

"Whatever."

Her flippant response made him smile despite his effort not to. Not only was Allie ballsy, she was also stunning.

Her deep red hair was pulled back in a high ponytail, which showed off the delicate line of her jaw and her long, elegant neck. The longer he stared at the pulsating column of her throat the more he ached to play out the things his devious mind imagined him doing to her.

A light sprinkling of freckles danced adorably across the bridge of her nose. They were, surprisingly enough for a fair redhead, the only freckles she seemed to have. Her baggy low-rise jeans and white tank top accented her trim, yet curvaceous body. A wide strip of a flat stomach peeked out from between the bottom of her shirt and the waist of her pants. He wanted to trail his tongue along that exposed flesh. His body hardened when he noticed her navel was pierced.

What he found incredibly frustrating was that she didn't have the sense to be scared of him.

"I know you won't kill me."

Sebastian frowned in confusion at her announcement until he realized he'd said that aloud.

"Did Raphael tell you that?"

Her smile wiped the smirk from his face.

"No, Sebastian, a Templar trying to earn redemption wouldn't sacrifice his soul by killing a human."

Sebastian stalked her, forcing her backwards until the wall was at her back. Her breath caught in her throat when he bared his fangs. "You may not have to fear death at my hands, but there are other things I can do that could make your blood run cold."

He sensed the fear in her, yet she stood her ground with a courage he found vastly impressive.

"Fine. You're right. You made your point, now back off."

She shoved at him hard, but he didn't budge.

"What where you looking for under my bed?"

When she didn't answer, he slapped his hands on the door next to her head. He leaned in close enough to see the brilliant gold flecks in her eyes and repeated the question.

This time, she wisely answered him.

"I dropped something and it rolled under the bed."

"Obviously." He slowly backed away and dropped his arms. "Go get it."

She went reluctantly, bending down in way so he wouldn't have another chance to appreciate her lovely posterior. Like a child caught with her hand in the cookie jar, she tried to hide whatever it was behind her back.

Reaching around her, Sebastian pulled her hand out. They had a brief battle of wills until he finally managed to pry her hand open

"Here, take it before you break my fingers."

She dropped the object into his hand. It was his family ring.

Absently, he pushed the ring onto his right ring finger and glared down at her. Damn it all, why did she have to come here? She should have stayed the hell away from him instead of coming here, into his home with that fucking gardenia scent. He was drowning in it, the aroma playing havoc on his senses.

Constantine was right; Allie filled a person with her spirit. Sebastian hadn't understood what he'd meant until now.

"Were you nicking my ring?"

"Of course not! I never stole a damned thing in my life." She looked genuinely hurt by his accusation. "I was only trying it on. It slipped off and rolled under the bed. I'm sorry."

Her apology cut through him. He knew she wasn't stealing his ring, only wanted to push her to see her get all hot and bothered. He hadn't meant to hurt her feelings.

"Then what were you doing poking around my room?"

"Raphael said I could come here and investigate the manor. With you still home, it's no wonder I don't feel anything." Her voice held an accusatory grouch.

Sebastian wished he could say the same. Only it wasn't paranormal activity he felt. It was lust and it was damn hard to control around her.

"Maybe Randall Manor isn't haunted, Allie. Did you ever think of that?"

She snorted right in his face. "Yeah, right. Good one, Sebastian." She ducked under his arm and gave him a radiant smile. "Anyway, it was nice to see you again."

Allie changed gears so fast it made his head spin. Her enchanting smile not only made him forget about her transgression, it also had him forgetting his conviction to ignore his attraction to her.

His silence killed her smile. "Or not." She replied flippantly. "I hoped we could finally make nice and be friends." She shrugged. "I guess that's not going to happen."

Instead of letting her go and being done with her, he did something completely out of character.

He forced her to stay.

She stopped dead and spun back to face him, obviously surprised, when his hand clamped down on her arm. Before he could think better of it, he leaned down and kissed her right on her pretty mouth.

Taking advantage of her gasp, Sebastian swept his tongue in her mouth, tasting the sweetness. He felt no fear in her, only a desire for him that robbed him of reason.

She inflamed him, making him remember what it was to be alive. Everything about her intoxicated him. Her spirit and her audacity rivaled any Templar's.

Sebastian wrapped an arm around her waist and crushed her against his chest. With his other hand, he pulled her hair free from its confines. The fiery waves spilled over his arm and trailed down her back, settling at her waist.

Cupping the back of her neck, he held her head still as he devoured her mouth in a kiss hot enough to sear them both.

She placed her hands on his cheeks, her tentative touch reaching down into him, to the place where his soul once resided. He couldn't remember the last time he'd been touched as tenderly.

Tearing his mouth away, he cut a path down to her neck and shoulder with his lips, stopping to tease with the sensitive flesh with his tongue and fangs.

Bloody hell, her flesh tasted too good for him to resist the temptation to sink his fangs into her and drink from her. Open to him, she was ripe for him to not only take in her blood, but her glorious lifeforce as well, infusing him with her very being.

Traveling down a dangerous path, Sebastian knew he had to end this before he crossed the point of no return. After three hundred years of a self-imposed celibacy, his need for Allie could quickly burn too hot to control. He tightened his hold on her, trailing his tongue down the column of her throat to her collarbone. Her breasts, so close to his mouth beckoned him, yet Sebastian didn't dare to pull down her tank top and explore them as he longed to. Pulling away from her, Sebastian almost died all over again when he saw Allie's dreamy expression. She gazed at him with hooded eyes, her cheeks flushed becomingly. No woman ever looked at him in such a way, not in life and certainly not during the relentless centuries of his death, as if no other man but him mattered.

Reality, as it always did, invaded the serenity of a perfect dreamlike moment. The thought of Jude Sommers, her self-absorbed and pompous boyfriend, lifted the veil of lust.

Suddenly cold again, Sebastian noticed her lips were swollen from the force of his kiss. He also saw the smear of blood on her bottom lip and swore loudly.

Startling her, he grabbed hold of her chin. "Open your mouth."

She slapped at his hand and backed away from him. "Are you nuts? What's wrong with you?"

Not about to be waylaid he advanced on her as she stepped back. "There's blood on your lip."

Touching her bottom lip, she inspected the tiny drop of blood on her finger. The tip of her tongue licked away the blood, which had him biting back a groan. At this point he didn't think his body could get any harder.

"Your fang must have nipped me, that's all. No need to go all apoplectic about it."

The woman was unreal. How could she not mind the fact that, not only was she good and kissed by a vampire, but said vampire hadn't been careful with his body parts and cut her lip. Obviously Allie failed to realize how easily he could have lost control and fed from her.

Given the scars on the right side of her neck, and knowing how close she'd come to death, he doubted she would welcome any more drinking of her blood. Not that he could blame her. From what Constantine and Raphael related to him, Allie was beaten badly before the vamp took a bite out of her. If Constantine and Raphael hadn't gotten there when they did, she'd be dead.

Those first few nights after they brought her to Seacrest Castle had been touch and go. To save her, they'd each given her small amounts of their blood to help her body heal.

Almost from the moment he saw her Sebastian was dangerously attracted to her and knew he had to do everything within his power to avoid her. Somehow, however, his perfect plan of avoidance didn't always go smoothly. Especially when he had two bored troublemaking Templars constantly trying to get them together.

What a bloody fool he'd been to think he could go on pretending he wasn't attracted to her, much less ignore her.

Allie was a woman a man brought to his bed and kept there until the stars burned out. Only a damn fool would avoid a woman such as her.

Sebastian was no fool.

* * *

Raphael raised a brow when he saw Allie's Passport. Though he arranged this, he sensed the tension coming from within the manor and wondered if he'd made a terrible mistake.

Constantine clearly sensed the tension as well. "I'll kill him if he ate her."

Raphael laughed as he parked his silver Jaguar. "I doubt Sebastian ate Allie, he's too damn civilized for that."

Constantine snorted. "Sage is no more civilized than I am."

Knowing the man Sebastian was in life and who he was in death, Raphael agreed with Constantine's assessment of him. "You got me there. Sebastian just hides it better than you."

"I don't try to hide what I am," Constantine announced as he got out of the Jag.

No, he didn't. Everything about Constantine proclaimed his lethal nature. He may be on the same path to redemption as they rest of them, but he veered off the road too many times to count.

As was Constantine's style, he stole into the manor as stealthy as a thief. Raphael followed, slamming the door loudly behind him.

"Allie better be in one piece, Sebastian."

Striding down the hall, he climbed the stairs first. Without a hint of tact, the two Templars peered into Sebastian's bedroom, spotting Sebastian sitting on the bed. His head in his hands, he looked a mess. He raised his head and pinned them with a tormented glare.

"*I'm going to cut you both up and leave you for the sun.*"

Sebastian put the threat directly into Constantine's mind, not wanting Allie to hear what he had to say to the two scheming bastards.

"*I dare you to try,*" Constantine retorted.

"Bugger off," Sebastian said aloud, wanting to strangle them. Needs raged in him, which lay dormant for centuries, threatening to shatter the thin thread of control he had on them. He stood and ran a hand over the short stubble of hair. "I can't believe you did this to me."

"Where is she?"

Constantine's demand held a note of accusation Sebastian didn't care for in the least. If Allie weren't still here he'd beat the Dragon senseless for the implication in his tone.

Biting back his indignation, he motioned to the bathroom door. "In there."

"In one piece?"

"Bloody hell!" Sebastian stood and strode over to the fireplace. He slapped his palms again the black granite mantle in a rare burst of emotion. "Of course in one piece, you bloody bastard."

* * *

Allie's body might be intact, but her mind was shattered into a million pieces.

Good God, the man can kiss!

Needing to clear her head, she splashed cold water on her face. Sebastian's kiss left her as close to drunk as she'd ever come. He worked her mouth with the expertise of a man who had centuries to perfect his form.

Pulling down her bottom lip, she saw a nice gash. He caught her good with those razor sharp fangs of his. Amazingly, she hadn't even felt it happen.

Letting go of her lip, she dismissed the cut, assuming accidents were bound to happen when you had fangs hanging out of your mouth.

A wonderful shiver passed through her, as she wished she were still lost in his kiss. His raw masculinity woke everything feminine in her. He was all grace and beauty, with a deadly ferocity simmering under the cool façade he presented to the world.

After tasting a small sample of Sebastian's fire, Allie was left shaken and wanting more. Not even Jude, a handsome man in his own way, moved her as Sebastian did.

What a shame it wasn't going to go much beyond this kiss.

Though embroiled in the same nocturnal world, they walked vastly different roads. Allie couldn't imagine the two of them mixing well together since he was of the dead and she of the living. It might work with just a friendship, as it did with Constantine and Raphael, but anything more could end in a huge mess, leaving her with a broken heart.

Though if a woman was to have her heart broken, she could do worse than a man as sexy and mysterious as Sebastian.

Ripped with thick cords of muscle, he oozed strength and sex appeal. Everything about him appealed to her, from his shorn head to the dragon tattoo on his upper arm. He was sexy as hell and it drove her insane how he pointedly ignored her when all she wanted to do was rip his clothes off.

As someone who was tattooed herself, she was dying to get a good look at the dragon piece that covered his upper arm and some of his neck. She doubted she'd ever get the chance unless she tied him down and had her way with him.

Not a bad idea if I do say so myself.

Turning off the water, she heard Raphael's voice coming from the bedroom. Quitting the black marble bathroom, Allie threw open the door that connected to Sebastian's room and waved at her friends.

"Hey guys. Here." Fishing around in her pocket, she pulled out Raphael's key and handed it to him.

At the same moment, Constantine's gaze shot to her bottom lip. He sniffed at the air, a vicious snarl curling back his upper lip. "Why the fuck is she bleeding?"

Unfazed by Constantine's furious demand, Sebastian threw him a glare. Before things got out of hand, as it easily could when dealing with vampires, Allie waved a hand through the air dismissively. "It's nothing. We were making with the nice-nice and Sebastian's fang accidentally caught my lip."

Three male jaws practically hit the floor when she carelessly threw out that tidbit.

Oblivious to the murderous glares Raphael and Constantine were directing at Sebastian, she turned around and glanced in the mirror hanging over the black lacquer dresser. "See? The bleeding already stopped."

Turning back, she finally noted how furious her friends were. Obviously it didn't seem to matter that he clipped her by accident. By their reaction one would think he tore off a chuck of her lip and was still gnawing on it when they burst in on him.

She also noticed Sebastian looked like he wanted to wring her neck.

Raphael was the first to snap out of his stupor at her flippancy. Given that his anger was now directed at her, Allie wished he was still struck dumb.

"I've known you for five months and not once did you *'make with the nice-nice'* with me. You're around Sebastian for five minutes and you're making out with him."

Allie rolled her eyes over his argument. "Don't go getting your panties in a bunch about it. Just because I never swooned at your feet when you tried those ridiculous lines on me doesn't mean I was immune to you. Jeez, Raphael, look at yourself! You're gorgeous. How could I not be attracted to you? But you're my friend. And I don't know," she shrugged, "I don't see you in a sexual way."

Constantine raised a brow at her. "So what am I? Dog shit?"

Allie closed her eyes and pressed her fingers to her temple in exasperation. "I am not having this conversation."

When she opened her eyes, she saw Sebastian casually leaning his hip against the fireplace looking entirely too amused. "This is all your fault."

He stabbed a finger at his chest and shot his brows up in askance. "Me? How the hell am I at fault here?"

Her hands going to her hips, she matched the glare he was giving her with one of her own. "If you didn't go and kiss me, I wouldn't have kissed you back and I wouldn't have to try to convince two furious vampires that I think they're hot."

She went to storm out, but Sebastian prevented her dramatic exit when he moved with the speed of lightening and grabbed her. Again.

"Allie," he said too calmly. "Did it ever occur to you that those two," he motioned to Constantine and Raphael, "wanted us to get together?"

Why would it take her friends this long to work their scheme if they could have executed it months ago? Ready to dismiss Sebastian's presumption, she peered over his shoulder to see two guilty-looking vampires suddenly vastly interested in the dark gray rug.

"They knew I was going to be home tonight."

Allie laughed at how guilty they looked—even Constantine—which shocked the hell out of her. "You sly dogs."

Yanking her arm from Sebastian's grasp, she went over to Constantine, giving him a good shot to the arm. "I didn't even see this coming."

"That's because you're too damn trusting."

"Maybe," she retorted with a shrug. "I gotta go. You guys can deal with Sebastian's anger on your own. I'll see you tomorrow night."

Unbeknownst to her, three men watched intently as she flounced from the room.

* * *

Once she left, Raphael looked to Sebastian. "Well, Sage, how pissed are you?"

Sebastian ignored him, instead going after Allie. Constantine let out a grunt of satisfaction. "Something tells me he's not half as pissed as he wants us to believe."

Raphael slipped him a sly grin. "Think if we bother him enough about it he'll tell us all the juicy details?"

Constantine shrugged. "Doubt it, but I'll see if I can get into his head and find out."

* * *

"Wait." Sebastian called to Allie.

She froze and turned on the darkened steps. "What is it?"

With the night wrapped around her, she looked vulnerable swallowed by the shadows of the staircase. "I don't want you to leave thinking I was sorry for what passed between us."

The emerald fire in her eyes nearly scorched him. "Don't worry. I don't."

"Good," he said gruffly. His body reacted violently when he saw her lick her lips. Thoughts he had no business entertaining about exactly what he wanted her to do with her tongue—and lips and teeth—hardened his body painfully.

The quick, yet infinitely tender kiss she placed on his lips squeezed at his dead heart. Reminding him what it felt like to beat with life, he'd never missed being alive as much as did then.

"Good night, Sebastian."

This time, when she turned to leave he let her go. Unable to move, to speak, he was struck dumb by the wealth of affection he felt in the gentle touch of her lips. He knew only one thing for certain right at that moment—now that he tasted her passion and affection, he wasn't going to let her get away.

Not when her kiss gave the promise of life denied him for seven hundred years.

Chapter Four

Hidden in the shadows of the trees, the vampire had an unobstructed view of Randall Manor. The front door opened and out marched a tiny and attractive redhead. He knew her, or rather, he knew *of* her. Though he'd only been in Damascus for a short while, it was impossible not to have heard about the notorious ghost hunter.

This was an extremely small town where most everyone knew each other, which was why nearly every place he went, human and supernatural alike knew her name.

Crazy Allie, yet he sensed she was anything but insane. Her eyes were open, seeing the things that lurked in the dark. Everyone else remained blissfully unaware of the dangers stalking the living, unseen in shadows as they waited to strike—as he was now.

Unfortunately for her, her mind was elsewhere, her eyes closed to the danger of him.

Surprisingly, she was prettier than he expected. He found the fall of her distinctive long hair appealing. Even from this distance he felt her lifeforce. No wonder the Templars kept her around. Every vampire needed a pet whore. Even now he had his own hidden away in various abandoned properties scattered all over the vast county of Pennsylvania. What a fine addition she would make to his collection.

Detecting the scent of Sebastian of Rydon, he tensed, prepared to battle the enigmatic Templar known as the Sage. No sooner did he catch the scent that he realized the smell was coming from Allison. His stink was all over her, overpowering the aroma of gardenias scenting her skin.

Watching her stride over to a gray SUV, Stephan felt overwhelmed by her spirit. When she climbed into the driver's seat of the truck and started it, the sudden blast of loud rock music pained his sensitive ears. Even after she sped away, the radiance of her lifeforce lingered, lighting the balmy summer night.

Dismissing Allison for the time being, Stephan sniffed at the air, detecting nothing but the aromas of nature around him. The target of his revenge was absent from the manor, not that he expected to find him home with the night still young.

He'd come here to see where Lucian of Penwick spent his days hiding from the sun.

A slow smile revealed his fangs as he thought about his plans. He'd set the trap well, leaving enough of a trail to lead Lucian right where he wanted him. Come dawn when he returned to this place, his sanctuary, Stephan would make sure Lucian found no solace here. The things he'd do would haunt the noble warrior for as long as Stephan allowed him to continue to exist.

Turning away from the manor, Stephan moved silently through the trees, heading back to his car, which he'd left down the road. Anticipation rode him as he sped toward the abandoned house he and his men occupied for the past few nights. Always one to enjoy a kill, what would make this one sweeter than the others was what might await him hidden deep within his victim.

Following the signs other vampires ignored, Stephan selected the women he'd collected with great care. Though he had no desire to take the power he sought for himself, he was a man of his word and meant to reward those who served him with the promised prize.

What use did he have for the ability to walk in the sun? He cared not for ultimate power, not when all he wanted was Lucian. Revenge fueled him, burning within as the ages crawled over him, putting him further out of God's grace with each night that passed.

Once a devout follower of the Lord, he'd planned on giving himself to the church. Lifetimes ago, he blindly believed God protected His children from the demons in the dark. One night of horror proved how wrong he'd been.

The Lord he'd put such faith in abandoned him, leaving him and his family at the mercy of a monster of His own making.

The time was finally upon him to extract his revenge for all that was stolen from him and for what he was forced to become.

His revenge would last for ages.

* * *

Sebastian kicked Raphael's door open, the need to beat Rogue near to death riding him hard. Raphael, in the process of undressing, seemed unfazed at the intrusion and merely cocked a brow at Sebastian in question.

"Did you want something?"

Sebastian bared his fangs in a ferocious snarl. "You are such a bloody bastard."

Raphael had the gall to smile. "Actually, my parents were wed when my father tossed up my mother's skirts and begat his spawn on the poor woman."

Sebastian wanted to punch the arrogant prick in the mouth. "You had no right to interfere in my affairs."

"And you have no right to be such a brooding bastard. It's beginning to wear on the rest of us."

"I don't brood."

Raphael turned away from him and stripped off his jeans. He threw them at him, but Sebastian caught them in midair before they hit him full in the face. "Yes, you do, and it's bloody annoying."

Sebastian tossed the jeans on the floor. "Stay the hell out of my business, Raphael."

Naked, Raphael faced him without a hint of shame. "You of all people should know better than to allow emotions to get the better of you. Selena was centuries ago. Move on."

"This has nothing to do with Selena and everything to do with you sticking your goddamn nose where it doesn't belong."

Raphael snorted as he pulled on a pair of sweatpants. "Bugger that, Seb. You stay away from Allie because of what happened to Selena and we all know it. What happened wasn't your fault. Stop blaming yourself and put it to rest."

Sebastian backed down when he realized Raphael's obvious concern for him compelled him to be a meddling bastard. Constantine on the other hand, probably only went along with Raphael for shits and giggles. He'd deal with that asshole later.

"Stay out of things you know nothing about."

Raphael rolled his eyes. "How is it everyone but Allie knows you keep your distance from her because of your attraction to her?"

Sebastian strode over to Raphael, going nose to nose with him as he let out a feral growl. "I'm warning you only once to stay out of this."

Turning his back on him, Sebastian stalked from the room, slamming the door behind him. He knew all the warnings in the world weren't going to keep Rogue from sticking his nose in his business. Nor would it pay to bother with issuing a like warning to Constantine. That ornery bastard did whatever the hell he wanted, all warnings be damned.

Heading into his room, he let out a curse when he caught Allie's scent lingering on the air. Grabbing a handful of shirt, he sniffed it loudly, letting it go with a muttered curse.

Shit, even I still smell like her.

The scent of her was all over both his room and person.

Raphael was wrong, he didn't avoid Allie because of what went down with Selena. He put her to rest the moment they put her in the ground. No, he avoided Allie because she made him remember what it was to be alive and that was a torment worthy of the sadistic jailers at Chinon.

Slipping off his family ring, he tossed it on the dresser, wondering why he bothered to keep it. The large ruby winked under the glow of the candles he'd lit earlier. As long as his body bore her scent he'd never get control over the needs thundering threw him. Not that he believed a change of clothes could erase her from his body and mind, but it would help calm him not to be surrounded by her.

Leaving a trail of clothes behind him, Sebastian stripped before quickly replacing them with fresh ones that didn't carry the scent of gardenias. With a muttered curse, he knew he needed to feed before he became a danger to everyone around him. Grabbing his keys and his baldric, he slammed out of the house with no particular destination in mind. As soon as he hit the warm night air, he thought he sensed the faint scent of vampire. With his senses a mess and still filled with Allie, he passed it off as nothing more than his mind playing tricks on him.

Once in his souped-up black Charger he hauled ass away from Randall Manor, needing to put as much distance between himself and any trace of Allie as possible. Although Sebastian suspected if he traveled clear across the globe it still wouldn't be enough space between them for him to get a grip on himself.

* * *

What a way to end a perfectly crappy day.

Allie crawled into bed and hugged her pillow, still unable to believe how her day ended. Jude ending things with her after ten wasted months was nothing more than a forgotten dream after the kiss Sebastian laid on her. A kiss that would have never taken place had Jude not broken things off with her. Talk about perfect timing. Never would she have thought such passion burned beneath Sebastian's icy surface. Always the epitome of calm, cool, and collected, Sebastian didn't seem the type to have such fire simmering beneath his surface. Nor would she have suspected his cold lips could melt her with the slightest touch.

With nothing but a kiss, Sebastian of Rydon managed to shake her right down to her soul.

As all the Templars did, Sebastian carried the weight of his sins on his shoulders, allowing them to define his existence. The burden of their sins were heavy, their past as much a part of them as the present.

Unable to grasp what it must be like for them, Allie didn't even try. Growing up in a vastly different time, she couldn't comprehend the life they'd led. The events that shaped the Templars as living men influenced who they became in death, which said much for the nobility running strong in each of them. Far from brutal killers, the Templars never veered off the road to redemption. Their oath to God stayed with them every moment of their existence.

Sleep a long way off, Allie's mind drifted as her body hummed from Sebastian's touch. Thankfully she'd managed to keep her feelings for Sebastian hidden from Constantine and Raphael. God help her now that her attraction to him was known. Doomed, she wasn't being overly dramatic by wanting to dig a hole and hide away from them. She knew they were going to torture her and Sebastian mercilessly.

Wayne Arnold, the older brother from *The Wonder Years*, had nothing on the two of them when together.

Closing her eyes, Allie cuddled into herself. Usually alone was good since it kept her heart safe, yet after Sebastian's scorching kiss and finding out what it felt like to be in his arms she wished he was here.

After tonight, Allie wondered if she could go on pretending her indifference toward Sebastian. Doubtful, she was a realist with no time for games. She'd played one for five months, the effort exhausting her. Previously she believed only Constantine knew the depth of her feelings for Sebastian. Though it embarrassed her to know her attraction was now public knowledge, she was glad she didn't have to hold back anymore.

The drawback to being a realist was that she was a firm believer in never fighting for a person's affection. Her own parents taught her it was a losing battle. Still, she secretly harbored feelings for Sebastian for five torturous months. Learning from five medieval warriors that some battles were worth the fight, she wondered what it would take to chip away the ice Sebastian surrounded himself with to get to the fire beneath it.

With a deviousness that would do Raphael proud, Allie came to the conclusion it was high time the Sage came to learn that sometimes, being burned wasn't such a bad thing after all.

Chapter Five

The moment Lucian of Penwick entered the old, abandoned house the stench of blood and fear hit him like a brick.

The place, a hellhole in every sense of the word, was littered with mountains of garbage and other debris. Death crept through him, wrapping around his bones. If he wasn't careful, he'd be pulled down by the weight of it.

The family who once lived here left behind a few pieces of well-worn furniture, remnants of life gone by. From the condition of things—graffiti covered walls, discarded used condoms, empty crack vials and scorched pipes amid the refuge—it was obvious local kids had been using this place for a hangout.

Stepping over the mounds of waste, Lucian went up to second story. The closer he got to one particular bedroom, the stronger the stench of blood and death was.

Blood splattered the floor and smeared the walls of the small bedroom. The sight of all that blood woke the hunger in him. Fighting to keep it under control, Lucian let his gaze cut through the dark, coming to focus on a girl strewn carelessly on a mattress in the center of the room. Nude, her body was a mess of bruises both faded and new. Her body and hair were covered with blood and things he didn't dare want to know.

Her open eyes stared unseeing at the ceiling. In them was a reflection of the horrors she suffered at the moment of her death. It was obvious this was no simple feeding, but a gross brutality that had lasted for days.

Knowing she was tortured before her pain finally ended, Lucian remembered well a time long ago when he'd suffered much the same. After enduring three years of imprisonment in Chinon, his slow, burning death had been a welcomed relief.

Little did he know what awaited him beyond death.

Lucian detected the distinctive scent of renegade vampires. The bastards hadn't even tried to hide their stink. If anything they made damn sure their stink was detectable over the other odors.

Sworn to respect life, Lucian had to do right by the woman.

More over, the circumstances of her death needed to be concealed. No trace of a vampiric killing could be left behind. Whoever did this knew it and counted on her being found and disposed of.

Assailed by the stench of her death when he lifted her from the mattress, he carried her outside.

A gross injustice, the senseless slaughter pained him more than he liked to admit. Placing her body on the ground, he pushed aside the long, leather coat he wore to conceal the Templar sword sheathed at his hip. Pulling the weapon free, he stabbed it into the ground. Gripping the handle, he nestled his hands between the cross pattee pommel and the steel crossbar. He genuflected beside her, suffering the burn in his mouth and throat as he whispered prayers for her.

Though they rolled off the tongue of a vampire, scorching it black with each holy word he spoke, he hoped God would accept these prayers. Someone had to pray for her, even though with no soul she'd be caught between Heaven and earth.

Finishing the Lord's Prayer, Lucian ignored the blood seeping from his mouth and the awful burning of his tongue. He stood and pulled his sword from the ground. He scanned the area, searching for whatever kindling he could find, and arranged a small funeral pyre around her.

After touching the tips of his fingers to his lips he placed them on her forehead and whispered a plea for forgiveness. Rising, he pulled a Zippo lighter from his pocket and lit the debris. He lingered long enough to watch the girl's body begin to burn.

No soul would be released to God since the vampire who took her life stole her soul. Seeing the flames and smoke rise into the night sky, he knew it would only be a matter of time before someone noticed it and called the fire department. Lucian bowed his head, said one final prayer, and returned to his silver Maserati Spyder.

He knew he'd never forget what he saw here. He'd carry the girl with him for the rest of his nights.

Through his remembrance of her, Lucian would give her the only form of immortality he could. Someone, even if it were only a vampire, would make sure she was not only avenged, but remembered throughout time.

* * *

By the time Lucian arrived at Seacrest Castle his mood turned foul enough to have Tristan taking a step back when he stormed into the great hall.

Tristan Beaumont, the unofficial leader of the Templars, was the proverbial older brother to them all. The one they all followed in life—and nothing changed in death. He shouldered the heaviest burden for their redemption and not one night passed when any of them forgot it.

Crossing the hall, a perfect replica of the Beaumont's ancestral home in Northumberland, Lucian stalked to the hearth. Attempting to find some small warmth from the fire, he didn't know why any of them bothered anymore. As long as they were without souls they'd never know warmth.

Turning away from the dancing orange flames, he pinned Tristan with a frosty stare. "Another girl was killed tonight."

Tristan swore under his breath. "Bloody hell!" He let out a heavy sigh of regret. "This makes two now, does it not?"

"As far as we know."

Tristan pursed his lips and shook his head sadly.

"Have you told the others?"

"No. I came straight here."

"I'll call them and tell them." Tristan sat on one of the chairs positioned before the hearth. He stroked his chin thoughtfully before letting out a long and drawn out sigh. "Where did you find her?"

"Off Blackwell Road. Almost everything was the same as the first, except this girl had to have been held prisoner for days. Days, Tris!"

"*Jesus Christ*. Do I even want to know?"

"No, you don't." Lucian shook his head curtly. "Let's leave it at, 'it was bad'. They didn't merely feed from her. They tortured her and stole her fucking soul."

Tristan closed his eyes, fighting back the fury the image evoked. More so than the others, he couldn't lose himself to emotions. Their salvation hinged on his ability to always remain in control.

Once his emotions were reined in Tristan opened his eyes. "You think these two murders are connected to the Daystar?"

"What else am I to think?" Lucian sat on the couch between the two chairs. "What other explanation can there be for the sudden surge of renegade activity? I tell you, Tris, these vampires aren't only feeding. It's more than that. The bastards are searching for something."

This area of Wayne County was extremely rural and sparsely populated. The summer was short, the winters long and severe, hardly a place to attract a large vampire population. Yet here they were, coming in droves since it was a hotspot of paranormal activity.

Most vampires kept to themselves, feeding quietly and staying under the radar. Their discretion was what kept the Templars from hunting them down and taking them out. As long as the renegades, the lowest form of vampire in the nocturnal hierarchy, behaved they had no need to rekindle an ancient war put to rest centuries ago.

Besides, a good old-fashioned vampiric war might attract too much unwelcome attention into their world.

"They tortured this girl trying to get information from her."

Lucian wanted to agree with Tristan but he knew the girl's torture ran deeper. "No. I think I was more than that."

A deep frown furrowed Tristan's brow. "What do you mean?"

Lucian shook his head in frustration. "I can't say. It's something my gut is telling me."

Tristan slapped him on the knee and stood. "Dawn is coming. I feel your hunger and it's doing you no good. Feed, then go home and get some rest. I'll tell the others we'll meet here tomorrow night." He gave Lucian a level look. "We'll find out who did this and there *will* be justice."

Lucian rose and nodded to Tristan, who looked worn tonight. Haggard. They all knew his burden and none envied him it. "You look like shit, Guardian. Take your own advice and go take care of business."

"I'm fine."

His curt tone told Lucian he was anything *but* fine. Not wanting to press him, Lucian clapped a hand on Tristan's shoulder. "I'll see you tomorrow night."

He quit the hall, heading back to his car with a heavy heart. Shit was about to go down—and it was going to go down hard. A war with the Obyri was fast approaching. The Templar's fate hung in the balance of the outcome of such a battle.

Driving through the courtyard, Lucian couldn't help but steal a quick glance at the small chapel set in the far corner of the bailey. He felt the call of the power it housed, thanking God renegades weren't susceptible to the power of the relic. The last thing they needed was a war with both renegades and the Obyri, another faction of Templar Vampires.

Hell, they were good, but no one was *that* good.

Relief came to him only once he was through the gatehouse. He didn't know how Tristan managed to hold fast to resolve in the face of such temptation.

Speeding toward Edessa, Luc knew Tristan called it right, the bloodlust was upon him, and if he didn't feed quickly, with dawn approaching he'd lose the chance.

Exhausted in body and mind, he knew sleep would bring him no peace this day. Warm brown eyes staring lifelessly at him would haunt his dreams until night came and he woke to his damnation, his only solace, the knowledge that when he found the renegades responsible he'd get the chance to make them suffer for their actions. Though, unless they found the Daystar, renegades were going to keep coming and continue killing. With only one lead to go on so far, Lucian was afraid things were going to get awfully ugly before this whole thing came to an end.

Chapter Six

Allie and the Templars sat around Seacrest Castle's massive dining table. Her gaze kept going back to the smiling face of Jordan Brewster. The girl's picture was slapped on the front page of the Damascus Daily Herald after her body turned up burned outside of an abandoned house. It too had been burned, though who set the fire none of the Templars knew.

Someone obviously went back to the scene of their crime and set fire to the house once Lucian left.

Opening the paper to the second page, Allie read the brief accounting of events, trying desperately not to look at the picture of Jordan's distraught parents. The article stated Jordan recently turned twenty and worked at Cherry Ridge Veterinary Hospital. She went missing three days prior to the discovery of her body last night, which was identified by her perfectly intact wallet on the ground next to her. Now, all they had to do was verify her identity through dental records.

Whoever killed her wanted authorities to know who she was. Blaming her kidnapping, and ultimate death, on transients, the police suspected someone burned her body in order to get rid of evidence.

Well, at least that much was true.

Lucian was left with no choice but to clean up the renegade's mess. Bad enough Josh and Nick, the two brothers who owned the paranormal magazine Allie worked for, were already breathing down Allie's neck to investigate the "recent surge of vampire activity in the area", none of them needed the cops to come sniffing around as well.

All it would take was the slightest whiff of strangeness to have Wayne County's finest knocking on Allie's door. As far as everyone was concerned, if anyone would know weird it was Crazy Allie.

Not that they'd be wrong on that account. Weird and Allie went hand and hand. If the cops came to her, they could easily trace her steps back to the Templars, something to be avoided at all costs.

The rules governing the Templars were clear and concise. They were not to kill a human unless their existence was threatened. All bets were off then and they were free to do whatever was necessary to preserve their existence and the relic they protected. That meant if the police came around and started poking their noses into the Templar's affairs, well, needless to say, there'd be a few less cops on the force.

Unable to look at the picture of Jordan's smiling face next to the one of her grieving parents, Allie put the paper down. Glancing down the incredibly long table, she noticed Sebastian trying everything in his power *not* to notice her.

So be it. If he wanted to be a baby, fine by her, she'd indulge his silly game for now since she wasn't willing to disrupt the meeting by making a scene.

Instead, she took in the hall and the beauty of the castle, which never failed to take her breath away. As always she glanced above the entrance, where the Latin words *For the Glory of God* were carved directly into the stone. The same maxim was engraved on the inside of Sebastian's ring.

The dais the table set upon separated the dining area from the rest of the cavernous hall. Museum quality tapestries depicting Crusade scenes hung on the gray stone walls. The long, pointed windows were covered with heavy black drapes, which, when drawn, kept out every shard of daylight.

Since it was imperative to keep Seacrest looking as normal as possible, already a difficult thing given it was a castle, building it sans windows would have definitely raised a brow or two. As if a castle sitting as bold as you please in the Pennsylvania wasn't already weird!

A fire burned in the massive hearth as it always did, adding to the heat of the night. Keeping her discomfort to herself, she wished she could inconspicuously to get rid of the sweat pooling in her cleavage.

Gathered at Seacrest Castle, they were trying to work the renegade problem and formulate a plan to locate the Daystar. Though she made every effort to pay attention, her mind kept wandering back to Sebastian. Besides, how did anyone expect her to concentrate on the business at hand when surrounded by five gorgeous Templars? Way too much male gathered within the same room, their raw masculinity worked havoc on her senses.

Tristan, who sat at the head of the table looking worn from worry, could almost pass for normal if he had some color to him. With his long, sandy hair tied neatly back in a queue, a steel gray tee shirt and black jeans, he nearly looked like an ordinary man—insanely gorgeous, but ordinary nonetheless. His eyes were what gave him away, that and his fangs.

No, that wasn't quite right.

None of the Templars could ever pass for normal.

They may dress in today's styles, had, for the most part, adopted modern characteristics, but the truth was, they were far from ordinary. Replace their modern clothing with chain mail and horses for cars, and they'd looked every bit the medieval warriors they were born to be.

Hell, they still carried their swords.

None of them spoke about their lives and Allie didn't ask. Once, Raphael confided in her about how they died and were damned as vampires, but after seeing his pain when he related the awful tale to her, she decided to never force them to relive such things. She loved them all too much to bring back the agony that came with talking about their lives.

Most of what she knew came from Internet research on the Knights Templar. She knew they were in France when King Philip ordered the arrest of the French Knights. Imprisoned at Chinon for three years, they were among the fifty Knights burned to death in Paris.

Raphael talked about it with her only once, and not in any great detail. His pain was obvious when he told her Michael took them from the flames at the moment of their deaths and damned them as vampires.

They'd lost their faith yet continued to fight and kill in the name of God. For that grievous sin, Michael took their souls and denied them entrance into Heaven. He spoke no more about it once he told that to her. She sensed he wanted to—maybe even needed to—but couldn't. The pain of the memories must have been too awful to dwell on.

She never asked any of them about the past again.

When Allie looked over at Sebastian, sitting with his brow furrowed in a frown and his hands steepled under his chin, she was tempted to make a scene to get his attention. The way he pointedly refused to look at her was rude and annoying. If the mood wasn't so somber she'd flash a boob at him to crack his icy veneer.

"Now that we've concluded the renegades finally got the balls to come out of hiding, does anyone else agree with what Lucian said?"

Tristan's voice pulled Allie out of her musings. "Why would renegades force our wrath by deliberately leaving those girls here for you to find?"

Allie looked to Lucian when Raphael asked that. The Knight sat stiffly and threw Rogue a glare. "If you saw the way they were left you'd need not ask that."

"Yes well, I didn't see them and we're talking about starting a war here. Not exactly the smartest thing to do."

"Luc's right." Sebastian threw out. "It's obvious this is about more than just the Daystar."

Tristan sighed loud and long, his gaze going to the picture of Jordan's smiling face. Seeing the flash of sorrow in Tristan's eyes, Allie turned the paper over. "This is the last thing we need right now."

Constantine nodded somberly. "Our time is fast approaching."

Though Con's statement made no sense to Allie, it obviously did to the Templars. By their agreeing nods and heavy sighs, whatever was "fast approaching" was one of those things she wasn't privy to. If they were keeping her in the dark about it, chances were good it was something bad.

"Now that we've established their deaths were overkill and about more than the Daystar, what do we do about it? Go to war and hope we can take the entire renegade armies before Victor comes sniffing around?"

Allie didn't know who the Victor was Sebastian mentioned, nor was she going to ask.

"A full on war will bring too much attention. That's something we can't afford." Tristan announced.

"So, we can't sit back and do nothing," Raphael added. "Can't say I agree with that option either."

"I'm not saying we should do nothing."

"We should wait," Constantine, the most bloodthirsty of them all, stated. Allie found it shocking he wasn't calling for war between the factions. "The fuckers will get sloppy and slip up. When they do we strike hard."

"Did you see a vision about this?" Sebastian asked.

"No. I don't need a vision to give me common sense." He retorted sarcastically. "We go to war, it's the five of us against hoards of renegades. Not to mention the Obyri will come and stick their noses into it. We'll lose and we'll go to Hell and I'm not going out like that."

Though Allie didn't know too much about the Obyri, she did know they were also damned Knight Templars. Though where God believed the Templars were worthy of redemption, not so the Obyri who were colder and more vicious than any renegade.

"Until we find the Daystar, renegades are going to keep coming," Lucian predicted. "If we wait to act, we might be too late to do a damn thing."

"Not to mention whoever killed that one," Raphael pointed to the paper, "got their jollies doing it."

Tristan nodded heavily. "We can't go to war. That's not on option. And though Constantine is right about waiting, Lucian has a point as well. The longer we sit around waiting, the more destruction these bastards are going to cause." He leaned back in his chair, for the first time Allie saw the fire of battle burn in his eyes. "I say it's time to bring the fight to them."

"But you just said no war."

"You're right, Raphael. I'm not saying war. I'm saying small battles. We take it to them one by one until we catch the bastards."

A devilish gleam lit Lucian's eyes. It was obvious he was gunning for the blood of the vampires killing these women. "I'll continue to go out hunting until we find them and end them."

"You do that. I need you two out there as well." Tristan pointed to Constantine and Raphael, as if they needed to be told to go spill some renegade blood. To Sebastian, he threw a long, meaningful stare. Allie had no idea what the look meant. "I hate that I'm trapped behind these damn walls."

"Yes, well, we need you here," Raphael said to him. "Don't worry, Guardian, I'll give one a good beat-down with your name all over it."

Tristan's lips curled back to reveal his fangs. "I hate to say it but, I miss a good fight."

Allie shifted uncomfortably in her chair, again drawing Sebastian's attention. Seemed he couldn't keep his gaze from going back to her.

For the past hour, every time she looked away from him, he couldn't help but let his gaze linger on her. Though he knew he should be paying attention to the meeting, Allie was a terrible distraction to him. He loved that she wore her hair up tonight since it showed off her throat. The artery pulsating with every beat of her heart held his attention long enough to mesmerize him. Focusing his hearing, he listened to the rush of blood through her body. His mouth watered to taste her again as the rich scent of gardenias filled him.

Like a deafening roar, Allie was not to be ignored. Whenever they were together, her presence stole his attention. Even tonight, when he should be concentrating on what was being said, his focus was instead on Allie.

She must have felt his hot stare since her gaze drifted back to him. Catching him watching her, she gave him a small, secret smile that hit him like a fist to his gut.

"Allie."

Tristan calling her name for the third time earned him both her and Sebastian's attention.

"Huh?" She looked adorably dumbfounded.

"Are you alright?"

She nodded at Tristan. "Yep. Why?"

"You were a million miles away." An amused grin played at Guardian's lips, telling Sebastian he knew exactly where her mind had been.

"That's strange since I've been paying attention the entire time."

Raphael's cough sounded suspiciously like the word *bullshit*, for which he'd get himself a thorough beating. Constantine's snort and Lucian's knowing grin confirmed the fact they'd *all* known Allie was daydreaming.

"Fine, you all caught me. I zoned out. Big deal. I got the gist of things."

Sebastian loved that she held her own against them. Not many people could—supernatural and human alike. Alone, each one of them was imposing in their own right. Together, they were a force to be reckoned with. Though they were the baddest things this side of Hell, Allie had no problem standing up to them.

Suddenly deadly serious, Tristan leveled them all with a meaningful glare Sebastian knew all too well. "You have to be our eyes and ears during the day."

"Haven't I always been?"

Tristan nodded solemnly. "You have to be careful, Allie. Don't take unnecessary chances that might get you killed. I won't have your picture slapped on the front page of the papers. Do I make myself clear?"

"Don't worry. I promise I won't get into too much trouble," she assured him with a wink.

Everyone at the table shot Allie incredulous looks. Constantine's very loud, and very rude, snort proclaimed what they were all thinking. Not one of them believed she wasn't going to end up knee deep in a shitstorm of trouble, since trouble followed her like a doom cloud.

With their business concluded, Raphael announced he had to go out and play, his way of saying he needed to feed. Sebastian felt sorry for the human female population in this area. Before Rogue was done here, it was likely he would have bedded and fed from every attractive and available woman in the region, leaving a sea of broken human hearts behind.

True to his word, Lucian went to a cabinet set in one corner of the hall and loaded up on weapons to take with him on his hunt. Since guns were useless against a vampire, Templars made sure they were strapped to the nines with blades. Aside from their swords, the same weapons they'd brandished in life, an array of daggers could also be found on their person at any given time. It was convenient in a fight but hell to take off for play—or so Raphael bemoaned.

Constantine, always ready for a good battle, joined Luc while Raphael stalked from the hall to hunt down his own prey. Either way, blood would be shed.

Standing, Sebastian pulled on his baldric and grabbed the duster slung over the back of his chair. He threw out a curt farewell to Tristan and Allie as he strode from the hall without so much as a backward glance.

Knowing his action would irk the hell out of Allie, he did it to get her alone for a few moments. He also wanted to rile her a bit because she looked adorable when pissed off.

He wasn't disappointed on either account.

He didn't even make it out the door before she caught up with him. All she had to do was curl her fingers around his arm and he stopped dead.

"I thought you said you didn't regret what happened last night." Her tone held enough reproach for him to know she was furious.

"That's right."

His pants felt as if they'd shrunk only in the groin area at the reminder of their kiss.

"Yeah, well, you're making me feel like I have the cooties or something."

He raised a brow at that. "Cooties?"

Allie rolled her eyes. "Oh please! Everyone knows what the cooties are, even a vampire as old as you, so don't play stupid."

Pushing her dangerously close to the limit of her exasperation, he knew he was jeopardizing a vital part of his anatomy if pressed her much further.

"Of course you're not diseased."

"Then why are you avoiding me?"

Cupping her chin in his palm, he stared deep into her eyes, loving the golden fire burning in them. "How could I avoid you when we were sitting at the same damn table?"

She snatched her face from his hand. "Whatever." She turned sharply and went to leave.

He wasn't amused anymore.

Much to his chagrin, Allie had dismissed him. A man of his status and stature did not get dismissed. Ever.

Though she strode quickly through the door and down the ten steps leading to the courtyard, Sebastian caught her easily. "Why do you do that?"

The woman had the sheer nerve to look bored. "Do what?"

He actually felt his teeth clench with frustration. "Walk away."

She shrugged off his hold. "I don't like games, Sebastian."

"So you walk away from someone? Have you any idea how bloody rude that is?" He dropped his voice to a menacing hush. "And I do not play games."

She gave him a level stare, in no way backing down. "I'm well aware of how rude walking away is. Why do you think I did it?" she drawled matter-of-factly. "I won't stand here and have you throw bullshit at me. That's just as rude."

"I didn't throw bullshit at you."

She snorted. "Oh come on! You didn't bother to say hello to me when you got here. Then, I sat at the table with you for over an hour and you didn't look at me once, not even to politely acknowledge me when I spoke. Do you know I actually considered flashing you to see how you would manage to continue to ignore me?"

Now *that* would have gotten his attention.

The idea of her flashing those breasts at him got him even harder. He gave credit to denim since he was putting the fabric to the test tonight.

Dropping his gaze to her breasts, he liked the way they strained against her tee shirt. Not too heavy nor too small, they were the perfect size to fill his hand.

No, he wouldn't have minded at all if she whipped them out for his viewing pleasure.

Of course, he couldn't be held responsible for what he did to her if she dared such a thing. Propriety be damned, he wanted to throw her down on the ground and take her right there on the ground like a barbarian.

"Um, Sebastian?" Allie's voice pulled him from thoughts of her stretched out beneath him on the grass, his body sliding slowly in and out of her until... "I'm up here." She was pointing to her face.

Caught gawking at her breasts, Sebastian was far from embarrassed by it. He gave her a mean scowl. "I know bloody well where you are," he snapped. "Don't point out your breasts if you don't want attention drawn to them."

"I wasn't pointing them out!" She pointed directly at them. Catching herself, she rolled her eyes at her action and lowered her hand.

Smiling at her exasperation, he admired the furious flush coloring her cheeks. "Obviously not."

Allie looked ready scream. Much as she did last night, she massaged her temples with her fingertips. "Oh God, I'm back in Bizzaro World again." She groaned dramatically, which had him biting his lip to keep from laughing— not a smart thing when one had fangs. Dropping her hands, she shook her head at him. "You make me crazy, you know that?"

The condition was mutual, though he was loath admitting it.

"I have to go." That came out brusquer than he intended.

"So do I." She glanced at the watch on her right wrist. "My sister should be at my house by now."

Surprised, he didn't know she had a sister. Then again, he made a point to know as little about her as possible. He thought it would make keeping his distance from her easier. Now he realized it only made him more intrigued to discover all the things he didn't know.

"Sebastian?"

His name on her lips was the sweetest sound he'd ever heard.

"What?" That too, came out harsher than he'd meant it. Painfully aroused, every moment spent in her company was torture.

"I hope we can be friends, that's all. Don't you think it's time, especially now with everything that's going on?"

Hanging between them, going unspoken, was their attraction for each other.

The smile she gave him when he told her they were already friends reminded him of the sun he hadn't seen in hundreds upon hundreds of years.

Sunshine.

That's what she was—a blinding midnight sun cutting through the darkness of his existence.

Chapter Seven

"Tell me, pet, do you have anything hiding in there?"

She knew his name was Stephan since that's what his followers called him. Prying open her mouth he peered inside as if looking for something. Wanting to shake her head and free her chin of his hold, she knew better than to try that twice.

All she could do was glare daggers at him, which earned his amusement. With a laugh he petted her head like she was a goddamned dog. And maybe by now she was, reduced to the name he liked so much to call her.

Pet. Dog. Both the same meaning though different words.

Hungrier and thirstier than she'd ever been in her life, she thought she was going to go insane from it. Mostly though, she was afraid, trapped in a nightmare she couldn't wake from.

At first she tried to count the days since she was kidnapped and brought here, but had given up. Three, she believed, though she couldn't be sure since there were no windows and no clocks. Only her captors' comings and goings marked the passing of time.

Not knowing how she lasted this long, she had moments when she felt more dead than alive. Given the things he'd done to her she wondered why her body wouldn't give up, especially since she knew her mind had.

She wanted to go home and see her mom and dad. She'd give anything to be back with her family, though she knew she was never going to see them again.

Home was a million miles away and so far, God wasn't listening to her prayers to rescue her.

Why the expression "shit in one hand, wish in another" came to mind, she couldn't say, but it did fit the situation. The shit was definitely filling up fast and her wishes of making it out of this alive lessened with each passing moment.

Her father's greatest fear was his only daughter would go out with friends and never come home. Her dead in a ditch, was what he told her kept him awake at night. Looking around the disgusting room, she wondered if being dead in a ditch wouldn't have been a better fate. A nice, quick death, over and done with before she even knew what hit her. Instead, she was beaten, bitten, and drained of blood until too weak to fight.

Coming out of work, she had been dragged into a van and restrained by two vampires who tormented her relentlessly during the long ride to where she was being held captive.

She knew she was in the mountains due to the popping of her ears. For someone who'd been born and raised in the Appalachian Mountains, she had to be awfully high for her ears to pop. High enough not to be found before the vampire killed her.

The house was filthy, with flies buzzing all around her. Bugs crawled the floor and walls, coming in to feed on the mounds of old trash decomposing throughout the rooms. Thick, repugnant odors of rotting garbage, blood, and sweat still made her gag.

When she thought of Hell, this was what she imagined it to be. Not a place with lakes of fire and a pitchfork-wielding devil with a forked tail and horns. That was the hell of make-believe. Real Hell was here in this house.

The devil didn't have horns and red skin. No, his skin was as pale as death and his razor-sharp fangs the stuff of nightmares and horror movies.

When their leader wasn't around, Stephan's henchmen took turns torturing her, each bringing his own twisted style of torment. A vicious bunch of vampires who took genuine delight in each and every whimper and scream they pulled from her, they were careful not to hurt her too badly. After all, they had to save something for their leader.

She was taken for a reason, though she didn't know why they'd targeted her. Stephan believed she might have something he needed and no matter how many times she told him he was wrong he refused to listen. Instead, he played mind games with her, until she felt herself slipping into the abyss of insanity, her only escape from the things he did to her.

Over the last days she found herself contemplating the wildest things, like maybe after she was dead coming back as a ghost to visit her family one last time—or haunt the vampire who killed her. Crazy Allie believed in ghosts, so maybe there was a chance it might be possible, not that she ever held much faith in the things Allison Parker believed in before now.

Maybe Allie wasn't so crazy after all.

Facing Stephan, it boggled her mind that he looked no older than her own twenty-three years. Since he liked to scare her with what he was, he reminded her more than once that he'd been around since the medieval age. Almost seven hundred years to be exact. Needless to say, it was a chilling concept to know this—thing—had seen nearly a thousand years go by.

He'd had a long time to perfect his methods of torture and murder.

"Please," she begged, though for her life or a quick death she didn't know anymore.

Regarding her curiously, he tilted his head to the side, his glowing silver eyes cutting through her. Strikingly handsome, his looks were deceiving. He looked like a guy she would be attracted to had she met him on the street.

His face wasn't that of a cold-blooded killer, nor the face of a demon. Yet beneath the guise of handsome young man lay a soul which belonged in the deepest recesses of Hell.

"Please, what?" His voice was a low, almost seductive purr. When he spoke she could see his fangs.

She doubted she'd ever get used to feeling those fangs biting her. Nor would the sensation of him pulling at her blood ever fail to stir her revulsion.

"Please kill me already."

Her words passed through a throat raw from screams and damage done by his fangs.

He ran his hand over her dirty and knotted blonde hair. "Where's the fun in that, love?" His English accent lent him an air of sophistication.

Too tired to fight back her tears, she shivered with disgust when he tenderly wiped them from her face. She knew better than to pull away. She dared that once. On God she swore she'd never do it again. The pain he inflicted upon her was too much to bear a second time.

"Don't do this. I don't have what you want."

Over the past days he asked her if she had "it", though he never said what it was he thought she had.

Knowing he could take whatever it was he wanted from her whenever he wanted, she knew he refrained solely because he found sick delight in tormenting her.

"I think you do."

Shaking, she shifted on the dirty mattress. The rope tied around her wrists and ankles cut deeper into her torn flesh. "I don't have anything," she wept.

He pushed her back on the mattress. She lay trembling violently as he slowly untied the rope around her ankles. When he nudged her legs apart she thought she was going to be sick all over herself. Behind him, standing in the doorway, were four other vampires watching and snickering.

"Oh, you have *something* I want."

He crawled up her body, fangs bared. She couldn't stop the scream rising from deep inside of her. Only his hard slap shut her up when she released it.

He took hold of the rope around her wrists with one hand, pinning her hands over her head. His other hand settled on her throat in a crushing grip. "Now we play, pet."

She slid her eyes closed and willed herself to another place and time, back to when she was a young girl and her parents took her and her brother to

Disneyland. What a fun time they'd had, enough to make lasting memories. She always wished she could go back to that place again...

Even if only in her mind, she took herself out of the dirty hovel of a house, away from the evil touch of the vampire. She lost herself in the memory of her family as the vampire took her body and robbed her sanity.

The last sight Amanda Driver saw was of his fangs lowering to her throat.

The sweet oblivion of madness took her then, finally giving her peace as a monster invaded her body.

Chapter Eight

Allie blinked against the harsh intrusion of sunlight. Grudgingly, she allowed the day to break the wonderful dream about Sebastian. Certainly not the first of such dreams, she doubted it would be the last. The man crept into her brain five months ago and refused to leave. Not that she objected to having him running wild in her mind. Although there were worse things to occupy her mind than a gorgeous medieval warrior.

Reluctant to abandon the coziness of her soft bed, Allie yawned and stretched, the harsh daylight invasive to eyes used to the night. When one ran with vampires, one rarely—if ever —saw the morning.

With a quick glance at the clock, Allie groaned and forced herself to get moving when she saw it was already two o'clock. Her body screamed in protest for more sleep when she dragged herself out of bed.

Shuffling out of her room, she went down the hall to the bathroom, the house as silent as the grave. Disappointed she didn't hear Lexine about, she assumed her sister had gone out to catch up with her old friends. She missed her kid sister, who she hadn't seen in three months. She had been hoping to spend some time with Lex before the investigation she had scheduled for today.

Catching her reflection in the mirror as she brushed her teeth, Allie barely recognized herself. Though usually pale, her complexion looked downright dead. Her hair was a mess and she moved beyond circles under her eyes into something resembling the hollowed out sockets of a skull.

I look like a corpse.

What she needed was a long hot shower to help her feel human and alive again.

With summer here, maybe it was time to get herself a tan. A tan meant sunlight. Sunlight meant waking earlier. Waking earlier meant going to bed earlier, which was something she couldn't do since it would take time away from the only family beside Lex she had.

Her parents didn't count as family to her.

Though it rarely made it past the ninety-degree mark in this area, lately it'd been unusually hot. Searching through her closet for something weather-appropriate to wear, she picked a black tank top and old, faded jean shorts. Leaving her heavy hair free, she didn't even want to take the time to tie it back. Not when the need for caffeine rode her probably about as hard as the bloodlust did in vampires.

She wished her sister hadn't left before she woke. She would have liked to see Lex before she had to run to the Millers.

If she hadn't gotten in so late last night, Allie would have gotten the chance to see her sister before she passed out from exhaustion. By the time she got home, Lex was already asleep. Ever the older sister, Allie checked in on her and gave her a quick kiss on the forehead before crashing for what remained of the night.

Her damp hair hanging free, Allie hurried downstairs. Passing the peeling paint, she wished her place was nicer. Unfortunately, the run-down house was all she could afford, and even then just barely. The floorboards creaked beneath the old, ugly, brown carpet. The paint on the walls was chipping away and the windows drafty but at least it was neat and clean. Most importantly, it was hers. This shabby yellow house meant freedom from David and Marie Parker.

As she came down the stars she smiled wide when she caught sight of Lex sitting on the scraggily beige couch, laptop balanced on her tanned legs.

Two years younger than Allie, Lex lived with their parents in Florida. Hence her deep, dark tan, which gave her a look of vibrancy and life. Since Allie crawled the night and Lex worshiped the sun, the two literally looked like night and day. One as ashen as a corpse and the other tanned to a golden bronze, they were opposite as sisters could be. Allie's red hair and green eyes favored their mother, where Lex's black hair and stormy vivid blue eyes took after no one. Allie was of average height, Lex a tiny thing, standing all of five-feet-one.

Even their personalities were different. Allie, as ballsy as they came, was an in your face person. Lex was the sweetheart, generally soft spoken and so still and quiet at times, it creeped Allie out.

Their brother had looked exactly like their father, which wasn't a bad thing since he'd been extremely handsome.

"Good morning, beautiful."

Lex gave her a radiant smile. Setting aside her laptop, she ran to Allie, all but slamming into her as soon as Allie touched down in the living room.

"Finally! I didn't think you were ever going to wake up."

Laughing, Allie untangled herself from Lex's bear hug. "Sorry, sweetheart, but I got in late."

"I know. I heard you come in but I was too tired to stay awake long enough to say hi. Did you go on a ghost hunt last night?"

"Unfortunately, no. I met up with a few friends, that's all."

As she walked to the kitchen Lex was right on her heels. She sat down at the table while Allie made a pot of coffee. "Was it the vampires?"

The eager note in Lex's husky voice made her cringe. Allie wished Lex didn't know about the company she kept. Unfortunately, Allie kept very few secrets from her sister, especially since they were all they had left when it came to family. After she'd been attacked, Allie had phoned Lex and told her everything, including the Templars.

Only after it was too late did Allie realize how interested Lex was in the darker aspects of her life. For the last months every time she'd spoken to her, Lex grilled her on the latest happening with the ghost hunting and wanted to know *everything* about the Templars. The ghost business was an open book. The Templars were not. Allie made sure she picked what she said wisely, trying to downplay Lex's rabid interest in them.

"Yes, I was with the Templars."

A fervent fire flared to life in Lex's eyes, almost reminding Allie of the eerie glow of a vampire's. "So? Can I meet them?"

The thought of throwing her sister in the mix with the likes of Raphael and Constantine had Allie shivering with dread. She trusted them absolutely, but also knew Raphael and Constantine well enough to know one would flirt shamelessly while the other would most likely try to scare the black out of Lex's hair.

"We'll see."

"You're no fun, you know that?"

Allie sat at the table and waited for her much needed coffee to brew. "Yeah, well, I'm more fun than Mom and Dad. Speaking of—how are the folks these days?"

Lex shrugged indifferently. "The same as always. You know nothing changes with them."

"Do they ever ask about me?"

Allie hadn't talked to her parents since the day she left Florida two years ago, having gone there to bury Christian. She never called them and they didn't care enough to call her. The only communication she had with them was through Lex, who she talked to at least three times a week, if not more.

"You know they don't. Jeez, Allie, they don't even bother with me and I *live* with them."

The coffee ready, Allie made them both a cup. After handing Lex the steaming mug, she laid out the sugar and milk, loving having Lex here to take care of. It reminded her of when they were younger, before they lost Christian, when she used to play mommy to them in lieu if their mother doing the actual job.

As a child, the responsibility of taking care of the younger two fell on her since their parents couldn't be bothered to do it themselves. No wonder she didn't want kids, she'd already raised two.

"How long are you here for this time?"

Lex took a sip of coffee before shrugging. "I don't know. Since school is done I'm in no rush to get back home."

Allie wanted Lex here indefinitely. She hated that her sister lived so far away with people who didn't want her around. At least here in Damascus Lex would be smothered with love.

Knowing only two things were powerful enough to influence her sister's decision, Allie was prepared to throw one out. "You want to go on a hunt with me?"

Lex practically beamed with excitement. "You know I do! When?"

"In a couple of days. Steven and Georgia Miller bought the Thomason's old place and converted it into a bed and breakfast. Supposedly, they had a few run-ins with a ghost and wanted the place investigated. I'm going tonight to do a walk through, real boring stuff, but I'll take you when I do the actual investigation."

What Allie failed to add was, she didn't think the place was haunted. Her gut told her the Millers were lying in order to gain some publicity for their fledgling B&B.

After what went down with Mr. Bishop's place, that sort of exposure would definitely give their business a boost.

A year ago Allie made a reference in one of her articles about Old Man Bishop's being among the top five haunted houses in Wayne County. Big mistake since it brought a shitstorm of people, all gunning to get inside the house and see a ghost for themselves.

Who would have thought *The Specter* was so widely read? Certainly not her.

To this day Mr. Bishop wouldn't even look in her direction without throwing her a nasty look. She hoped once the stragglers stopped coming around the hostility might end. She'd even retracted her claim months ago—jeopardizing her reputation to do so. What more did he want from her, blood?

The recent surge of vampire activity would force her to keep a close eye on Lex. Still, being here was safer for Lex's well-being than returning to Florida.

Look what prolonged living with their parents did to Christian.

Their brother had never been strong enough to withstand their parents' indifference. Their apathy broke him. He turned to drugs as a means to put an end to the pain. They nearly lost him to his heroin habit, only to truly lose him once he got his life together. A hit and run took his life and left Allie with a hole in her heart that would never heal.

Resolved to do whatever was necessary to keep Lex here, Allie knew it was only a matter of time before she broke on the matter of keeping her kid sister and the Templars separated.

Now all she had to do was prepare Lex for the inevitable. Though Allie doubted all the preparation in the world could prepare *anyone* for coming face to face with Templars.

Lord knows even she was still getting used to the idea of them.

* * *

Everything about The Gate was dark in order to give it a Gothic feel. Black walls, black ceiling, and black floor certainly achieved the effect. Behind the long black bar, lined with metal stools, glass shelves were stacked with bottles of expensive liquor. The cheap shit they used for the overpriced drinks was *under* the bar and out of sight.

The shelves were backlit with black lights, giving it a beautiful effect.

Scattered around the large club, tall tables accompanied by equally tall chairs gave it an artsy look. In the cages set on high black pedestals, gorgeous scantily clad girls danced proactively to the thumping music.

Having arrived early, as soon as Allie saw Constantine muscle his way past the throng of bodies on the dance floor, all gyrating and grinding to the hypnotic beat of a Type-O-Negative song, she let out a loud laugh. His tee shirts were an ongoing joke between them since she bought him a novelty one as a goof a few months back. The one he was wearing tonight read *I leave bite marks*.

"Cute," Allie remarked with a nod to the shirt.

His breath ticked her ear when he leaned in close to talk. Unlike him, she was merely human, lacking his exceptional hearing. "I knew you'd appreciate it." He gave her the slow once over, something he *never* did. "I like."

Her cheeks burned hot at the complement. Unused to wearing the getup she had on, she'd felt like an idiot when she left the house, despite Lex's assurance she looked "hot".

Given the way his tone oozed suggestively, it was no wonder the ladies liked his whole bad-boy thing. He worked it to perfection.

"Where's Raphael?" Choking back her embarrassment, Allie craned her neck to peek around the club.

"Otherwise engaged."

That meant he was with one of his ladyloves tonight. Lucky him. Though better if Raphael were here, Constantine was more than capable of protecting her if the shit hit the fan.

The club was jumping tonight, at least for this part of the world. More than fifty people in a club constituted "a crowd" in the mountains. Hopefully that meant a renegade or two would show. The plan was to use her as bait—not something she was too pleased about—giving Constantine the chance to extract information from the renegade about the Daystar and the recent murders. Knowing how brutal the Dragon could be, she almost felt bad for the creature should one take the bait.

Hoping to fit in at the gothic club, Allie dragged Lex to Hot Topic after she finished at the Miller's. She felt ridiculous in the pleated black miniskirt, black satin bustier, and black knee-high boots. Also extremely uncomfortable, she wondered how the gothic crowd went around dressed like this all the time.

Laid-back when it came to fashion, she was the jeans and tee shirt type of woman, usually sporting no make-up, with her hair pulled back in a messy ponytail. Basically, the complete opposite of the heeled-platform-boot wearing, leg-and-cleavage-baring vamp-bait she was acting as tonight.

The Gate, a popular Gothic club in Scranton, was where local renegades were known to hunt. The Templars simply called the place the "Supermarket" since this was where the pickings for victims were abundant.

"Tonight is going to be a fucking waste of time."

"Don't I know it," she agreed. Renegades had a way of never being around when you wanted them to, and being a bother when you didn't.

Though vampires usually sensed each other, a crowd like this made it difficult to focus on the sensation. Unfortunately, it put Allie in the middle of a dangerous situation since Constantine wouldn't detect the scent of a renegade until it was too late. Still, it was worth the risk if they were able to save even one innocent life.

"Go do something. Draw attention to yourself. I don't want be here all goddamn night."

Allie laughed, arcing her arm to indicate the crowd. "Look around you, C, what can I possibly do, besides whip out a boob or something, to draw attention to myself?"

"Talking about your tits again, are we?"

Gasping, Allie spun around to see Sebastian standing directly behind her. As usual, he looked gorgeous all in black. She shot Constantine an accusatory frown. "You didn't tell me he was here."

Constantine shrugged and looked out into the crowd. "You didn't ask."

If she thought she could hurt him, she would've given him a good shot to the nads.

"Nice outfit." Sebastian's slow appraisal made her feel naked even with clothes on.

"I'm only wearing it to fit in."

He cocked one brow as he took in her black leather boots. "Shame, really. Those boots should be worn more often."

"Be my guest," she offered sarcastically. Given how she usually dressed, she felt a bit insulted that he liked her decked out in this costume. "You can have them after tonight. I doubt they'd fit you, but hey, you can always try."

His eyes narrowed on her. That's not what I meant," he growled into her ear.

"I know."

Stiffening when she felt his hand brush against her naked thigh, she knew he did it on purpose. Somehow, his cool touch managed to send heat through her. "I'm sure your boyfriend likes them."

The rancor in his tone startled her. "I don't have a boyfriend. Jude broke up with me two days ago."

Sebastian's powerful stare nearly burned her. She could have sworn she felt him brush her thigh again. "I thought you were still together."

Now *that* was insulting. Did he think so little of her character to assume she was a cheater? "I wouldn't have kissed you if I was still with him. I may have a rep for being nuts, but I'm loyal, even to an asshole like him."

"I didn't think otherwise."

Laughing at his gruff tone, she gave him a good shot to the arm. "Yes, you did, but I'll give you a pass 'cause I like you."

Did he actually fluster at the wink she threw at him? Oh, that was priceless!

"Now I don't have to worry about breaking your moral fiber when I get you in my bed wearing nothing but those boots."

Oh sweet God…

Well now, *that* was a healthy splash of honesty murmured seductively in her ear.

Though he was teasing her, she secretly wished otherwise. Pathetically, all Sebastian would have to do is crook his finger at her and she'd be his, body and soul. Allie should be ashamed of herself for falling at a man's feet, but it was Sebastian for God's sake. He wasn't the average man, which helped to salvage a bit of her pride—or at least that's the crap she liked to tell herself.

"With you two hanging over me, no vampire in his right mind is going to take the bait. I'm going over there to make myself available. I suggest you two stay here and try not to get into any trouble."

* * *

Watching her walk away, Sebastian admired the gentle sway of Allie's hips. She didn't know how wrong she was. One vampire here already took her bait.

Though he loved how Allie worked a pair of jeans, she also rocked the Goth getup she was wearing tonight. Other eyes focused on the source of his fascination and he resisted the urge to throw his duster around her to hide the sight of her from other men.

Even Constantine couldn't stop staring.

Sending his elbow into the Dragon's ribs was a good way to get his attention off Allie's ass.

"Why the fuck did you do that?"

Sebastian was unmoved by Constantine's fierce scowl. "Take your eyes off her."

Constantine regarded him with cool curiosity. "We've staked our claim, have we?"

Reluctantly dragging his gaze from the appealing sight of Allie, he pinned Constantine with a lethal glare. "You sure you want to go there, Dragon?"

"See me quaking with fear?"

Right then Sebastian couldn't think of a single reason to allow Constantine to continue to exist. "You and that other asshole knew I would."

Of course he was referring to the "claim" thing. He might not have wanted to, but when it came to Allie he found himself feeling things he couldn't fight. Especially the possessiveness he felt toward her. That ran deeper than a basic need to protect a friend. Much deeper.

"You're too brooding." Constantine's indifferent shrug had Sebastian dangerously close to dragging the Dragon out of the club in order to beat him bloody in the parking lot.

Exasperated, Sebastian grunted and slapped his hands against his legs in frustration. Either do that or do some damage to Constantine. "Again with the brooding shit. Coming from you, who made being an irritable prick into a bloody art form, isn't that a bit ironic?"

Constantine's grin held no real humor. "Exactly. I own it. You don't."

Needing to look away from Constantine before he gave in to the barbaric urge to slap the taste out of his mouth, he stared across the club and watched Allie perch herself on a high chair at one of the round tables. A waitress hurried over to her to take her drink order. Sebastian didn't need to hear her to know she ordered water.

Even wearing the uniform of every other Goth-queen in the club, somehow Allie owned it and made it her own. She stood out in the crowd of people trying to look dead.

Only a few minutes passed before someone approached her and tried to hit on her. The kid looked ridiculous in his puffy shirt with lacy sleeves and deep blue velvet frock coat. His hair was dyed black and he wore black eyeliner and black lipstick. Sebastian found himself baffled over why humans believed a male vampire would look like that. It was insulting, actually, and a sting to his male pride.

The kid wore a *frock coat* for God's sake.

When the bartender came over to ask the Templars if they wanted drinks, Sebastian didn't even bother to take his eyes off Allie when he curtly declined for both of them.

Suffering this place was bad enough. Neither of them wanted to add to the torture by forcing liquid down their throats.

Watching the kid intently, Sebastian snarled when he made himself at home on the chair opposite Allie. He leaned across the table to talk to her as if she cared what he said. What the kid failed to notice was the way she threw Sebastian and Constantine an exasperated look.

When the waitress returned with Allie's bottle of water the kid reached into the inside pocket of his silly coat and passed the waitress money. Once the waitress walked away, Allie spoke to him and pointed to Sebastian and Constantine.

Constantine winked and the kid almost fell off the chair.

Flustered, he jumped up, said something to Allie, then lost himself in the crowd. Allie held up her water at them in a mock toast, laughing before taking a long swig.

Moments later another guy approached her. Disappointingly, he too was of the living. Again, Allie made quick work to get rid of him, keeping herself available to any dead who happened to decide to show.

She cocked a brow at Sebastian and shrugged, wiggling her foot.

"She said to tell you it must be the boots the boys like."

Knowing Allie put the sarcastic comment into Constantine's mind, Sebastian arched a brow regally. "Did she?"

Allie watched him warily when he stood and strode over to her. He whispered in her ear. Her eyes went as wide as saucers and her breath caught in her throat.

When he returned to the bar, leaving Allie shaken at the table, Constantine looked at him. "What did you say to her?

"None of your goddamn business," he shot back smoothly. "Trust me when I say Allie will never look at those boots the same way again."

* * *

After another hour of wasted time, Allie got tired of watching Sebastian watch her. Besides, her ass went numb from sitting on it for so long, always an indication it was time to wrap the party and go home.

What a waste of a perfectly good night.

Allie stood and stretched before maneuvering her way through the crowd back to the Templars. The bomb Sebastian dropped in her ear earlier still rang loudly in her mind.

She glanced down at her boots and laughed, knowing she'd never look at them the same again.

But she was damn sure she'd wear them again to torture Sebastian for what he'd said.

"Tired of getting hit on by boys in puffy shirts?"

She gave Sebastian a face that clearly proclaimed she was not amused by his sarcasm. "Just plain tired, actually."

"Here I thought you were enjoying all the attention."

"Clearly, you don't know me." She squeezed herself between the two hulking men so she could leave the empty water bottle on the bar.

"Clearly I don't."

The truth of his statement hit her as she stared at him. He knew no more about her than she knew of him. Though practically strangers, they had an undeniable bond since the first night they'd met.

Constantine was eyeing a pretty brunette standing alone at the other end of the bar. "I'm keeping your Charger. Hitch a ride with Allie."

Before Sebastian agreed or not, Constantine was already making his way toward the girl. By the time he reached her, the girl looked all but ready to jump him right there in the club.

Women obviously loved his whole badass look, since with nothing more than a lifting of his brow and a crook of his finger Constantine turned them to jelly.

Allie threaded her fingers through Sebastian's, the calluses on his palm scraping against her soft skin. She tugged him toward the door. "Come on. I promise to play nice."

Sebastian caught her easily before she moved away. He wrapped his arm around her waist and pressed her against his chest. Leaning into him, she loved the feel of him.

I can't make that promise, sunshine." His rich voice was a purr in her ear.

Allie shivered, his portentous words sending wonderful chills dancing all through her body. Lifting her arm, she reached behind his head to lightly caress the nape of his neck. She smiled wickedly at the tiny shudder she felt rip through him at her touch.

"I didn't think you would."

Chapter Nine

Sebastian stepped behind her when Allie went to fit the key into the lock of the driver's side door. His strength at her back, his arms coming around her, caused her hand to go limp and her breath to catch in her throat. The wonderfully cool feel of him against her caused everything in her body to come alive, especially when he traced the exposed part of the tattoo on her back with the tip of his finger. His tender touch nearly undid her.

"A Templar sword."

He sounded mystified by what was inked onto her back.

That he never noticed the pommel of the sword bore a red cross pattee surprised her, but then she remembered how little they were together since they first met and how he avoided her when they were. Besides, it was only recently warm enough to wear tops revealing enough to show the tattoo.

"I got it after Constantine and Raphael saved my life." She shrugged as if it wasn't a big deal when in fact, it was. Getting the tattoo was an incredibly emotional experience, every moment of the ordeal lost in the moment when she thought she was going to die and her friends rushed in and saved her life. "I wanted to honor them. A Templar's sword seemed the best way."

"It's beautiful."

The way he said it sent tiny chills traveling over her skin. "Thank you."

Unable to resist the temptation, Allie stepped back into him. It felt so good to have his strength at her back.

"Do you have any idea how badly I want you?"

Sebastian's voice was thick with need. His words wove their way through her body, settling at the juncture of her thighs. It caused a delicious pressure there, which she desperately needed him to relieve.

Allie hoped he wanted her as much as she wanted him. "I think I can imagine."

She threw her head back, resting it on his shoulder and groaned. The movement exposed her throat, which Sebastian caressed. He rubbed his cheek on her hair, breathing in deeply, smelling her. When she felt him grind his erection against her ass, her knees went weak. If he wasn't supporting her with the arm wrapped around her, she would have crumbled to the ground.

The way he held her, she felt how huge he was—and how hard. Her body undulated for him, for what she knew he could do to her with the long length of him.

His voice wove through her when he spoke quietly. "I want to use my entire body to bring you pleasure."

Oh God…

Allie's mouth ran dry and her legs nearly buckled at the images racing through her mind. It was any woman's sweetest fantasy come to life. All she had to do was reach out and grab it.

Her limited sexual experience couldn't even begin to comprehend all the wonderfully wicked things he could do to her, but she was more than willing to find out.

"Sebastian…"

His name came out on a sigh as his fingers traveled over the column of her throat.

"I love my name on your lips." His head dipped and he placed a feathery kiss on her bare shoulder. His cool lips made her shiver with a delicious thrill. "Do you know what I would love even more on your lips?"

Allie was beyond words. All she could do was shake her head.

He traced the line of her jaw with his thumb. "My mouth."

Oh dear God…

Sebastian turned Allie around and looked down into her flushed face. The temptation of her parted lips was too much for any man to resist.

He certainly wasn't just any man.

Being celibate for three hundred years was a hell of a thing when confronted with his desire for Allie.

With the resolve of a warrior heading into battle, Sebastian knew it was time to stop the bullshit and claim what belonged to him.

Letting go of the invisible chains binding him, he refused to hold himself back any longer. Looking into her eyes, he hesitated for only a moment before he claimed her mouth in a fierce kiss that rocked them both. The keys slipped from Allie's fingers, landing at her feet. She gripped his shoulders, her fingernails biting into the flesh as she whimpered into his mouth.

All civility was stripped from him when he engulfed her in his arms and crushed her against him. Her soft breasts pressed into him, her heartbeat strong enough that he felt it pumping wildly against his own chest. The scent of her desire came to him in rich waves, filling his senses as he fought the losing battle of control.

Realizing Allie was forced to stand on her tiptoes to accommodate his height, he leaned forward so she was again flatfooted. Once she had her footing she wrapped one leg around him. The heat of her seeped through their clothing to touch the part of him he ached to bury deep inside her.

Growling into her mouth, Sebastian inhaled deeply, taking her breath into himself. Needing more contact with her, he gripped her leg and held it against his hip. He crushed his pelvis against hers, the bare flesh of her thigh under his calloused palm warm with life.

It would be so easy to slip off her panties, unzip his jeans and slide into her. The thought of taking her body under the night sky, the moon lending an alabaster glow to her flesh moved him closer to madness.

Lost in her, in the taste of her mouth and the feel of her body against his, Sebastian felt her need throbbing through every part of her. Her desire for him was a physical hurt in his own body as he ached to sheath his length in her. He needed to feel the warmth of her body surround him.

As his sexual need for Allie reached feverish heights, the bloodlust rose in its wake. Groaning when it hit his gut with the force of a truck, his mouth ran dry at the same moment. A splash of reality, it brought him out of the raging desire. Reminded him that they weren't alone, but in full view of the road and the small group of people who stumbled out of The Gate.

If they didn't stop now, they would pass the point where he could.

As much as he liked to think he was in complete command of himself, around Allie, he had little to no control over his raging desires.

Sebastian pulled away from her grudgingly, smiling at the way Allie fell back against the car breathlessly. She stared at him with eyes hooded with desire, a smile on her swollen lips.

"If you keep kissing me like that I'm going to club you over the head and drag you back to my lair like some horny cavewoman."

Though he tried to hold it back, Sebastian let out a hard laugh. Leave it to her to say something like that.

With some distance between them, he was able to focus his senses on things other than her. The night crept back into him, had him focusing on the things he missed when he was lost in her.

The pump of the club's music and the loud din of voices took the place of the thundering sound of her heartbeat. He felt the impact of Constantine's bloodlust and sexual need come at him, heightening his own.

Yet beyond all that, past the scents and sounds of the night, Sebastian felt something else moving through him. A subtle shifting in the air, faint enough that he knew if his senses weren't so aroused he might have missed it entirely.

Instantly on guard, Sebastian bent down and retrieved Allie's keys. Once he handed them to her, he went to push her behind him. She held her ground, a concerned frown drawing her brows together.

"What's wrong?"

He glanced over the roof of the SUV. If he had to get her out quick her truck wasn't going to cut it. Glancing at his Charger, parked clear across the large lot, he knew they couldn't reach it in time, especially not when four renegades emerged from the thicket of trees across the narrow road.

Four against one was hardly a challenge for Sebastian. Yet, with Allie here he wasn't going to attempt to go at this one alone. Having been in enough battles throughout history, he knew firsthand how quickly things could get out of control. He'd not take a risk with Allie's life, no matter how badly he'd love the chance to take these ragtag bastards out—just for the sport of it.

His upper lip curled back, his fangs bared fiercely. "Looks like our party is about to be crashed."

"Vampire?" The tremor in her voice was the only indication she wasn't as calm as she appeared. His woman put on a brave face that would do any warrior proud.

"Renegades." He clarified, pluralizing the word.

"Shit," she swore, stepping closer to him. "How many?"

"Four."

"Leave it to a renegade to ruin a good time."

If Allie said that at any other time, Sebastian would have shown her how much he appreciated her dry humor. With four vampires quickly approaching them, now wasn't the time.

The vast expanse of shadowy woods across the road made an ideal hideout. The renegades must have been lying in wait for the perfect victim to come stumbling drunkenly out of the club. They should have kept on waiting, since it was their foolish mistake to think to take him on.

The assholes had to sense his strength, which meant they arrogantly thought to try to take out a Templar.

Peering through the dark of the Pennsylvania night, Sebastian watched them meander across the road and into the parking lot. He growled out a warning they foolishly ignored. Grinning evilly at they way they walked like they were the big bad, everything in him wanted to make them bleed for their arrogance.

He sent out a silent call to Constantine and pushed Allie behind him. She ducked behind him and pressed against his back.

"That's one fine piece of female you got with you," the leader of the bunch remarked.

The vampire looked no more than eighteen years old. With his heavy Western drawl, all he needed was a six-shooter and some chaps to look like he stepped out of a history book.

Sebastian felt cold fear run through Allie. Her hands fisted into his duster. "Guess he likes my boots too," she whispered.

Ignoring her remark, he shrugged off his duster, which she caught before it hit the ground. Unsheathing his sword, he threw the vampire a cold glare. "She's mine,"

The vampire sniffed at the air at the same time a surprised look crossed his young face. "Holy shit, boys, we got ourselves one of them Templars."

Sebastian cocked a brow. "Now what the fuck would four shits like you know about Templars?"

A dirty looking kid, obviously hung to death given the rope burns around his neck, puffed out his chest and notched his chin arrogantly. "I know enough. He don't look so tough. Does he, Poor Pete?"

That was bullshit and each one of them knew it.

Pete, the young blond standing next to him, spat on the ground. "Naw. Bet we can take him out and grab ourselves that beauty hiding behind him."

Sebastian threw the vampires a cold smile. "Please be that stupid and try."

"Aw, hell, Buck, he got him a sword. I ain't gonna go and get my head lopped off for no woman."

"Shut the fuck up, Gavin," Buck snapped. "We got no quarrel with you, Templar. Give us the girl and walk away."

Sebastian almost admired Buck's arrogance. Almost. For the most part, he found it irritating enough to have to kill him for it. "I don't think you understood me, Buck." Sebastian replied calmly. "I said the woman is *mine*."

He made sure to put enough of a promise of death in his words to have Gavin wisely looking like he was going to drop from fear.

Buck shrugged. "Have it your way. But you're outnumbered."

"Albeit not out-skilled," Sebastian threw back.

"Oh good. A fight," Constantine remarked blandly as he strolled through the parking lot as if he hadn't a care in the world.

"Holy shit." Pete's eyes widened in horror. "That's the Dragon."

Constantine inclined his head. "Always nice to meet a fan."

Pete pulled on Buck's sleeve. "Let's go, Buck. I ain't fucking with that one. She ain't worth it."

Buck backhanded Pete. "Stop being such a pussy. You got any idea what killing these two will do for our reps?"

Gavin backed away, shaking his head. "Poor Pete's right, Buck. I ain't tangling with two Templars. One maybe, but not two, and not *that* one." He jabbed a finger at Constantine.

Sebastian sighed dramatically. "Bloody hell! Why is it everyone shits themselves at the sight of you even though I'm the one holding the damn sword?"

"I look meaner."

"You are meaner," Allie supplied, peeking out from around him. Her comment earned her a nasty look from Sebastian. "Sorry, baby."

"I took out twenty Saracens when Constantine was too busy getting the shit knocked out of him to lend a hand."

Constantine grunted. "And God help us all, you've been riding that moment of glory for centuries." He nodded toward the renegades, who looked like they were going to either vomit or pass out. Pete looked like he might do both. "Let's do this quick. I'm fucking starving and I left a very willing female waiting."

Constantine reached down into his boots and pulled twin daggers free. Gavin made a sick sound in the back of his throat at the sight of those deadly blades. Poor Pete looked like he was going to drop dead from fright.

The quiet renegade, clearly too terrified to act the fool and egg on the Templars' wrath, backed up until he was practically back on the road. Only Buck was stupid enough to puff out his chest and raise his chin in an arrogant stance, which only worked to piss the Templars off even more.

Sebastian pushed Allie away. "Stay back."

She nodded. "Don't gotta tell me twice."

Hurrying behind a parked car, Allie felt it was far enough away from where the fight was going to go down. She wasn't about to get caught in the middle of this one. She may be a ghost hunter, but her skills didn't extend to fighting renegades. That's what Templars were for. They could mow those renegades down like grass. Clutching at Sebastian's duster, she held onto it as if holding it close to her was the same as holding *him* close to her. Crouched low behind the car, she peered over the hood so she could watch the fight and see her boys ending those arrogant bastards.

"We didn't mean no offense. I swear it. We got no fight with you," Pete stammered nervously.

"Bugger that. Weren't you all just talking shit?" Sebastian slowly advanced on the ragtag group.

"Look, we only wanted a quick meal."

"Instead you're going to get a quick death." Sebastian promised in a menacing tone.

Sebastian bared his fangs and gripped his sword tighter. Eager to spill blood, the centuries melted away and he was back in the Holy Land, on the threshold of battle.

A quick glance at Constantine, showed the Dragon felt the same rush of adrenaline. Every muscle in his body strained as he barely held himself in check, needing to bleed the ground with their enemy's blood.

"This is going to be too fucking easy," Constantine rasped out, his voice thick with lust for the coming fight.

In a flash of movement, the Templars attacked.

Sebastian went for Buck but Gavin got in the way. He brought his sword up, catching the young renegade across the middle. The vampire's eyes widened in shock as Sebastian's blade cut clean through him. Gasping, he fell to the ground, nearly sliced in two. Bleeding, his insides falling out, the renegade clawed at the ground in a futile attempt to get away.

Without a hint of remorse, Sebastian kicked him over and planted his booted foot on the gaping wound in his chest. The fires of battle blazing in his eyes, Sebastian sneered with evil delight as he took Gavin's head in a brutal, but clean, cut. The vampire ended in a burst of ash.

Turning, Sebastian swung at the vampire who struck at him with the katana he had hidden under his filthy macintosh. "What's your name, boy?" Sebastian asked as he countered the kid, who had the nerve to actually think he was a match for Sebastian. Though the kid wielded his weapon well, he didn't have the skill to cross blades with a medieval knight who had centuries to hone his prowess.

"Ethan."

Sebastian smiled. "Good to know. I hate to turn a man to dust without at least knowing his name."

While Sebastian and Ethan continued their fight, Constantine impaled Pete in both shoulders with his daggers. The kid, too terrified to fight, howled in pain and staggered back. Constantine slapped him to the ground before giving him a solid kick that had Pete curling into a fetal position.

Coming down on him, Constantine grabbed him by the front of his hair. "The least you could do is put up a fight."

Pete didn't even try to defend himself against the legendary Templar. He lay with his eyes closed; accepting the death he knew was only seconds away. Constantine couldn't stomach a coward.

Pulling the daggers out of Pete's shoulders, Constantine grunted in disgust, using them to take Pete's head. The vampire disintegrated into dust.

It was Buck who gave the most fight. He might not have been on the level the Templars were, but he at least had the balls to back up his smart mouth. He dared to take on Constantine in a hand-to-hand fight. Though he did his best to knock the blades from the Templar's iron grip, that wasn't going to happen.

Nothing was ever going to willingly separate the Dragon and his weapons again.

Shrugging, Constantine sheathed his daggers. "We gonna throw hands? Good. More fun for me. I get to beat the shit out of you before I end you."

Constantine proceeded to do exactly that.

As Allie watched, awed at how easy the Templars made it seem to take down four renegades, Constantine literally beat Buck near to death. If Buck were human, he wouldn't have survived even half the battering Constantine was laying on him.

Constantine hit him so many times and with such brutal force, Buck stumbled backwards. He tripped over his own feet and landed hard on his ass. He tried to fend off Constantine's booted foot. Unfortunately for him, he wasn't strong enough or fast enough to avoid being kicked until his bones cracked.

At the same time, Sebastian slowly advanced on Ethan. Even from a distance, Allie saw the glint of enjoyment glowing in the depths of his eyes. For the first time since she found herself part of the Templars' world, she saw a glimpse of what lay hidden beneath the façade of modern man to the warrior he'd been in life. He was a warrior fighting with the fires of Hell in his eyes and the strength of survival running through his body.

A swipe of Sebastian's sword cut down Ethan before he severed the vampire's head in one fluid motion. Reducing him to a pile of dust, Sebastian tossed the katana to Constantine. Dragon's branded right hand shot out, catching the weapon easily and using it to make quick work of Buck, not bothering to toy with the arrogant vampire before ending him.

The fight was over fast enough to make Allie's head spin. Knowing Constantine's penchant for violence, the quickness of the battle must be killing him.

Bending down to retrieve his blades, Constantine grunted with frustration. "I miss the days when we had worthy opponents to fight."

Sebastian wiped blood from his face, keenly aware of Allie watching from only a few feet away. He looked over at her. She was holding on to his duster for dear life. "So do I. Just not tonight."

After using the bottom of his shirt to wipe the blood from his blade, he

Midnight Sun

sheathed it before going over to Allie, making sure he was thoroughly in check when he did. The last thing he wanted was for her too see the bloodlust in him after a kill.

"Here." She handed him his duster. "You were amazing."

He threw her a lopsided grin. "I've had some practice."

Her small laugh and the hand she ran over the taut muscles of his arm managed to quiet what was left of his raging fury. It amazed him how she calmed him with nothing more than a touch.

"I bet you have, Templar."

As the fury abated the bloodlust hit Sebastian hard and fast. His gut contracted painfully and his mouth felt filled with sand. Everything remotely human inside him was overpowered by the vampire's need for blood.

He couldn't even look at Allie without seeing the faint blue veins pulsating beneath her flesh. Her heartbeat sounded loudly in his head as the smell of her blood called to him, promised to relieve the agony of need burning him from the inside out.

His fangs ached with the need to pull her to him and take her life into him. "Allie," he rasped out thickly, "I have to go."

She nodded in understanding, glancing at Constantine, who was cleaning off his daggers before replacing them in his boots. "I understand. You stay here with Constantine." He felt her dejection even as she made an effort to keep her tone blithe.

"No."

He wasn't going to let her drive away alone when there was a chance more renegades waited for the chance to strike.

That's how those pricks rolled, in groups, released in waves. A great battle tactic for success, it was also a pain in the ass as far as the Templars were concerned. They never knew if the fight was over or if an ambush lay in wait for them.

"Suit yourself, just don't think I'm giving up a vein if you lose your shit." She unlocked the driver's door then hit the master lock control. "Remember,

-89-

they'll kill you if you bite me."

Sebastian knew the "they" she referred to were the Templars. He didn't need the warning since he had no intention of feeding from her.

"Dent my car and I'll beat you to death," he threw at Constantine, who was already heading back to the club

"I'm so scared, Sage," he retorted without even a glance back before he disappeared into The Gate.

"I mean it, Dragon."

"Go away."

Sebastian relented and climbed into the truck. Arguing with Constantine was the equivalent of ramming your head against a brick wall.

Allie was already in the truck and had the radio on. An Evanescence CD was playing, the music haunting and somewhat soothing. Hopefully he'd be able to make it back to Randall Manor without the hunger completely taking control of him.

As Allie sped off down the road, taking them further away from where he could feed, he almost felt a sense of panic come over him. He leaned back against the seat, gritting his teeth as wave after wave of the bloodlust coursed through him. The rhythmic beat of the music wasn't helping him when it came to maintaining control.

"Talk to me." He pushed the words out from between his clenched teeth.

"What do you want me to say?"

Staring out the windshield, he ran a hand over his head, for a brief moment wishing he still had hair. He wondered what it would feel like to have Allie's hand run through the long brown hair he'd had before the jailers finally sheared it off.

"Anything. I don't care. Talk to me to get my mind off the hunger."

She didn't hesitate to oblige him. "Next Monday makes two years since Christian was killed."

That blurted out bit of news surprised him. Allie rarely talked about her family, especially her brother. He didn't even know how he died, only when and where it happened. "I'm sorry."

What else was he to say? What could the dead say to ease the hurt of the living when someone they loved crossed over to God?

"Don't be." He noticed her fingers bit into the steering wheel, telling him why she never spoke about her brother. The pain of his death was still tearing her apart. "He'd been addicted to heroin for years, hence my hatred of drugs. We thought we were going to lose him so many times, always dreading finding him dead somewhere. Thank God he got tired of being a slave to his addiction before he got AIDS from a dirty needle or killed himself from an overdose."

Allie, usually so animated, spoke now in dull, lifeless tones. He sensed the pain coursing through her as she related Christian's life and death to him. He knew this was something she had been keeping within her, letting her emotions fester for years.

"He entered rehab and worked the twelve step program for a year before feeling confident enough to venture out and try life as a sober man." She looked sad. It left him helpless, unable to take the sorrow from her. "He met a girl who didn't judge him about his past. She even came to his funeral. I like to believe she genuinely cared for him."

Sebastian couldn't speak, robbed of words as he sat, watching her talk. Her pain cut through him, forced away the bloodlust and replaced it with her grief.

"They were out on a date when he slipped into the street and was hit by a car. The doctors said he never knew what hit him. I don't know whether that's true or not. I hope it was. It kills me to think he was aware of getting hit and rolled under the car."

Her broken heart reached out to him, begging him ease its pain. "I'm so sorry, sunshine."

He saw she was holding back tears. "So am I," she whispered. "He was a sweet boy. But he was lost, Sebastian."

"You don't have to explain him to me, sunshine. I'm not judging him. How could I? Look at what I've become?"

Someone not judging Christian would be a first. Everyone judged him.

Including her, Allie thought guiltily.

She spent years hating him for his addiction, not merely unable but *unwilling* to separate the drug from the person. Even now, she still hated him for the lost years and the memories they would never have.

"Sorry I'm the buzz kill." She smiled weakly. "I shouldn't have gone on like that."

"Don't be, sunshine. You needed to talk about it and I needed to listen."

Changing hands on the wheel, she steered with her left, her right going to rest on Sebastian's knee. "Thank you."

"For what?"

She absently rubbed her thumb back and forth. "For being you."

Out of the corner of her eye, Allie saw the small smile pulling at Sebastian's lips. She meant what she said, she was glad the events of her life brought her and Sebastian together. With all of the Templars, actually. Funny how God took one brother and gave her back four.

The rest of the ride to Randall Manor seemed to take forever, yet it wasn't nearly long enough.

Allie was reasonable enough to know she couldn't—nor shouldn't—keep Sebastian from feeding. He needed to do it to continue his existence, even if it galled her to know he'd be taking the blood from another woman. The fact of the matter was, if she wasn't willing to let him tap a vein she better step aside so he could go do what he had to in order to survive.

It didn't mean she had to like it, however.

By the time they arrived at the manor it was plain to see the bloodlust returned to him in full force. He looked as if he was in terrible pain, which he likely was since she knew the hunger hurt them. It was also clear Sebastian didn't want to leave her when he made no move to get out of the truck after she pulled to a stop in front of Randall Manor.

"I have to go."

Reaching out to lightly stroke the side of his cheek, Allie gave him an understanding nod and a small smile. "I know, baby."

A rumbling growl came from deep within him when Sebastian cupped her chin. He captured her mouth in a hard, fast kiss. "I want it to be you, Allie," he ground out against her lips.

As soon as those words left him, he was gone.

She sat and watched as he took off on the back of his black and silver custom chopper. Her entire body was numb except for her heart. That particular part hurt so badly she wished she could claw it right out of her chest.

Tears in her eyes, Allie drove away, trying hard not to imagine Sebastian running his hands along another woman's body, coaxing her to open for him and give the one thing Allie couldn't.

She shook her head to dispel the vision, but it was no use. Her Templar bringing another woman pleasure, his mouth pressed against her neck as he took her blood into his own body, branded on her mind.

By the time she reached her house the thin thread of control she clung to in order to keep her emotions in check snapped. She hated the tears falling freely from her eyes and the pain that tore through her. This was the reason she always kept her heart to herself. It couldn't be broken if she kept it to herself.

But she had given it away. Before she even realized it happened, Sebastian owned Allie's heart. And now it was laid bare and cut to the core, the pain of it coursing through her as she dragged herself in. Through her tears she saw Lex sitting crossed-legged on the floor typing furiously away on her laptop. Barely sparing her sister a glance, she headed toward the stairs, needing the sanctuary of her room to hide away in until she could get a grip on her emotions.

When Lex looked up, the welcoming smile faded, as did all the color from her face. "Allie? What's wrong?"

Allie shook her head. One word was all it would take for that thread to snap. Taking the stairs two at a time, she only wanted to get to her room and shut herself away from the world.

Lex followed her, wringing her hands nervously. "Please talk to me, sis. You're scaring me."

Allie tossed her keys on the floor and sank down on her bed. "I'm being stupid, that's all."

She was fighting hard to hold in her tears. She didn't want to cry, afraid if she started she'd never be able to stop.

"Are you hurt?"

Allie shook her head. "Not physically, no."

It was her heart that was bleeding.

She gave her heart to Sebastian, who through no fault of his own, managed to shatter it into a million pieces.

Allie peeled off her uncomfortable Goth outfit, slipped into a large tee and men's boxers, and then climbed into bed. Lex settled in next to her. Her sister's love and support was her undoing. The thread of control snapped and a floodgate of tears spilled forth.

As Allie wept, Lex held her, rocking her gently. She whispered soothing words in her ear, as Allie had done when it was Lex who needed comfort.

That's how they stayed for the next hour. Allie in Lex's arms as she cried out her frustration and hurt over what Sebastian was out doing.

Neither of them heard the hum of the motorcycle engine coming from the open window.

Chapter Ten

Storming into Seacrest, Lucian slapped the newspaper down on the table in front of Tristan. "Another girl is missing."

Buried under a mountain of bills, Tristan looked from the picture of the young woman on the front page to Lucian, who could barely contain his frustration.

"So I've heard. I believe they said her name is Amanda Driver on the news."

"This can't go on, Tris." Lucian began pacing back and forth beside the long table. Though he couldn't age, the stress caused him to look well past the twenty-six years he'd been when he died. "If only I could get a fix on the bloody bastards! Constantine can't either. Somehow, they've managed to block themselves from us."

Tristan leaned back and steepled his fingers under his chin. "Either that or they're mobile, jumping from place to place."

"So they can go on like this indefinitely." Lucian looked about to explode with fury. Such a powder keg of emotion was never a good thing in a vampire.

"I understand your frustration, Luc, believe me I do. But now is the time to remain levelheaded. Too much is on the line for you to go off half-cocked. We have to stay focused and keep pushing the search."

Lucian stabbed his finger at the face of Amanda. "Tell that to her," he thundered. "If she's not fucking dead already."

Remaining calm in the face of Lucian's fury, Tristan stood and clapped a hand on Lucian's shoulder, stilling his furious pacing. "Most likely she *is* dead, or else wishing to God she was. All we can do is continue on and hope no other women are going to die before we locate the Daystar."

Lucian turned on Tristan. All the rage inside him was reflected in the abysmal depths of his eyes. "The Daystar could be nothing more than a bloody myth for all we know." He let out a frustrated, but empty, breath.

"You know full well we wouldn't have been sent here if the Daystar was mere myth. You of all people know how important it is to hold fast to faith. Don't go down that road again, Knight. Only Hell awaits you at the end of it."

Lucian's eyes took on a haunted glow as the memories of the past came back to him. Those long tortured years at Chinon, their death and damnation, they all rushed to him until he felt as if a hand were squeezing his dead heart.

Fighting past the sensation, he leveled a glare at Tristan. "I'm being played with and you know it," he ground out roughly. "I don't like someone headfucking me."

"And I do?" Tristan rose and faced off with him. For the first time in years Guardian's civility stripped away to reveal the vampire beneath the façade. "Think you I don't want to rush headlong into war with this scum? I'd love nothing more than to cut down the legions of renegades until every last one of them is in Hell where they belong." He calmed somewhat, backing away as the silver fire ebbed in his eyes. "But that's not going to happen, since all I can do is stay cloistered behind these fucking walls with my hands tied as innocent lives are taken and souls stolen."

As the Guardian, he couldn't stray too far from Seacrest or stay away too long. Not when all of their souls depended on him to fulfill his duty and guard the relic he was chosen to protect.

In the face of Tristan's vehement frustration, Lucian sank down on a chair and dropped his head in his hands. His long, dark brown hair fell forward, curtaining him as he fought back his anger.

Shaking off Tristan's hold, he turned on him with fangs bared. "You didn't see those girls, Tristan. You didn't see what they did to them. You didn't feel the emptiness of the absence of their souls." He lifted his head and rubbed his hands over his eyes, trying to dispel what he saw. "Jesus Christ, I can still see the vacant look in their eyes."

"Easy, Luc."

Lucian stood, feeling the night crawl over him, hand instinctively curling around the hilt of the ever-present sword at his hip. He cut Tristan with a blazing gaze filled with retribution. "When I find who's responsible for this, I won't leave enough pieces of them for the sun to burn."

"Like I said, we'll find them and set free the women's souls. You'll have your vengeance for their lives. We all will."

God pity the monster once the Knight found him, for no Templar would.

Chapter Eleven

Five long and lonely days passed since that night at The Gate. Five seemingly endless days since Allie last saw Sebastian and all she could think about was how much she missed him.

Unfortunately they'd all been busy with their own tasks as they desperately tried to narrow the search for the Daystar while turning Damascus upside down in a mad dash to find Amanda Driver. It kept Allie and Sebastian from finding time to meet during the night.

The upside to the situation was she got to spend the days with her sister. Having Lex around gave her such a sense of peace she wondered how she'd get through a day once she returned to Florida—if she returned, that is.

Though she hadn't seen Sebastian in nearly a week, they talked by phone every night. Right before dawn he'd call her, drowsy as the new day robbed him of strength and consciousness. He wanted her voice to be the last he heard before he slipped into death-like sleep. Allie stayed awake until he called, before collapsing into bed to catch a few hours sleep before she had to wake and begin her search for the Daystar all over again.

All her hours spent searching the Internet, hunting down ancient texts, pouring through tomes, produced the only new fact thus far, that the Daystar was Druid in origin. Besides that, she found no other information.

The Daystar was buried so deep in history it was like trying to find the proverbial needle in a haystack.

Much of her research brought her back to the Order of the Knights Templar. Their own history was steeped in mystery, which left them open to crossing paths with other avenues of history, the Daystar being one of them.

With so many questions swirling in her head about the Order, it nearly killed her not to ask. First and foremost she burned to know if the Knights Templar truly possessed the Holy Grail. Next was the Arc of the Covenant and King Solomon's gold, which would explain away where all their wealth came from, a strange thing given the monks all took a vow of poverty.

Basically, the Templar vampires could, in one conversation, end centuries of historical debate.

Unfortunately, even with all of their knowledge, none of them knew jack-shit about the Daystar.

Long hours were spent scouring the Internet trying to find where the legend of the Daystar began. She hoped if she learned that, she'd eventually travel down a path which would lead to the object itself.

Since time was against them, she doubted she'd find out enough to save Amanda's life. That was left to the Templars, who went out each night trying to find her. They left no stone unturned, no abandoned structure unexplored. Still, they found nothing, as if the poor girl simply vanished into thin air.

Lying on her stomach, arm hanging off the bed, Allie cracked open one bloodshot and bleary eye. It took a second for her to focus on the clock but when she did, she groaned long and loud. As usual she'd slept the morning away, which meant she'd have to skip eating and rush around like a maniac to get to the Miller's bed and breakfast.

The B&B was in Galilee, which was the next town over from Damascus. Still, she couldn't be late, so she'd have to hurry to get there by four.

If the stereo blasting down in the living room was any indication, Lex was awake already. With Lex in tow, she'd be glad for the extra pair of hands. Working alone, it was hell dragging in and setting up all her equipment, which was why she usually only used the hand-helds. Lord knew half the stuff she'd spent a small fortune on she couldn't even lift.

After the Millers, Allie had one more appointment scheduled for the day.

One with a sad, lost, and lonely old lady whose mind, hopefully, was fully functioning when Allie got there…

* * *

Once the sun dipped bellow the high Appalachian Mountain range, Sebastian woke feeling no better for having slept the day away. If anything, he felt worse than last night.

He spent the days tossing and turning restlessly, the dreamless death-like sleep evading him. When he did manage to slip into unconsciousness, he still wasn't given a reprieve from the hurt on Allie's face. His sleep was haunted by tear-filled emerald green eyes that reflected the betrayal infecting her heart.

Rolling onto his back, Sebastian let out a low groan, every bone in his body aching. His head pounded as if someone was banging on his brain with a hammer, always a wonderful feeling, he thought grumpily. Lightheaded and weak, if he weren't already dead he'd swear he was on his way to the grave.

The condition he was in now was exactly how he felt after a particularly long and brutal battle back in his living days. Sore as hell, bone-weary, and miserable. Only difference was, back then he enjoyed the feeling since it meant he survived another battle with all his body parts intact—for the most part anyway. He didn't count the gaping wounds Tristan or Lucian had to sew closed to save his sorry hide from bleeding to death. He didn't dare let Constantine or Raphael anywhere near him with a needle. He'd rather do battle with a Saracen than have either of them stitch him.

As much as Sebastian enjoyed the modern conveniences of this age, he didn't belong here. This wasn't the world he was meant for. None of the Templars were. They came from a time when a man's hand was made for a sword. When battle meant having to look into your enemy's eyes before you killed him. A brutal time filled with violent men and, it was a world he'd always belong in.

He missed the feel of good horseflesh and the quiet that came from the lack of machinery, which was so much a part of the modern day-to-day living.

The land had a newness to it back then, when the earth was still largely untouched by the hand of man.

Born into a long line of warriors, he was trained from birth to hold a sword. He could sit a horse before he learned to walk. He was as out of place in this cushioned era as a modern man would be in his. Hell, half the men born today wouldn't last a day in his time.

It felt like only yesterday when his father took away his wooden training sword and gave him his first real blade. The pride that pumped through his young body was something he'd never forget.

On that day, he'd gone from child to man in the span of one breath to the next. From that moment on, he trained every day, year after year, injured, broken, and sick near to death—none of it mattered. Nothing would keep him from knowing a single day without the feel of his sword in his hand.

For years he pushed his body past almost inhuman limits for the chance to face off against his sire and know the son surpassed the father. It was what he trained for, what he bled for, and on the day he bested his father on the lists, Sebastian knew true glory.

That same night he left Rydon Castle to follow Tristan on Crusade.

Only sixteen when they went off to fight for God halfway across the world, in today's time it was unthinkable. Neither boy could resist when Guy Sinclair, a charismatic young lord, passed through their lands in search of able bodies to join his army. They'd relinquished all they'd had, willing to sacrifice even their own lives, to travel to the Holy Land in search of glory.

To this day, he never returned to Rydon Castle.

The trek to the Holy Land was one Sebastian would never—could never—forget.

They traveled for six grueling months to reach a place so hot and dry, Tristan often joked Guy was leading them right into Hell. In retrospect, Tristan hadn't been off the mark about that.

Hell was exactly what they found.

The things he'd been forced to do while serving in the Order haunted him to this night. The blood he'd shed, both guilty and innocent alike, still stained his hands. When he closed his eyes he saw the mutilated bodies of those he'd killed in the name of God—even long after he stopped believing in the Lord.

Their damnation came with few restrictions, unlike when they'd been in the Order. There were times the lack of sex damn near drove him mad. Thankfully, abstinence wasn't among their current precincts. Forcing his body to move, Sebastian dragged himself out of bed. He flinched as the pain shot through him. *Jesus Christ*, he wanted to kick himself right in the ass for putting himself through this torture. One quick feed and the pain would go and he'd be back to his full strength.

Sad green eyes kept him from it.

His body needed the blood of more than just the small and sickly animals he'd been feeding from these past nights. He needed strong blood. Human blood. Nothing less would ease the pain and fully sate his hunger.

Feeding from animals left him weak and vulnerable, which was a dangerous state given the threat all around them.

It forced him to feed more often. Every night, actually, and still it wasn't enough.

Nevertheless, he couldn't bring himself to feed from a human. No matter how much his body needed it, he couldn't imagine touching any woman but Allie. The thought made his skin crawl with revulsion.

He missed her.

She was doing everything within her power to find the origins and location of the Daystar. Her perseverance was impressive. The woman was relentless.

The Templars, meanwhile, went out every night in search of the renegades responsible for the murders of those women. So far, they found nothing, which meant tonight was one more night Sebastian would have to go off and feed to have enough energy to go with the others on the hunt.

Heading into the bathroom, Sebastian took a hot shower, standing under the blistering water long enough to almost chase away the cold.

Almost.

Until God gifted him his soul back, the cold was part and parcel with the whole damnation thing. Only human blood had the power to ease it, and then only for a short time.

In the middle of getting dressed, Sebastian felt Allie as keenly as if she were right beside him. He didn't bother to question the elation her presence filled him with.

A moment later he heard the doorbell ring. He felt the anticipation surge through Allie as she waited none-too patiently for someone to let her in. He was about to go and do exactly that when he heard Raphael's door open and bang shut. He stomped down the stairs, muttering about needing more sleep as he went.

Like the storm she was, Allie blew into Randall Manor. "Hey, Red." Raphael sounded shot to hell with exhaustion. "You're a welcome sight to wake to."

In her excitement, Allie pushed right past Raphael. She didn't even catch his complement. "Do you want to know how Paul Buckman died?"

Raphael, still groggy, rubbed the sleep from his eyes. She tried to ignore that he wore only dark gray sweat pants, the rest of his body on display in all its medieval muscular glory. Thank God her affections lay elsewhere or else Allie would be a goner.

Her gaze went directly to the puckered scar over his heart. She tried not to stare at the spot where Michael pierced him and took his soul.

All of the Templars bore the scar, same as they shared the identical brand on the top of their right hand.

"Who the hell is Paul Buckman?" His voice was still gravelly from sleep.

"Alice Buckman's husband." Seeing he was still clueless, she added, "Alice as in *Grandma* Buckman."

His brows shot up in surprise. "Kenny's grandmother?"

She brushed past him, striding through the house. "You know another Grandma Buckman?"

Passing the stairs, Allie couldn't help but give a quick glance up them, wondering if Sebastian was awake yet or not.

God, how she missed him. If she possessed half the mettle she pretended to have, she'd march right into his room and lay claim to him once and for all.

The awful truth was, when it came to Sebastian, Allie was all bark and no bite. Drop her in a haunted house at midnight and she'd be fine, thank you very much. Put her alone in a room with Sebastian and she was awkward and unsure.

Storming into the kitchen, Allie flipped on the dim overhead and dropped down on a chair at the small, round breakfast table. "I paid Grandma Buckman a visit today. Can you guess what I found out?"

"I've no idea."

Raphael sat on the chair across from her. He ran a hand over his face, looking like she did when she was in need of a strong cup of coffee.

She leaned in close, as if she were about to reveal the secrets of the universe to him. "Her husband was killed by vampires. They came for a scroll he bought at an antique shop a year prior to his murder."

"Let me guess. This would be the same scroll that piece of parchment came from?"

Surprised to hear Sebastian's voice, Allie darted her gaze to the doorway. All the breath left her lungs when she saw how gorgeous he looked. Tired, but gorgeous.

A black button down hung open to reveal a smooth expanse of pale, muscular chest. Her gaze locked on the scar over his heart long enough to wish she could kiss it away.

The snug blue jeans encasing those massive tree-trunk legs rode low on trim hips. Following the length of those jeans down, she saw he was barefoot. Normally Allie couldn't stand feet, but seeing Sebastian's, she wasn't at all surprised to see even his feet were nice.

As she drew her gaze back up, she couldn't help but notice the bulge of his groin. The man was certainly blessed, she thought wickedly, remembering the feel of him when he'd ground his body into hers.

When she dragged her eyes back to his face, she nearly died of mortification at his knowing grin. Leaning back, Allie did her best to maintain her composure after getting caught gawking at his crotch.

"You bet it is. When vampires tried to take the scroll, Paul fought them. In the scuffle, the bottom corner tore away. It's the same corner Kenny found."

Not a hint of reaction passed over Sebastian's features. His expression might as well have been set in stone.

"What else did Grandma Buckman say?"

Forcing her hungry gaze from Sebastian, Allie looked back at Raphael to answer his question. "Nothing. As quick as her memory came, is as quick as it went. I was surprised I even got that much out of her. Do me a favor, guys. If I ever get that bad when I'm old, put me out of my misery. Don't let me suffer like that."

Her saying that finally put some expression on Sebastian's face. A flash of irritation crossed his features. "How did she know it was vampires who killed her husband?"

"The poor woman went on and on about the demons who killed her Paul," she explained, ignoring the way Sebastian practically barked the question out at her. "She claimed they had unholy glowing eyes and fangs. I think it's safe to say she was talking about vampires."

Raphael sat back in the chair and stretched out his long legs. "So, what do we do now?"

"Nothing. We're back at square one," Sebastian announced, his tone laced with frustration.

"How so?" Allie countered. "At least we know there's a scroll floating around out there. That's more than we knew this morning."

He cocked a brow at her. "Care to tell me where to begin looking for it?"

Good point. "Okay, so we're back at square one,"

Raphael stood and slapped his hands against his thighs with a huff. "Well, I'm going to get dressed. You'll be home tonight, right, Sage?"

If Allie didn't know better she would swear Sebastian threw Raphael the hairy eyeball.

"You're not going out with them tonight?"

Sebastian released a long, drawn out sigh after a short, yet pregnant pause, almost as if he were resigning himself to the answer he planned on giving her. "No, I'm not."

"Oh."

After Raphael left to get dressed, Allie suddenly felt shy with Sebastian staring down at her. "I guess I'll go,"

She made no motion to stand. He made no motion to walk away. "How's your sister?"

"Good." Allie was pleasantly surprised he remembered that her sister was in town. "She wanted to go out tonight but I told her that wouldn't be a good idea. The last thing I need is for her to be running around unprotected."

"I'm sure she wasn't happy about that."

"Actually, once I told her about what's been going on, she understood."

"Smart girl."

"Yeah, well, Lex is the smart one." She stood; ready to leave Sebastian to whatever it was he planned on doing tonight. "Out of the two of us, I got all the balls and she got all the brains. Guess that's why I'm Crazy Allie."

"Prove it."

"Huh?" Allie was clearly bewildered.

Sebastian stalked over to her. He leaned down close to her ear and she shivered deliciously. "The logical thing would be for you to leave, sunshine. It would take balls for you to stay here with me."

His hand reached out to her, the seal burned into his flesh drawing her attention. The stark reminder of his past and what he was might have frightened another woman. But not Allie. Looking back into his face, the sight of the fangs, which he made no attempt to conceal, caused her heart to race with excitement.

Any hint of resistance quickly melted away at the look of raw need burning in the depths of his silver eyes. The fire was for her, and with all of her soul, she wanted to be burned by it.

His eyes narrowed and he offered her the shadow of a wicked grin, holding the promise of the pleasure he planned on bringing her. At that moment she knew she'd rather be here with Sebastian than anywhere else in the world.

Taking his hand, she followed him up the stairs. Passing the closed doors, she heard the Templars within moving around as they readied themselves for their hunt. Allie felt a stab of awkwardness at the fact that they weren't alone. Sebastian must have felt her unease since he gave her hand a gentle squeeze of reassurance.

When they reached his room, he released her hand and stood aside to let her pass. She crossed the threshold with the distinct sensation things were never going to be the same for her after tonight.

Chapter Twelve

Finality came over Allie when Sebastian closed and locked the door to his room. She felt lost to the world. Only the two of them mattered when he turned to her and pinned her with his profound stare. A single brow lifted at her, a silent dare. He waited to see what she would do, change her mind and leave or stay and open herself to him as he brought her deeper into his world.

Too deep to leave once this night played out.

The glow from the candles he'd lit gave a cozy atmosphere to an otherwise austere room. The vanilla aroma wafting from them, combined with the wonderful spicy scent belonging to Sebastian filled her head and made her giddy with anticipation. The erotic art of Luis Royo staring down at her lent a wonderfully wicked feel to Sebastian's lair.

And Sebastian himself…

He was everything dark and mysterious, her most secret fantasies brought to reality in the form of a man so handsome it left her breathless. Raw sex and strength, she wished to hold to this moment, a calm before the storm, always.

"You can leave, Allie." His deep voice, resonating, flowed through her like a wonderfully warm wave. "I'll never keep you here against your will."

"I know."

"I'll never hurt you."

She smiled. "I know that too."

He moved to the entertainment center dominating the wall opposite the bed, the focus of which was a huge plasma television. He turned on the stereo and Live's "I Alone" played low. One of Allie's favorite songs, it sang of all the things she felt but didn't dare to tell him.

He turned back to her, head lowered, and regarded her through intense eyes. Right then she knew exactly how prey felt being stalked by a predator.

"Come here."

Of course Sebastian would want her to come to him. More than merely his arrogance demanding it, he asked her for an acceptance of what he was that ran deeper than mere words.

She went to him without a hint of reservation.

Stepping into his arms felt like coming home. He wrapped around her in an embrace and she melted into him. Slipping her arms around his waist, she wanted to touch all of him to make sure this was all real.

To make sure *he* was real.

Allie was half afraid she'd wake alone in her room, this having been nothing more than a wonderful dream. The thought terrified her. Finally where she wanted to be, she hugged him tighter, wishing she could hold on to the moment forever.

Standing in his arms, Allie felt as if a million butterflies were let loose in her stomach. Now that she was here with him, she had no idea what to do. This was no ordinary man. He had centuries of sexual conquests to his credit. She didn't have an impressive list.

Her rep as a nutball limited her in the sex department to the loser she gave her virginity to and Jude. Neither was worth bragging about, nor did she have such extraordinary sex with them that she walked away having learned a trick or two.

His much more…extensive…sexual experience intimidated the hell out of her. What could she possible do to him hundreds of women before hadn't already done? What pleasure could she bring him that wouldn't seem mundane in comparison to what he must have known before her?

Leaning away, yet keeping her in his hold, he frowned. "I can feel anxiety in you. Why?"

Allie blushed, hating that he could sense her emotions. "I'm being silly, that's all. No worries."

He clearly wasn't buying the bullshit. "Talk to me, sunshine. What's bothering you? Do you want to leave?"

She felt him tense as he waited for her answer. "No, of course I don't want to leave," she assured him. "Look, the thing is, I may be daring about the paranormal stuff, but when it comes to sex I'm a big coward."

He cocked a brow at her. . "So, I've discovered the one thing with the power to unnerve the fearless Allison Parker."

Fearless? Hardly. *Nervous?* Definitely.

"What can I say? Not all of us have centuries of experience under our belts. Sorry if I'm not all calm and cool about this."

He seemed to be weighing what to say next. "Neither have I."

His quiet admission knocked the wind right out of her. "You haven't?"

Sebastian shook his head slowly, a tortured glint flaring in his eyes. "I've had my share of women, Allie, I won't lie about that, but for the past three hundred years I've been celibate."

Allie thought she actually felt her jaw hit the floor. Closing her gaping mouth, she tried to appear unfazed, but she was stunned. *Three hundred years?* She couldn't begin to fathom what could make him decide such a thing. "Are you serious?"

"Decidedly so."

This was too incredible. "Why in the world…?"

He cut her off by placing a finger over her lips. "Now isn't the time to talk about this."

Biting back the million questions that demanded answers, she had to agree with him. The time for talk would come later.

He removed his finger from her mouth, but not before gliding it over her bottom lip. She tucked said bottom lip between her teeth and worried it as he stood staring down at her as if he expected something from her.

God, she felt so unsure of herself. "I don't know what you want from me."

Sebastian leaned down and softly rubbed his cheek against hers. She heard him inhale deeply. He smelled her hair. "Everything you have to give me, sunshine." Raising his head, he trailed a finger along her cheek and jaw. "I've wanted you since the night I first saw you."

For the second time, Allie's mouth dropped open in shock. The man kept dropping these bombs on her. "You've got to be kidding me."

"I'm deadly serious."

"Then why the hell have you been ignoring me all this time?"

He placed a feathery kiss on her forehead before answering. "You were a temptation I didn't dare give in to."

His fingers slid down to the column of her throat, causing a wonderful shiver to pass over her. She fisted the back of his shirt in her hands, clinging to him desperately as he slowly lowered his head and captured her lips. His mouth was so cool, yet in his kiss was a fire that burned hot enough to set them both ablaze.

Needing to feel him all over her, Allie stepped into him and pressed herself against Sebastian's body. Every part of him was wonderfully hard and extraordinarily unyielding. Under her hands his body felt like stone come to life. She felt small and delicate with him, things she didn't think any man would make her feel.

She'd never had the luxury to be anything less than strong. With parents like hers and a brother and sister who relied on her, weak was not something she could afford to be. Yet with Sebastian, she was able to let it all go, trusting in him enough to relinquish her control.

Bringing her hands around to the smooth expanse of his chest, she laid her palms against his bare skin. He sucked in a hard, yet empty breath. How strange she felt no heartbeat under her hand or no warmth of a living body. Yet he was gloriously alive.

Unconsciously, her fingers went to the scar over his heart. He pulled away from her sharply. "Did I hurt you?"

"No, you didn't hurt me."

He made no effort to tell her why he jumped back. He looked tortured for a moment, but quickly pushed that emotion aside.

"I wish I could take back all of your pain."

He came back to her, shaking his head. "I don't. I wouldn't be here if my life played out differently."

He couldn't have said anything to impact her more. She felt as if her heart was going to beat clear out of her chest as a lump of emotion lodged in her throat at the magnitude of his profound declaration.

She swallowed down her emotions and blinked back her tears until they stopped threatening to spill down her cheeks. "Well then, I hate to say it, but I'm glad you're here too."

Only his Allie would be glad she was here with a creature such as himself.

He kissed the tip of her adorable nose. "It wasn't that bad."

That was a lie and they both knew it. Still, Sebastian felt it was a necessary one in order to wipe away the sadness etched over Allie's face.

Sebastian gathered Allie close, close enough for him to feel her heartbeat. As her life pounded against his chest, he recaptured her lips in a searing kiss that had her moaning into his mouth. She snaked her arms came around his neck, her fingers biting into the nape of his neck.

The scent of her need filled him, pushing him further away from civility and closer to the edge of sanity. With nothing more than the touch of her lips, she drove him dangerously close to madness.

He lifted her, forcing her to wrap her legs around his waist. Tiny, she weighed next to nothing in his arms. As he carried her to the bed, he felt a stab of anticipation, wanting this with her for months. He'd never felt the like before, never known the thrill of expectation when it came to sex.

His past dissolved in her kiss. War, death, and all the horrors he'd witnessed vanished from his mind the moment he kissed her.

Before he took his vow, sex was nothing more than a means to relieve his body's basic need. The women he'd bedded nameless and faceless, less than even a memory. Everything was different with Allie. He wanted to get lost in her, to loose himself in her lifeforce.

He broke the kiss only long enough to lay her down on the bed. Her hair spread like fire over his crisp white sheets. She reached her arms out to him, a silent plea for him to come back to her and he swore he felt his body spark to life.

No woman ever reached out for him. Only Allie. *His* Allie.

Her desire was so strong it emanated from her in rich waves that took hold of his senses and robbed him of reason.

"You aren't still nervous."

Not a question, it was a statement of fact he needed confirmed before he touched her again.

Allie validated what his senses already told him. "No, baby, I'm not nervous."

All he needed to hear, he inhaled the air, the aroma of her arousal was all around him. He climbed on the bed and kneeled over her to marvel at her beauty.

She was a gift from God.

Needing to feel her bare flesh against his, Sebastian peeled off his shirt and threw it to the floor. He flashed his fangs in a wicked grin when Allie sucked in a sharp breath. She devoured him with her eyes, making him so hard for her it hurt.

"Like what you see, sunshine?"

She cocked a brow at him arrogantly. "Hell yeah."

He laughed, loving how she matched his arrogance. He never thought a woman would exist who would dare.

He wanted to touch all of her at once. Taste every inch of her. "I don't even know where to start on you."

"Saying that was a good start."

Afraid to hurt her with his large and calloused hands, it was with an infinite gentleness born out of hundreds of years of learning how to control his strength that he was able to caress her body so carefully.

He inched Allie's tee shirt up, a smile playing on his lips as he fingered the steel hoop that pierced her navel. He loved that small ring, finding it extremely sexy.

Allie sat and reached her arms above her head so he could take off her shirt, which he did with great relish. He threw her shirt away and kneeled, dumbfounded, staring at her breasts. The white lace bra barely covered them.

"You're so small,"

Gasping out a laugh, Allie gave him a shot to the arm. "You don't tell a woman she's small when staring at her chest. It's rude. Imagine if I said that while staring at your—well—you get the idea."

His badly timed comment finally dawned on him. "I didn't mean it like that."

She gave him a small, shy smile he found adorable. "I know."

He gently ran his hands over her arms. Her skin was soft and smooth. "You're just so much smaller than me, sunshine. I don't want to hurt you."

"I'm tougher than I look and you know it."

He did know it.

What she lacked in physical strength she more than made up for mentally. His Allie was a woman with strength of wits to spare.

Sebastian's hands shook as removed her bra. As if he were opening a gift, he peeled away the bra, marveling at how beautiful her body was. Her breasts fit perfectly in his palms as he knew they would.

Her petal soft, pale pink nipples pressed against his rough palms, pulling a small whimper from her. His touch caused her eyes to close and her head to drop back. He rolled her nipples in his fingers, pinching them gently. Her throaty moan was a sound so erotic he'd sacrifice his life a thousand times over to hear it again.

Wanting no barriers between them, he rid them of the rest of their clothes. Though she was a bit shy, Sebastian quickly let Allie know he wouldn't tolerate her holding back from him. He wouldn't allow her to be shy about her body.

Her flesh was smooth and pale, her tattoos standing out in sharp contrast to the flawlessness of her. If he weren't so damn hot for her, he would take the time to examine each piece of art on her in great detail—with his fingers and tongue as well as his eyes.

But not now when he was too far gone with need to hold himself back any longer.

Pushing her back on the bed, Sebastian covered her with his body, making sure to catch his weight on his arms. God help her if he actually gave her his full weight. He'd crush his fiery ghost hunter.

This was exactly as he'd imagined her in his fantasies, warm and open to him. Her arms came around him and he felt all his strength dissolve in her tender hold. That she could be so abrasive with the rest of the world and so feminine and gentle with him made him almost feel as if his heart was going to splinter apart from emotion.

Never a man given to strong sentiment, it was a wonder to him that Allie could pull such strong feelings from him, and in so short a time. Astounded by her, it said much for the impact she had on him.

He settled himself between the warmth of her thighs as her hands traveled over his back. She tickled him with her nails, grazing his flesh until he had chills running through him and he was damn near shaking with need.

He seized her mouth in a deep, bruising kiss. Her nails bit into his back and he growled low in his throat. Snaking an arm under her, he lifted her hips and ground into her. Her heat made his cock so hard it hurt. He wanted to thrust into her to ease the pain of his desire and feel her wet warmth close around him.

Still, Sebastian forced himself to hold back until he tasted the one thing that pushed him past reason.

Allie's blood.

He caught her with his fangs again. In the back of his mind he wondered if he hadn't done it on purpose to get a taste of her.

"I'm sorry," he ground out from between clenched teeth as he fought for control.

Allie was clearly baffled. "For what?"

Sebastian wiped away the small smear of blood on her chin. "I cut you again."

The look she gave him said she thought he'd lost his mind. "You stopped kissing me for that? And they call me crazy!"

He licked at his fangs. So, his woman didn't want him to stop? Who was he to not oblige her?

He kissed a trail down Allie's throat, lingering at the furious throb of her vein. He could hear the roar of her blood as her heart hammered wildly. They were the most amazing sounds he'd ever heard. They were the sounds of her life and he wanted—no, he needed—to take a piece of that vitality into himself.

He used his entire mouth to make a path down to her breasts. His lips, his teeth, his tongue, dragged small whimpers from her. When he caught her hard nipple between his teeth she nearly shot off the bed. He held her down and rolled his tongue around it until she cried out and palmed the back of his head. She arched her back, pushing herself against him, needing more of his touch.

When Sebastian trailed even lower down her body, to flick light kisses over her stomach, she closed her eyes and giggled. "That tickles." It came out as a breathy whisper as he played with her navel ring.

He ran his hand up her thigh, nudging her legs open. Sebastian felt her stiffen. "Easy, baby."

The delicious scent of her desire filled his senses. The beauty of her body overwhelmed him. With his senses filled with her, he was dancing on a dangerous edge of control. When he covered her sex with his mouth, the taste of her delicious, she said his name on a sigh. The sound was amazing and urged him on to tease her with his lips and tongue.

Allie let out a guttural moan and threw her head back against the pillow. One hand fisted in the sheets next to her thighs, the other cupped the back of his head. Writhing on the bed as he laved at her, he nearly came undone over her unbridled response to him.

Needing more of her, Sebastian grabbed her ass and lifted her hips higher. It gave him better access to her body, opening her so he could devour her at his leisure.

Struggling to maintain his control, he marveled at how sweet and rich her taste was. It reminded him of the honey-treat he'd snuck when he was a boy.

Well rewarded for his effort to worship her with his mouth, he felt her thighs tremble as she neared her peak. The force of her pleasure overwhelmed his senses.

Knowing she was close enough to climax that all he had to do was nudge her a bit further, he wanted to turn her desperate whimpers into cries of passion. Smiling against her body wickedly, the warrior in him came to the forefront and pushed aside his civility. Like when he used to charge into battle, he strengthened his resolve and pressed forward, driving her to soaring heights with his entire mouth and a few fingers.

The cry he pulled from her when she reached orgasm echoed throughout the quiet manor.

Beyond thought and words, Allie shivered as wave after wave of pleasure washed through her. She finally understood what she'd been missing.

If anyone was going to bring her body to such pleasure she knew it would be Sebastian. The man worked magic with his mouth, as she imagined he could. Reality set in a second later, shattering her bliss when Sebastian lifted his head from between her legs. She thought she might die of shame right then and there.

No man ever did to her what Sebastian had just done. She felt laid bare right to her soul and completely vulnerable. Though not an unpleasant sensation, she was still embarrassed nevertheless…

Until she saw the cocky grin on Sebastian's face.

He quite literally glowed with pride. Or rather his eyes did, sparkling with enough satisfaction to chase away the last of her shame.

"Aren't you the smug one?" she teased breathlessly, still feeling the effects of her orgasm.

He leaned over her with an arrogant grin still on his face. "Hell yes. And aren't you the well-pleasured lady?"

She smirked back at him, caressing the side of his face. "Yes I am."

He kissed her lightly on the lips, such a delicate touch it made her heart constrict. "You're mine, Allie."

"I've always been yours."

His mouth worked, yet no words came from him. Instead, he licked his fangs, staring down at her with eyes hooded with desire. "I want to fuck you so badly I ache."

A small whimper caught in the back of her throat at his raw need. She felt how heavy and swollen with desire he was when he settled on top of her. She cradled him between her legs, her own body undulating with need. When he pressed against the juncture of her thighs and rubbed the tip of him over her already sensitive folds she shivered deliciously.

Allie ran her fingers over his lips. She touched his fang, deliberately pricking her finger to draw forth a few drops of blood, which she let fall into his mouth. His body jerked at the moment he tasted her blood, his eyes sliding closed as he let out a low growl that raised the hairs on the back of her neck.

"You give to me," she whispered to him as he ground his pelvis into her, "I give to you."

"Allie…" Her name came from him in a broken groan. "I need you, sunshine. Now."

His eyes flew open, his stare hot and hungry. Allie knew she was in for one hell of ride.

Dropping his head into the hollow of her throat, he slowly slid into her until she sheathed him fully. She cried out at the feel of him deep inside of her as her body stretched to accommodate him.

Her nails gouging him, he sucked in a sharp breath, releasing it on a low groan. He nipped her shoulder as he rocked her body with long, hard, steady strokes. No gentle coupling, this was two bodies coming together in a desperate mating. Animalistic, raw, it was everything Allie knew it would be and more.

Sebastian took what she offered him, panting wildly as he pumped into her body. She brought her legs high up around his waist, allowing him to go deeper with each long stroke into her. She squeezed her legs together, wishing she could hold him inside her forever.

He grabbed at her thigh, his fingers biting into her flesh and held it against his hip as he buried his face in her neck. She felt herself begin to shatter as he pumped his body into hers. The pleasure was so intense, Sebastian was the only clarity in a world gone hazy with desire.

His fangs grazed her and she shivered deliciously. He lifted his head, hovering over her pulsating vein. She tensed. Waiting…

Anticipation thundered through her, causing her heart to race and her breath to come out in great rasps. When he made no move, Allie writhed beneath him, grinding her body into his. She felt as if she hovered on the threshold of something as incredible as it was frightening.

She placed her hands on his cheeks and brought his head back down to her neck, tilting her head to give him better access. He went to pull back but she held him fast.

"Please, Sebastian," she begged brokenly. She wanted—no, she needed—to share this with him. To give him her blood and a small piece of her life.

And then his teeth were on her, grazing the sensitive skin of her neck and she nearly came undone. He thrust into her body as his mouth opened. She went rigid, waiting for pain even as she clung to him and whimpered his name as if it were a prayer. She felt Sebastian's body racing toward his release with each long stroke into her, his rhythm growing more frantic. She could also *feel* the hunger flowing from him to her, a horrible ache in her gut.

He lifted his head and drew back his lips. Allie closed her eyes and dug her nails into his back, terrified it was going to hurt, but not scared enough to make him stop, which she knew he would with nothing but a word from her.

She had enough faith in him for both of them.

He brought his head down, his fangs piercing her and she screamed—not in pain, but ecstasy as her body found its release.

Liquid ecstasy, that's what her blood tasted like. Warm, full of life, it flowed into him as Sebastian pulled it from her neck, wanting to stop but knowing if he did he'd die from the need for more. He felt her body shaking, her fingers digging into him. Her broken cries were sweet music as he felt her coming around him in a wonderful flood of warmth.

Her energy and life infused him with glorious heat as he continued to pump into her body, taking what she offered like the greedy bastard he was. She was a force he couldn't resist, her blood a drug he needed to survive.

Incredibly, he felt her cup the back of his head, holding him against her in a tender embrace. As she allowing him to take a part of her into his body, he gave her a piece of himself as well when he climaxed into her, dying all over again as pleasure so intense erased centuries of darkness, cold, and pain.

With a harsh cry, he pulled his mouth from her neck. The brilliance of her spirit flowed through him, warming him, bonding them in way no earthly force could.

If he still possessed his soul, he knew without a doubt she would have laid claim to it right then. For what it was worth, she already had his heart—dead though it was.

Spent, the hunger sated, Sebastian collapsed on her. Her heart beat wildly against his still chest. Her ragged breath fanned his burning flesh as her blood worked through him. Her hands stroked his back. Comforting him. Calming him.

He wished this moment could be suspended in time indefinitely.

He heard Allie whisper something brokenly.

He pulled away, afraid his weight was crushing her, and stared down at her to see her eyes were filled with unshed tears.

"Oh God, I'm so sorry, sunshine."

Those words were ripped harshly from his throat, which was still coated with her blood.

She shook her head and offered him a weak smile. "There's nothing to be sorry for, baby. I wanted you to do it."

No? How could he not be sorry seeing her smeared with blood?

He felt like a fucking monster who stole her blood. He was the same as the filthy renegade who robbed a piece of her life in order to preserve his own foul existence.

He felt her body trembling, the loss of blood chilling her right down to her bones. Tears wetted her pale cheeks. "Then why are you crying?"

She looked at him curiously. "Didn't you hear me, Sebastian?"

He shook his head. This was the first time his vampire hearing failed him.

A look of such tenderness came over her that if he still bore breath in his body, he would have been robbed of it.

Her fingers splayed over his back and she gave him a gentle hug.

"I love you, Sebastian."

Chapter Thirteen

"I hate you."

Amanda spat it out as Stephan tenderly stroked her cheek. The grotesque mockery of affection pulled her out of the stupor she'd been blessedly drifting in and out of over the last hellish days.

"Ah, you're back." His voice was like a low rumble of distant thunder, ominous and evil.

She hated his voice, with its aristocratic English accent and low, hushed tones. She hated his face, perfectly handsome. She hated the feel of his smooth hands on her body, like that of a lover's right before the pain came.

She hated everything about him except his honesty.

No matter how cruel he was to her, how much he hurt her, he never gave her false hope. No, from the night she found herself in this Hell, he made sure she knew she'd never make it out alive.

The hope she held to was of her own doing, a torture all its own as the days and nights blended together in one long stretch of misery.

Amanda stared at the ceiling blankly, the stench of her blood and filth thick in the small sweltering room. She'd give anything for a burst of fresh night air to relieve the stink and remind her of the life beyond her prison.

To ensure no sunlight invaded his lair, Stephan had the windows boarded shut, black sheets nailed over the wood. She wished she could see the sunlight once more before she died, but she knew she'd never get the chance.

This was where she was going to die, in the dark, surrounded by monsters.

And God help her, she wanted that death if it meant the pain would stop. Yearned for it with everything she was. Prayed for it over and over, until her plea became a never-ending chant inside her mind.

"Just kill me already. Please."

Amanda never thought she'd beg for death. In her innocent mind she always believed death was the worst thing that could happen to a person.

Over the last long days she realized how wrong she'd been.

Her captor's hands on her made her skin crawl. Beyond fear at this point, she didn't think twice about slapping his hand away. He tsked at her, giving her an insulted pout.

"Do I have to restrain you again?"

Stephan allowed her ropes to be removed only because she'd lost her fight. She shook her head frantically, afraid he'd tie her back up. He smiled, obviously loving her fear. Out of the corner of her eye she saw his fangs. A shiver of disgust passed through her.

Amanda turned her head and stared down at him, resting his head on her shoulder, an arm draped over her stomach. The other was tucked between them. This was the sort of embrace two lovers would share.

She wanted to vomit from the intimacy of it.

Blinking her tired eyes into focus, she shivered when he lifted his head and faced her. He looked wrong, not like the monster she knew him to be. To her delirious way of thinking he had no right to be so boyishly handsome. He should look like a demon. He should be ugly, twisted and grotesque. He shouldn't have such nice brown hair or incredibly full lips. His voice shouldn't be so rich and smooth. He shouldn't look like a knight who stepped right out of the pages of history.

Amanda choked back the bile rising in her mouth at his touch. She stared deep into his glacial silver eyes and saw no mercy in their depths.

Over the past days he tortured her ruthlessly, doing it all with a charming smile on his handsome face. She didn't know if her body could take much more. God knew her mind couldn't.

"I want to die."

He laughed, sliding a fingertip over her swollen and cracked lips. "Do you, sweet Amanda? I don't think you do," he purred softly. "You know what I think? When you trap yourself inside your mind, all you dream about is going home. You think I don't know you dream of your family, but I do. Oh yes, love, you still hold on to the hope I'll let you go."

His hand trailed down to her bare breasts. He grazed her raw nipple and she cried out in pain, her body so battered that even his gentle touch hurt.

His hand went lower to her belly. He drew small circles over her skin.

She did the one thing she ceased doing days ago.

She wept.

"But we both know the reality is, I'll never let you leave here alive."

"Why me?" Her question was a broken whisper of despair.

He smiled sweetly, his fangs gleaming. "We went over this too many times already, pet. You know I had to see if what I need is hiding somewhere inside of you."

"But I don't have it."

"I know." His fingers traveled even lower. Amanda stiffened with dread. "But it was such fun to have you as my guest. I've enjoyed you very much."

The finality in the way he said that gave Amanda hope her release was coming.

His hand cupped her intimately. He touch was repulsive, and so icy a chill passed over her.

No one ever touched her in such an intimate way other than this monster. He stole her virginity in one brutal thrust of his icy body the first night she was here. Since then, he used her again and again, until her body was beaten and raw. Until her soul was broken.

He rolled on top of her. Through her tears she saw the familiar look of hunger come over him. Yet this time, she saw more in his frosty gaze than merely bloodlust.

Finally. She saw it. He was going to end this.

He came into her then, pushing his body brutally into hers. She held back her scream of agony as the pain splintered all through her. He grunted and bared his fangs. Grabbing her wrists roughly, he pinned them over her head. The abuse lasted only moments, yet to Amanda it seemed to go on forever. She wanted to cry but her tears were gone. Wanting to scream again, her voice would not come.

All she could do was lie there helplessly and be used.

When he spoke his voice was the harsh growl of a demon. "Are you ready?"

She looked at him gratefully and nodded. "Thank you," she said that softly only a breath before his teeth pierced her throat.

Amanda's last thought was of her mother's smiling face.

She carried that vision with her as the monster took her from her suffering and finally gave her peace.

Chapter Fourteen

Allie laughed softly at Sebastian's astonished stupor. By the look on his face, she had the distinct feeling if he'd been standing when she told him she loved him, he would have fallen right on his ass.

"Too bad I don't have a camera handy," Allie teased weakly, her voice a hoarse whisper. "The look on your face is priceless. I bet the boys would love the chance to see it."

All he seemed able to do was sit in amazement. "You can't mean it."

"Yes I do."

Stretching out on the bed, every part of her ached. The cold she felt from the inside out was something she knew the Templars suffered the last seven hundred years.

How awful to always be this cold.

Sebastian sat next to her on the bed. The sheet was tossed aside—thankfully onto her—leaving him to hang out in all his naked glory. The man definitely had no shame. Not that he needed any. With a body as gorgeous as his, covering it with clothing was a crime.

She finally had a clean view of his incredible tattoo. Black and gray work, the design was a classic Dark Ages dragon crawling down his shoulder. The tail wrapped around his neck, ending behind his ear.

When she sat, Allie dragged the sheet with her. Clutching it tight around herself, she wasn't exactly as immodest around Sebastian as he obviously was around her.

She placed her hand on his knee, shocked at how warm he was—as warm as any living being. Her life lent him a temporary reprieve from the cold. That alone made it worth it for her to put aside her reservations when it came to him feeding from her.

"I wouldn't have said it if I didn't mean it," she assured him. "Not to sound pathetic, but the truth is, I've been half in love with you since I first saw you."

Sebastian made a very male grunting sound and finally looked at her. His disbelief was evident. "How can you love me?"

The incredulity in his tone pulled at her soul. "How can I not?"

Sebastian was quiet for so long, Allie grew incredibly uncomfortable under his intense stare. He seemed to be trying to see past the surface of her and glimpse into her heart.

Without a hint of warning, he grabbed her by the back of her head. She sucked in a startled breath when his hand fisted in her hair and he pulled her head toward him. From the look on his face and the hungry gleam in his eyes, for a moment she swore he was going to eat her. Instead, his mouth came down on hers in a kiss meant to claim. To dominate.

She'd never forget this kiss.

Dizzy with passion when he released her, Allie was still in her right mind enough to raise a brow at the undeniable male arrogance oozing off of him. She wanted to say something witty, but was too dazed to form a single coherent thought.

Allie finally learned what it meant to be "kissed senseless".

"You make me believe miracles are real."

Nothing else he might have said would have made her feel more cherished. "Sebastian…"

Medieval warrior, damned vampire, Templar, label him whatever you wanted and it would make no difference. He was an incredible man and she adored him no matter what he was or the things he'd done in his past.

He'd been judged enough. Now it was time for him to be accepted and loved.

Throwing herself at him, she wrapped herself around him, bear-hugging him for all she was worth. He pulled her onto his lap cradling her. This time, it was her turn to steal some warmth from him.

He tucked her into him, resting his chin on her head as his fingers idly danced over her arm. Nearly lulled to sleep by the tender touch, she snapped awake when he spoke. "Did I hurt you? Before?"

Surprisingly he hadn't. Not like when that other vampire took her blood. "Nope."

His hand petted her hair, lulling her into a totally relaxed state. "Why did you let me take your blood?"

"It felt right." Though a part of her didn't want to know the answer, the question tumbled from her before she could stop it. "How many times have you fed since the night at The Gate?"

Sebastian didn't hesitate in his answer—unfortunately "Every night."

Gone was her relaxed state. Hurt and jealousy exploded through her like the shattering of glass. "Oh. I hadn't realized it was that much."

Not being the jealous type, this was all new to her and left her heart raw with pain.

Allie never thought herself a violent person, yet her heartache made her want to smack Sebastian right in the mouth.

Disgusted, she went to climb off his lap but Sebastian stopped her. He settled her back on top of him and placed a finger under her chin. He tilted her head so he could see her face. "I haven't touched another woman since the night I found you poking around my room."

Okay—now she was confused. "But you've been feeding."

He gave a small shrug. "Animals, Allie. I've been feeding from animals."

Her jealousy died instantly. "I thought vampires couldn't do that."

"We can, but it only quiets the hunger. It doesn't sate it."

The admission floored her. Five nights had gone by since the night at The Gate. Five nights he'd suffered with the hunger. It had to have been sheer torture and so much more than she expected him to put himself through.

"You didn't have to do that."

"Yes I did." He stroked her cheek tenderly. "The thought of my hands on another woman made me sick."

That statement was worth a million "I love yous".

She gave him a fierce hug and showered his face with kisses. "Thank you,"

He smiled and she saw his fangs peeking out from behind his lips. "You're welcome."

She leaned into him, resting her cheek against his chest and wrapped her hands around his waist. "Can I ask you another question?"

"You can ask me anything, sunshine."

She smiled at the way his voice rumbled through him, echoing within him. "What's it like?"

"What's what like?"

She licked her lips, hesitating for a moment. She didn't want to open old wounds, yet she felt it was time she began to see into his world. "Being a medieval warrior in this day and age?"

Sebastian had wondered how long it would take her to start asking about his life. The curiosity must have been killing her given her inquisitive nature. If their positions were reversed and she'd been the one to see history played out before her eyes, his curiosity would burn him to know what that must have been like.

"Wrong," he admitted without hesitation. "I look around at what the world became and I feel wrong here."

She pursed her lips together and nodded gravely. "I can understand that." She gave him a curious look. "You know? I don't even know your birthday."

So many centuries had passed since he marked the day, he had to think about it for a minute. "November nineteenth, twelve eighty-two."

Allie must have done the math in her head before letting out a soft whistle. "Wow. My boyfriend is six hundred and twenty three years old. Talk about a May-December romance."

Sebastian smiled at that. He liked that she called him her boyfriend. "I was only twenty-eight when I died."

"I can't even imagine all the things you must have seen."

If he stopped to think about it, even *he* couldn't imagine the things he'd witnessed. He'd stood in the presence of kings and queens. Stood in the shadows and watched historical events unfold right before his eyes. "One day I'll tell you all the wonders I've seen."

Her smile was radiant and her laugh infectious. "That'd sure make watching the History Channel a lot more fun." Then the bomb he dropped crept back into her mind. "Why were you celibate for so long?"

Cringing inwardly, Sebastian knew Allie wasn't going to let that bit of news go too long without an explanation.

He lifted her off his lap and set her aside. Lying back on the bed, he folded his arms behind his head. She scooted over to him, making sure she was still covered by the sheet. He found her modesty adorable considering what they'd just done.

She was a bloody mess and pale as death. Dark circles shadowed her eyes, the spark gone, leaving them dull and lifeless. His saliva already healed the two small punctures his fangs made, leaving behind bruises that would fade naturally.

It was exactly how she looked after being attacked by those renegades.

He had no words for how deeply it pained him to have done this to her. Even as his guilt knew no bounds, a part of him felt intensely satisfied to have been able to take the life she so selflessly offered him.

Her generosity and love humbled him.

"I drove a woman mad."

He gave her credit for how fast she snapped her jaw closed after it dropped open. "You can't be serious."

"I assure you I did. Her name was Selena Ashford. She was the daughter of a local lord back in Northumberland." He remembered the night like it happened only yesterday. "And only fifteen when I saw her running through the woods that separated Seacrest and Rydon. What a sight she was in that white gown. She looked like an angel.

"I made quick work of the renegade chasing her, though not quick enough. Selena saw me take the bastard out. She saw what I was, what I did. She saw me reduce the renegade to dust."

Allie looked baffled. The sentiment was reflected in her tone. "You saved her life."

"She lost her mind that night and I was responsible." Though he hardly ever thought back on that night, the recollection of the look in Selena's eyes still cut through him. "The renegade should have killed her. After seeing what she became, it would have been the merciful thing."

Allie placed her hand on his chest. Her icy flesh chilled him.

"No, Sebastian. Take it from me because I know, if you would have left her for that renegade you would have condemned her to Hell."

"You can't know that."

"Can't I?" Allie kept her voice whisper soft. "I was attacked remember? I know what it feels like to have a monster stealing from your body. That vampire wasn't only taking my blood, Sebastian, he was stealing my soul."

"Oh God," Sebastian said hoarsely. He sat up, his hands biting into her shoulders as he fought the need to give her a good shake. "Why didn't you tell me? I wouldn't have taken from you if I'd known that."

Allie's hands covered his. She pried them off her and held them down by threading her fingers through his. "I don't know. I never wanted anyone to know that."

Sebastian lay back and ran his hands over his face and head as he exhaled loudly. At that moment, feeling like a demon that crawled out of the bowels of Hell, he swore he could almost hear Lucifer's laugh cutting through the silence.

"You didn't drive Selena mad. Your takedown of the renegade obviously triggered what must have been there all along. You have to know that's true,

Sebastian."

When Allie lay down next to him, he gathered her close and held her against his side, wishing he could give her warmth back. He liked her in his arms, it was where she belonged. "I watched over her until the day she died. For twenty-six years I witnessed her suffering. I swore I'd never do that to another living soul. I only put myself around humans when I had to feed."

"That's because you're a good man." Allie snuggled closer into him. "What made you break your celibacy vow after all these years?"

He rolled over onto her. He wanted her again, but she looked like hell and he knew she wasn't up for another go. "You, Allie. Everything about you."

"I'm flattered."

He felt her love for him run through him. It lit him, burned him, made him wish to God he was alive with her, to share life with her not merely take it with nothing but death to give in return.

Though he didn't want to leave her, he had to. He had to put some distance between them in order to clear his mind and regain control.

"I'll be right back."

Getting out of the bed, Sebastian placed a kiss on Allie's forehead, loving the small, shy smile she gave him. He headed into the bathroom, stopping only long enough to pull on his pants.   After washing her blood from his face he brought her a wet cloth. By the time he got back to her, though only gone for a few minutes, she was already drifting off to sleep.

Her eyes opened when he began to wipe the blood from her. "Am I that much of a mess?"

"I'm afraid so." He felt guilty as sin for it.

She touched her hair and groaned. "I bet I look awful."

"You look beautiful."

"You're a good liar." Her laugh was weak at best, her eyelids already closing again. "My hair is a matted mess. It's the one draw-back of keeping it so long." She rubbed his shorn head and giggled, the first time he ever heard the like from her. "Guess you wouldn't know anything about that."

"No, I wouldn't." He ran his hand through her hair, working the knots free. "All better."

"Thanks."

Her arms reached out to him, beckoning him back to her. It was hell to resist what she offered. "I have to go for a bit, sunshine."

He expected hell from her. Obviously, his Allie was too tired to protest. "Hurry back, okay?"

"I will. Get some rest."

Her eyes fluttered closed, yet when he went to leave, Allie whispered his name. He turned back to her. "Are you coming back before I have to go?"

"Don't worry, Allie, I'll always come back to you."

She looked relieved as she snuggled into his bed and fell asleep almost instantly. Sebastian stood staring at her for the longest time, marveling at her.

His eyes cut through the dark as he quietly left the room and made his way down to the den. He needed to put some small distance between Allie and himself for her sake. Already he wanted her again and hoped being away from her would allow him to gain control over his body.

He felt Constantine's presence in the house. *Bloody hell.* The last thing he wanted was to deal with the Dragon.

Constantine reclined on the sofa, his jaw clenched and his anger palpable. The television was on but he wasn't watching it. He sat staring out into nothing.

"I thought you and Raphael were going out to hunt with Lucian," Sebastian remarked as he sank down on the couch.

Constantine slowly turned his head and pierced him with an icy glare. "You fucked her and fed from her."

Sebastian flinched at that harsh accusation. "That's none of your goddamn business."

"Cocksucker." Constantine fisted his hands. He was barely holding onto his fury. "I should fucking end you right now."

Sebastian cocked a brow at him. Of all the Templars, they were the most evenly matched. They both fought with the same level of ferocity. "You can try."

Fangs bared, Constantine leaned in close to him. "You had no right."

Yes, well, he already knew that, too bad he wasn't about to admit it to Constantine. "Believe me, C, she was more than willing."

A feral sound reverberated in the back of Constantine's throat. "I know. I heard."

Sebastian shifted uncomfortably. He didn't like that Constantine heard every one of Allie's whimpers and moans.

Letting out a loud sign, Sebastian leaned back on the couch. "I care about her, Constantine."

"No shit."

"You and that other asshole knew this would happen if you got us together so what's the fucking problem? You and Raphael got exactly what you were hoping for."

Constantine stood and went to stalk from the room. "Fate's a funny bitch. She always finds a way. All we did was give you both a push." His eyes were haunted when they met his. "She's too fucking good for any of us."

"Don't you think I know that?"

Constantine stopped in the doorway and looked back at him. "Something's going to go down big, Sage. Protect her."

Sebastian knew better than to doubt Constantine's warnings. "You know I will."

Constantine nodded curtly. It was his way of accepting the situation.

The Dragon left the manor silently after that warning. Sebastian shut off the television and sat in the dark listening to Allie's soft breathing. She was all over him. He could feel her lifeforce thundering through him. It made him feel alive again, and that was something he'd never come close to feeling since the night he died.

Actually, if the truth were known, he'd lost this feeling long before that day.

Sometime during his long captivity at Chinon, he lost his humanity alongside his spirit, a dead man years before they lit the fire and cheered his death. He died the night they broke him. The night his own screams nearly deafened him.

Tired of being alone, of fighting against his nature, Sebastian rose and went back upstairs. After laying out some things he thought Allie might need when she woke, he slipped into bed next to her. He felt an unfamiliar knot of emotion in his chest when she curled herself into him. He put his arms around her, holding her naked body against his.

It was as close to Heaven as he ever hoped to get.

Chapter Fifteen

Though Allie warned her against going out, Lex felt as if the walls of Allie's house were closing in on her.

With Allie gone for the night, likely out with the Templar vampires, she didn't want to be alone. Having no one else to call here, she tracked down Patricia Olsen. Not Lex's first choice of friends, still, Patricia would do in a pinch.

What a bad idea it'd been to get together with that catty bitch. All it served was to remind Lex how different she was from the girls she'd considered her friends when she lived here.

Not that things were much better in Florida.

No matter where she went and who she was with, seemed Lex was destined to feel like the odd man out.

She'd driven Allie's old Dodge into Edessa, the next town over from Damascus, taking the dark and twisting roads cautiously. She'd spent barely an hour at Patricia's before she needed to go. Her friend hadn't changed a bit since high school. She still had the power to make Lex feel awkward. Freakish.

Seeing Patricia was a harsh reminder of how far removed Lex was from the "normal" world. Unfortunately it left her with nowhere to fit in, since, thus far, Allie adamantly refused to allow her into the nighttime world where fairy tales were real and normalcy was the unusual.

Passing Our Lady of Grace church, located ironically on Church Street, Lex felt compelled to go in. Though it was late, she saw Father Phil smoking a cigarette outside the rectory and asked the friendly old priest if she could have a few minutes alone with God. More than happy to oblige a young person in their quest for the Lord, he'd opened the church to her.

This was the first time since her brother's funeral she'd been in a church. Lex didn't know why she stayed away from God so long. After all, she knew for a fact He existed. Allie told her all about the Templars, how they died and were reborn as vampires and how God cursed them, their souls taken by an archangel.

If that wasn't proof of God she didn't know what was.

On her knees, forehead to her clasped hands, Lex was beyond prayer and beyond thought. She long since settled into a wonderful state of perfect peace, not even realizing an entire hour came and went until finally her tortured knees took her out of her trance.

Looking down at her watch she cringed with dread when she saw it was nearly eleven o'clock. Though Allie wouldn't be home yet, her sister was bound to call to check in on her. If she wasn't there, Allie would have a coronary, rush home, find her gone and kill her for leaving.

An angry Allie was the last thing Lex wanted to deal with.

Rising from her aching knees, Lex stretched and looked around for Father Phil, thinking to thank him for letting her linger so long. Seeing he was nowhere to be found, she left quietly.

She was coming out of the church when saw him standing at the foot of the stone steps.

Lex felt frozen to the spot by the sight of the man. Good God, he was huge. The expression of his face was enough to chill her despite the warm, humid air of the summer night.

Tall, broad, dangerous, and handsome as all get-out, he looked like the poster boy for Gothic fashion. On him, the gothic clothes didn't come across as a costume. No, he owned the look, as if the whole look had been created solely for him.

He was staring at the church with oddest eyes she'd ever seen. They were silver and quite literally, glowed.

Oh God, he's a vampire.

By all rights Lex knew she should be terrified, knew she should retreat back into the church where she'd be safe. Yet her feet froze to the spot as excitement thundered through her.

How odd to find such a creature near a church. Weren't there rules preventing such a thing?

Maybe it was the fleeting look of dejection that passed across his face. He stared at the church as if she wasn't there, as if it were only God and him and nothing else existed.

She knew the feeling. She'd indulged in it for the last hour.

Unsure what to do, Lex stood staring down at him and noticed the jagged scar that cut down the left side of his face. It should have made him ugly. It didn't. If anything, it made him more appealing.

This was a man who shook off the perfection of youth and settled into the wear and tear of adulthood.

His frosty stare shifted and settled on her. He cocked a brow at her as his tongue ran over his bottom lip. "What have we here?"

His voice was low and smooth. There was a hint of amusement in his tone that she chose to ignore.

"Are you alright?"

"I am now."

Something about the way he said that made the tiny hairs on the back of her neck stand on end.

As if he wasn't a threat to her life, Lex let the door close and began down the stairs. She knew with every step she took toward him it brought her closer to her mortality. Yet she felt no fear. She wondered if he'd put a spell on her, but dismissed the idea when she recalled Allie said vampires couldn't do that.

Standing on the last step, she still had to look up at him. "What are you doing standing outside the church?"

"What are you doing coming out of church?"

Good question. Lex wished she knew. "I guess I needed God."

The same despondent look passed over him again. "Don't we all?" His tone was about as sarcastic as the shirt he wore that read *It's all about the pain (the ink and the jewelry are just souvenirs)*.

He looked like God was the last thing he needed. "I don't know. Do we?"

He actually seemed to think about that for a moment. "No. We don't."

By the way he said that, Lex believed he was lying. Though whether to her or himself, she didn't know.

Maybe he didn't know either.

She stood close enough for him to hurt her if he was of a mind to. And though she knew the danger she placed herself in, she didn't move away. Her curiosity about what he was and her attraction to him overrode common sense and kept her right where she was.

Normally someone who played it safe, who hid in the corner while life was lived all around her, something in Lex rebelled at the idea of retreating. She wanted to touch his pale skin, wanted to see if it was as cold as it looked. He stood so still it was creepy. And were those fangs peeking out from behind his lips?

He licked his lips. Yep. Those were definitely fangs.

Everything Allie warned her about earlier tonight came back to Lex in a rush. Still, something forced her to remain right where she was. In harm's way. She didn't want to leave him alone, not after seeing the lost and lonely look in his eyes. It seemed almost cruel to leave him. Like she'd be abandoning him.

"You're scared."

Well of course I am. Did he forget he was a vampire?

Yet a whispered voice assured Lex he wouldn't hurt her. As the melodious voice resonated in her mind an itch began right above her navel. She gave it a quick scratch though it did nothing to ease it.

"I know what you are, so yes, I'm afraid of you."

"Do you now?" One of his black brows rose in question. Then he looked at her all thoughtfully for a moment. "What am I, elf?"

"You're a vampire."

His eyes narrowed and his nostrils flared. "Someone's been telling you bedtime stories, have they?"

She swallowed hard when he leaned in close and inhaled the air around her. She swore she felt as if he was trying to push inside her mind. "Damascus isn't your average town."

"No it's not." Since he was so close to her, she was able to smell the scent of patchouli that clung to his pale flesh. She never been overly fond of the scent, but on him it smelled wonderful. "I don't want you to be afraid of me."

His voice wove through her, wrapped around her and touched her as if his hands were on her. She shivered as a delicious thrill crept up her spine.

If she weren't careful she'd give in to the odd sensations awakening within her, drawing her to him. "I have to go."

"So soon?"

She nodded, wondering if he was going to let her leave. "I have to get home."

He leaned in close. So close they were practically touching. "Stay," he whispered seductively in her ear.

Yes. Stay. She wanted to more than she was willing to admit. "It's bad enough my sister is going to freak since I went out after she warned me not to. If I'm any later she's going to kill me."

Lex didn't understand why she was treating him so casually. The man was a vampire. He was the very thing Allie warned her about.

The whispering in her head, a beautiful chorus of voices coming from somewhere far away, out of sight, told her she belonged in this moment.

These were the same voices that led her back to good any time she thought to veer from the path of pure. But not this time, now, they were telling her to stay with a creature who was sin incarnate.

Slapping a hand to her temple, she feared she was losing her mind.

And the itch—*Oh God*, the itch on her stomach was getting worse every day. A burning itch directly over her navel that no amount of scratching could relieve.

"Your sister is right. Bad things come out at night."

She let out a nervous laugh. "Does that include you?"

"Especially me."

Maybe the lyrical voices were wrong.

The movement of his hands caused her gaze to shoot a glance down, gaping in shock when his hand moved to cup his erection through his pants. His other hand, the top of which was branded, brushed through her hair. His touch was gentle, keeping her from running as her hair spilled over the pale flesh of his hand and arm.

"You can't begin to imagine the things I want to do to your body."

'Oh God…'

No, she couldn't imagine. She knew nothing of sex firsthand, having never even been kissed before. Those voices kept her body pure, yet now they drew her toward this formidable vampire. They compelled her to want things from him she'd never thought twice about with any other man.

She wanted to know those things he wanted to do to her. Yearned for him to show her, to bring her body to life. The mere thought of his mouth and hands on her were enough to make her heady with needs she never knew burned within her.

It took some effort but Lex remembered they were in front of a church and that he wasn't merely a man. Yet when she finally gained the ability to move, instead of heading back up the stairs she stepped toward him. As if he knew how badly she craved his touch, his hand left her hair. His calloused palm felt rough against the flesh of her arm when he took hold of her.

His touch came and went faster then the span of one heartbeat to the next. With fangs bared he let out a hiss that raised chills over her.

"*Christ*," he ground out between clenched teeth. "You're Allie's sister.

Lex was not surprised this vampire knew Allie, since most of the nocturnal population of Damascus did. From what her sister told her, even they knew her as Crazy Allie.

Pride rose in her, ready to defend her sister even at the cost to her own life. "Yes I am. And you better not call her crazy because she's not,"

"I know she's not crazy," he said quietly before sighing with resignation. "You have to go, elf."

Yes, I should.

Too bad she couldn't get her body to cooperate and walk her away from him.

She asked his name with no expectation of him actually answering her, and was pleasantly surprised when he did.

"Constantine Draegon."

"What an amazing name." She rolled it over in her mind, liking the way it sounded. "Since you know Allie, I guess you know I'm Lexine."

He inclined his head politely, licking his lips again, as if he tasted the air around them. "Good night, Lex."

"Good night, Constantine," she whispered back softly.

The moment was suspended in time with them simply staring at each other. Finally, Lex turned and rushed down the block to where she'd parked Allie's old car. Since the Passport wasn't in great condition, Allie kept the old Dodge in case the SUV broke down, though the blue monstrosity was in even worse condition.

Driving away, Lex felt as if something profound passed between her and Constantine Draegon.

***

Once the air no longer crackled with the intensity of her lifeforce the fingers squeezing Constantine's dead heart eased their stranglehold.

Bloody hell.

Allie's sister. How the hell didn't he sense that long before she came out of the church? He should have discerned her bloodline long before he touched her. Something prevented him from detecting such a vital piece of information about her.

He also hadn't been able to push inside her mind. No matter how hard he tried, it felt as if he kept hitting a brick wall. At first he assumed she made a deliberate effort to hide her thoughts from him, but that wasn't the case.

Lex hadn't kept him out of her thoughts.

Something else did. The force blocking him was stronger than any supernatural power he'd ever encountered. Yet she seemed oblivious to it. He believed she truly had no idea what was inside of her. Nor, he assumed, did Allie.

Bloody hell. This was going to add another complication to their already convoluted existence.

The possibilities of what the power within her was were endless. As were the consequences to her for possessing it.

Constantine lingered long after he watched Lexine Parker drive away, still feeling as if a piece of her was with him. The fact that she was Allie's sister twisted his gut and had him cursing Fate.

Seemed she was forever giving him the big cosmic "fuck you".

Pure. That's what Lex was. Pure. He felt the innocence of her body with an intensity that nearly knocked him right on his ass.

He wanted to taste that purity, take it into himself to know what it felt like to be so clean.

He thought the last true innocents vanished from this world long ago. He'd been dead wrong. And then to have such purity wrapped in a package of striking beauty made it nearly too tempting to resist taking her right in the front of God's house.

Looking at the cross gracing the steepled roof of the brick church, Constantine wanted to believe the day would come when he'd step out of the shadows and into the glory of God's love. Though it was doubtful. Creatures such as himself were doomed to Hell even before they took their first breath of life.

Now Lexine—God Himself would come down to personally escort her home.

With one last glance at the church, Constantine headed back into the shadowy park across the street. His run-in with Lex left his body hard and hurting. The bloodlust was quickly rising to a dangerous level. If he didn't feed soon things were going to get ugly.

With a bar located on the other side of the park, he always found one or two drunken women wondering around. Always good for an easy fuck and a quick meal, they'd do to slake the hunger and the sexual needs awakened in him by Lex.

Even as Constantine took another woman, he knew he'd be seeing Lex. The image of her was branded into his mind as deeply and permanently as the seal on his hand.

Eying a small group of women gathered around a bench in the center of the park, Constantine didn't find any of them attractive. Not one of them whetted his appetites. Nevertheless, they were perfect.

As they smoked and laughed, their words slurring drunkenly, he knew they'd be easy meat.

He would pick one and use her until dawn began its ascent. His needs would be sated and he'd return to the Manor to wait out the day.

Fuck it, why not take all three.

Hell, he'd need them all to satisfy the lust and the hunger one tiny blue-eyed girl woke in him.

Chapter Sixteen

"*Jesus Christ*," Lucian hissed when he caught the unmistakable scent of fresh blood and death permeating the air. "Not again."

They were already too late. Another girl was dead and the renegades responsible long gone.

"I smell it too," Raphael announced, walking beside him through the thicket of trees. "What a reek."

Lucian tried not to smell the blood on the air, fought hard to block it out, but couldn't. It drifted through him, letting him know beyond a shadow of a doubt when they found her it was going to be a gruesome sight.

They were heading toward an old, abandoned house hidden deep in the woods. Houses like it peppered the countryside, many little more than crumbling lean-tos, which was why the Templars were having such a difficult time locating the renegades. The bastards were jumping from house to house, and as long as they cleaned their trail, it was nearly impossible to track them.

Strictly by chance Lucian and Raphael came upon this place. They'd been heading back to Seacrest from a bar in Mount Pleasant when Lucian caught the subtle scent of human blood in the air.

Since they had to go deeper into the woods, they left the Maserati on the side of the road and went off on foot. They didn't get far before the stench of death mingled with the blood, causing Lucian's gut to twist. He knew what they were going to find when they came upon the source of those odors.

"Luc, look there."

Lucian's intense stare cut through the dark. "I see it."

The boarded up windows were a good indication that vampires had been here. Following the metallic scent carrying on the warm summer breeze, it led them to the door of the house. Though neither Templar detected the stench of renegades, they weren't taking any chances. Lucian kicked open the door, charging in with sword drawn. Raphael followed, battle-ready for what might await them within.

As soon as they entered the house, their vampiric senses were assailed with the odors of blood, terror, sex, and death. The evidence of renegades was everywhere, clear they left mere hours ago. Their scent was still strong, mixing with the more noxious odors. The place all but hummed with the remnants of their energy and their victim's fear.

Lucian led the way to the bedroom, already stiffening with dread, knowing what they would find.

Lying on a mattress was the naked body of a young woman. Her body was a map of pain, evidence she'd been tortured for a long while before finally given the release of death.

From her matted blond hair right down to the blood smeared over her inner thighs, Lucian felt her suffering run through him.

The only difference between her and the others was the look in her eyes. They held no terror, only a strange peace as they stared unseeingly at the ceiling. Her cracked lips gaped open, frozen on her last gasp. The entire left side of her throat had been viciously torn away by the monster who'd killed her.

Lucian instinctively knew they'd found Amanda Driver.

"Jesus Christ," Raphael whispered in horror as he came up behind Lucian. "How long do you think she'd been here?"

Seeing the condition of her body, Lucian wanted to hurt the bastards who'd done this to her. The need for retribution burned dangerously hot within him. "Too goddamn long."

He didn't understand why he gave a shit about these women. God knew he'd seen the death of innocents before. Hell, he'd even done his fair share of killing. Yet with every one of these girl's deaths he felt he lost a piece of himself.

When he found who was responsible, he was going to bring a reckoning to them and send every last one of them to Hell.

Raphael placed a comforting hand on his shoulder. "Come on, Luc, there's nothing left for us to do here. Dawn is coming. We have to go."

"Go wait outside."

"Lucian…"

Lucian ripped his shoulder out of Raphael's hold and pulled his sword free of its scabbard in one fluid motion. His fury pushed him nearly beyond reason.

Such a state of emotion was a dangerous thing. Even more so for a Templar, who was above the average vampire in strength and ability.

Raising his sword and holding it above his head in a battle-ready stance, Lucian bared his fangs in a ferocious snarl. "Don't question me on this. Get the hell outside. Now."

Raphael threw up his hands. "I'm going. But for God's sake, Luc, you have to calm down. You can't go back to that place again. Remember what happened last time."

Remember? How the hell could he forget? The night continued to haunt him even after seven hundred years.

Though, he couldn't rid himself of the blind rage that tore through him like a violent storm, Lucian lowered his sword. "I'll calm down when I take the heads of the bastards responsible for this."

"I know, Knight. Believe me, I feel the same way. But right now, we have to get out of here before dawn comes. You'll be no good to this girl if you're ash."

The threat of the sun calmed him somewhat. At least enough to have him lowering his sword. He felt the coming dawn like a million pinpricks on his skin. Nevertheless, he couldn't leave Amanda this way. After what she'd obviously suffered she deserved to be laid to rest properly, even if her soul was gone and wouldn't find peace until it was released to God.

"Go wait for me outside. Please."

It had to be the "please" that finally got Raphael to give Lucian a few moments alone.

As soon as he was gone, Lucian stabbed his sword into the floor. He tore down the cardboard that covered the windows. Amanda suffered long enough in dark.

He sat on the mattress next to her, struggling against his emotions and the hunger her blood woke in him.

He smoothed her dirty hair away from her face before running his hand down her smooth cheek. Her youth and beauty were radiant even in death. "I'm sorry I couldn't find you sooner."

He wrapped her in the sheet with infinite care. When he lifted her off the blood-soaked bed he saw something that chilled him to the marrow of his bones.

Written in blood beneath her on the mattress was his name.

Goddamn it.

As he suspected from the start, this wasn't about the Daystar. This was about *him.*

Lucian retrieved his sword and carried Amanda's body outside. Raphael was waiting for him none too patiently. "Find wood," Lucian barked, ignoring the incredulous look Raphael threw him.

The sensation of the approaching dawn made him uneasy. Nervous. The prickling at the nape of his neck had him wanting to tear away the flesh to ease the discomfort.

He didn't want to be here, the one to have to lay another murdered woman to rest. After witnessing too much death in his time, he was tired of it. The pain and suffering he'd seen, the destruction, it all took a terrible toll on him. He longed for the indifference the others had. Wished for it with everything he was, especially now.

His skin beginning to prickle as dawn inch closer, Lucian wished he were locked away in the dark where the deadly rays of the coming sun couldn't touch him. Couldn't burn him to ash.

They'd all been to that party and Lucian had no desire to do that dance again. Not ever.

With Raphael off finding kindling, Lucian laid Amanda out on the dirt. He wasn't going to tell Raphael about the sick present left for him. The less Rogue knew, the safer he would be—or so Lucian hoped.

After carefully arranging her body on the ground, he said a quick prayer over her. Again, he hoped God would accept the prayers that came from the tongue of a vampire.

He wanted Amanda to have peace; even though he knew her soul was gone.

Kneeling in prayer was how Raphael found him only moments later. They quickly constructed a small pyre with the wood Raphael found. Lucian placed Amanda's body on the pyre, reluctant to ignite it, to burn her to ash and destroy what God so carefully created.

"You alright?"

"I'm fine," Lucian gritted out tersely as he regained his feet.

Raphael was staring down at her as well, his sorrow and regret mingling with his own. "What a bloody shame."

What more could be said besides that?

There'd be no coming back for her. She'd have no chance at immortality. There wouldn't even be a Heaven or Hell waiting for her. With no soul, she'd be caught in limbo until it was released from the monster that stole it from her.

Even if it took Lucian forever, he was going to set not only Amanda's soul free, but those of the other girls as well. He'd not allow them to linger in that terrible plane caught between all realms of existence as lost-souls. Ghosts.

Lucian pulled the Zippo lighter from his pocket. With a flick of his wrist he ignited the lighter. He bowed his head, said one more prayer for her then lit the pyre. Snapping the lighter closed, he turned to Raphael, who was watching the flames flare to life.

"Let's go before someone sees us."

Raphael nodded glumly. "I don't know how you did this twice already."

"Neither do I, Rogue," he admitted honestly.

Human life was sacred to them all, and to see it torn away was torture for them,

And hopefully, one day, he would be able to join them in Heaven and find peace for himself.

* * *

Unable to stop his morbid curiosity, Stephan went back to the house to see if Lucian had been there. He needed to know firsthand if he'd struck another direct hit to the noble Knight. He had to absorb the anguish left behind in his wake.

While still a good distance away he saw the smoke and caught the scents of burning wood and flesh. He knew without a doubt the fire was Lucian's doing.

Lucian cleaned Stephan's mess as he knew he would. How damned predictable the Knight was. Holding onto his false nobility as if he had a chance at ever earning the redemption he fought for.

Stephan was never going to allow that.

He'd never allow Lucian the luxury of Heaven.

As he moved closer to the house where he'd held Amanda, he caught the scent of a second vampire. Sniffing at the air, smelling past the stink of Amanda's burning body, he detected another Templar had been here.

Raphael de Vere.

Ah, the Rogue. His reputation was well known throughout history. He cut a sexual path through the ages beginning shortly after his damnation. It continued right on down to the whispers he heard from the women in this area who claimed he could melt them with nothing more than a look.

All the Templars had names, he'd learned. Constantine Draegon was aptly dubbed Dragon. Even Stephan for all his furious need for revenge, wouldn't touch that one. To cross paths with Dragon was to seek out your own end.

Sebastian of Rydon was known as the Sage and Tristan Beaumont, the Guardian. He'd made a point to learn why they'd gotten their names and what their weaknesses were. Oh yes, he'd taken the time to learn his enemies well.

Coming upon the burning pyre, Stephan watched Amanda burn for a few moments, thinking what a shame he had to end her so soon. He would have liked to keep her around for a while longer. She would have been perfect for what he had in store for Lucian.

Unfortunately Amanda hadn't possessed the Daystar. He'd been sure she possessed the power of it. His frustration at having been wrong was what led him to be rougher with her than he had been with the others. Time was no longer on his side. He had to find the Daystar fast or he'd lose the chance to use it as a bargaining tool to keep his men with him.

Knowing he'd never be able to take on the Templars alone, he'd promised the Daystar to those who aided him over the years. With only one more lead left, one that brought him to the Templar's doorstep, he'd not take a chance at their wrath before he saw his plan through. He'd leave it to his men to fetch the girl once he had Lucian.

Harboring no desire for the power of the Daystar, all he wanted was to hurt the one responsible for destroying everything he held dear in life. His family, faith, and ultimately, his life.

He remembered the words of his brother, and carried them with him all these years.

Always remember, Stephan, a smaller strike in the right places can fell even a giant.

That's exactly what he was doing now. Smaller strikes at a stronger foe was slowly bringing his enemy down.

All the years of patience and planning were finally paying off. With each woman he killed he struck a brutal blow to his enemy. Not a mortal wound, it was a direct hit nonetheless.

All that was left to do now was wait for the perfect opportunity to land the final blow.

Chapter Seventeen

Allie lay nestled in Sebastian's arms long after she woke. Loving the feel of him, she curled into him, reluctant to leave him and face the day. Not after the incredible night she'd spent with him.

Opening her eyes, she lifted her head and smiled at the peaceful look on his face as he slept. She wondered if he dreamt, if he had nightmares of the day he died.

To think they'd all slowly burned to death while crowds of people cheered on cut through her heart and made her wish to God she could take the memory away. She wished she had the ability to let them relive their lives and prevent their deaths and damnation.

Since her arm was thrown around his chest, hugging him close to her, she felt his lack of heartbeat. Trailing her hand up his chest, she touched the scar over his heart. She wished she could give him back his soul and put life back into the heart Michael severed.

What he told her about Selena last night was awful. Not that the poor woman lost her mind, but that he felt responsible for it. What a burden he forced himself to bear all these years.

He of all people should know Fate was going to do her thing no matter what anyone did to stand in her way.

Unable to linger next to him any longer, Allie sat up, dizzy and weak from the loss of blood. Seeing the fire burning low in the hearth, she appreciated the small warmth it provided given how cold she still was from the inside out. Though it barely illuminated the room, it cast enough light for Allie to make her way around without slamming into every piece of furniture on her way to the bathroom.

She stood on shaky legs, making sure Sebastian was covered with the heavy blankets. Gathering her clothes from the floor, she practically ran into the bathroom. The last thing she wanted was for Sebastian to wake and see her naked ass as she tiptoed around, scurrying for her clothes.

Oh yeah, that was a dignified sight.

She dared a glance in the mirror, amazed the only visual evidence of Sebastian's bite was two bruises on her throat and her pasty complexion.

She also couldn't believe how awful she looked. Pale as death and dark shadows under her eyes was not a good look for her. Not to mention her hair being in knots was going to take forever to brush out.

She wondered what sort of women he would have been attracted to in his own time. Did she measure up to the medieval beauties, or all the other women he'd come across over the centuries? She looked at her freckles, her pale skin, and her red hair. She was okay-looking. Nothing spectacular. Nothing impressive enough…

"Stop thinking so bloody loud. You're fucking gorgeous and you know it, and even if you were a mutt, Seb would still adore you."

Allie gasped, throwing a hand over her moth to keep in her squeal of embarrassment when she heard Constantine's grouchy voice in her head.

"What are you doing listening to my thoughts?"

"As if I want to hear them. You sound like a goddamn girl."

"I am a girl."

"Bugger that, you don't have to sound like one. Now stop screaming in my head so I can sleep."

"Fine, I'll stop thinking."

Allie looked away from the mirror, her stomach twisting with dread as a mortifying thought crossed her mind. *"Constantine?"*

"What is it now?"

"Did you hear my thoughts last night?"

He hesitated. *"No."*

Something told her not to believe him. *"Are you sure?"*

"No, I'm not sure whether or not I heard you in my head."

"Constantine?"

He signed. *"For the love of God, Red, what?"*

"Does he love me?"

This time there was no hesitation. *"That's for him to say, not me. Now leave me alone so I can sleep."*

Allie turned back around and smiled. *"Sleep good, C."*

"Stay out of trouble, Red."

When Constantine was gone from her head, Allie glanced down at the sink and noticed a new toothbrush, towels, and soap laid out. Neatly folded on top of the pile was a small piece of paper.

Picking it up, Allie carefully unfolded it. There, in bold-as-you-please writing, were the words *"For you. Hope you slept peacefully. S".* Re-folding it, she put the paper aside so it wouldn't get wet when she washed.

Sebastian may look like a hit man for the vampire mafia, but he possessed a tender streak Allie knew not many people got the chance to see.

As much as she would love nothing better than to linger for the rest of the day and night with Sebastian, she had to get home to Lex. Quickly getting dressed, Allie made sure to tuck her note into her back pocket. She called her house on her cell phone.

Lex picked up on the first ring.

"Where the hell are you?"

Allie cringed, having never heard Lex yell like that. "I'm at Randall Manor," she whispered, so as not to disturb Sebastian.

"Randall Manor? Are you kidding me? I've been calling your damn cell every half hour and you're at Randall Manor."

Allie forgot she turned off the ringer last night. "I'm so sorry, Lex. The time got away from me last night and then I fell asleep. I just woke up now."

"I can't believe this." She still sounded pissed but the edge was off her anger. "Sebastian better have been one heck of a lay to have worried me like you did. That's all I'm saying."

Allie grinned wickedly as a delicious pressure settled at the junction of her thighs thinking about Sebastian's touch on her. "Oh, don't worry about that, sis. He was. My toes are still curled."

Allie actually heard the smile in Lex's voice. "Then I guess I have to forgive you, don't I? Don't ever scare me like that again."

"I promise I won't."

"You're forgiven then. When are you coming home?"

Before finally deciding whether or not to accept the job at the B&B, Allie wanted to do a preliminary walkthrough with her hand-held equipment. She wasn't going to commit to this job without some sort of evidence one way or the other that the Miller's weren't wasting her time.

Still, she owed it to herself to make at least one walkthrough. God forbid the place turned out to be haunted and Allie foolishly threw away the opportunity at an investigation. She'd never forgive herself for the wasted opportunity.

"In a little while. I have to get ready to go to the Millers. Are you coming with me?"

"Of course!" Lex squealed so loud Allie had to pull the cell away from her ear.

"Go get some rest. I'll be home in a bit."

"Okay. Love you, sis."

"I love you too, Lex."

Allie flipped her cell closed, replacing it in her pocket. She washed quickly, opting to take a shower once she got home. When she left the bathroom she saw he was awake, sitting up in bed, looking devastatingly gorgeous as usual.

"Thanks for leaving me…"

"Come here," he interrupted

Smiling at the arrogant way he said that, Allie crawled back on the bed and snuggled next to him. She laid her head on his shoulder and draped an arm across his chest. He wrapped his arms around her and held her as close as he could.

He may sound boorish, but he was incredibly gentle with her.

"Sorry I woke you."

He made a gruff sleepy sound. "I don't like you with clothes on."

Allie smiled. "What a nice thing to say." She kissed his pectoral. He squirmed. "I like you naked too." She slipped her hand under the covers and ran her hand over his six-pack stomach.

"If you keep doing that I'm not going to let you go home to Lex."

"You heard?"

"Vampire, remember? Extraordinary hearing comes with the package."

Was she to have no privacy, not even in the safety of her own mind? "Did you hear everything?"

He gave her a small squeeze. "What? That you think I'm a good lay? No, I didn't hear that."

Between Constantine and Sebastian's teasing she wanted to die from embarrassment. If she had more blood in her body she would have blushed bright red. "It's not polite to eavesdrop, you know."

He raised a brow at her. "This from the woman who I caught snooping around my bedroom."

Allie sat up and lifted her chin in feigned indignation. "I wasn't snooping."

His smile devastated her senses. "Yes you were."

"Whatever. Let's agree to disagree on that matter."

"If that makes you happy."

"Being with you makes me happy."

He made a very Constantine-like grunt of affection and kissed the top of her head.

She ran a hand over his chest. He closed his drowsy eyes and lay still, savoring her touch. It made Allie even more reluctant to leave. "I have to go."

Sebastian opened his eyes. "I know, sunshine."

She dipped her head and gave him a quick kiss. "Go back to sleep, baby. I'll see you later."

"I'd better."

His parting words, an unspoken admission that he'd miss her, filled her heart. For the first time in her life she was genuinely happy. She loved him, and though he hadn't returned the words, he returned the sentiment.

He could keep the words for she knew she had his heart

* * *

Once Allie left, Sebastian folded his arms under his head and closed his eyes. He still felt her blood flowing through him. Such a large part of her stayed with him, yet it also made her absence that much more keen.

He didn't like being trapped in here while she was out there unprotected. He worried about Allie, the concern cutting him to the core. He'd never worried about anyone before, not even Selena. With her, he'd felt responsible, believing he was to blame for what she became.

Remembering Selena in her last year, he recalled how she'd lost her will to go on. She gave up on life, growing tired of living in the prison of her own mind. By the time death took her, her madness had eroded her beauty, leaving her a withered shell of a human being.

He knew Allie would never waste away like that. She possessed too much life and she loved it too much to ever have it wear her down.

But as much as life burned within her, one day Allie *was* going to be taken by her mortality. Sebastian would be forced to watch helplessly as time aged her, suffering through each night knowing it brought him one day closer to losing her. And once she was gone and her midnight sun extinguished, he would again be lost and alone in the dark.

"*Dear God,*" Sebastian begged, "*please don't ever take her from me. Don't let me suffer in the dark alone anymore.*"

Sebastian fell back to sleep with Allie's warmth running through him and her love chasing away his relentless nightmares.

* * *

Before heading home, Allie stopped off at the supermarket to shop for the things she would need to make dinner for Lex.

Feeling horrible for having worried her sister, Allie hoped to make it up to her by cooking her favorite food before going out to the B&B. Too bad Allie was a lousy cook. Before she was done, Allie fully expected a few burns and setting off the smoke alarm at least once before she gave up and took Lex out for pizza.

As she came out of Peck's Supermarket juggling bags of groceries while she fished the car keys out of her pocket, she smacked right into Jude.

Her recent ex-boyfriend had the nerve to glare down at her like she was nothing more than shit under his shoe.

"Watch where you're going."

"Hello to you too, Jude," she shot back. "How's Denise?"

Jude threw her a haughty look. "We're both fine."

Sure, after some penicillin, Allie thought, almost laughing out loud.

"Look at you," he said with a wave of his hand. "You look horrible. You and those friends of yours. I warned you they were no good. I see I was right."

Allie might let Jude get away with insulting her. Hell, he made an art form out of it, but she'd be damned if he bad-mouthed the Templars.

She stepped in close to him, her voice a low warning. "Say one more nasty thing about my friends and I swear on God I'll make sure you'll be saying it to their faces."

The threat held enough weight to have him paling to a shade even whiter than she was. "Women are dying, Allie, did you know that? How do you know those men you call friends aren't responsible? For Christ's sake, the black-haired one with all those tattoos looks like a frigging serial-killer!"

Jude was about to pop a vein. How in God's name she tolerated this arrogant, judgmental, and very annoying man for ten months, she didn't know. She chalked it up to one of those stupid things a person did that they spent their life pretending wasn't their one regret.

"They have nothing to do with those murders. If you spew that bullshit to anyone, I'll personally make sure you regret it."

He rolled his eyes, completely ignoring her threat. "Go home and get some sleep. You look like shit," he spat out nastily.

Allie shook her head, knowing it wasn't worth the effort to argue with him. He was never going to change. Once an asshole always an asshole. "It's been a real pleasure. Let's not do it again sometime, shall we?"

Having to suffer him was the equivalent of having her eyeballs plucked clean and stepped on.

She pushed past him and climbed into her truck, driving off without a further thought of her ex-boyfriend. And why would she, when she had Sebastian to think about?

* * *

Jude hurried into Peck's and quickly picked up the refill of his and Denise's penicillin prescription. Heading home, having turned onto Route Three Seventy-One, he realized a big black truck was following him.

Though he tried to outrun it, he couldn't shake the guy on the narrow, winding road. Nor could he avoid it when the truck pulled beside him, heedless of any oncoming traffic. The driver, whom he couldn't see behind the black tinted windows, slammed into the side of Jude's Mercedes.

Careening to the right, Jude's car rolled into a deep ditch. By the time the car stopped rolling he was upside down but thankfully unhurt. He was still strapped into the driver's seat, though. Fumbling with the seatbelt, he tried everything to free himself short of attempting to bite his way out. His head snapped to the left when the mangled door was pulled open.

"Please…"

Never one too proud to beg, Jude did exactly that when a hulking bruiser of a man stalked to the car brandishing a syringe. Though Jude tried to fight the man, Jude was no match for his strength and easily subdued.

The man said nothing as he jabbed a needle into Jude's arm. Gasping, Jude yanked away his arm but not before the man pushed down on the syringe's stopper and injected him with the drug it held.

Whatever it was hit Jude instantly. His head spun and his stomach lurched until everything went black. He heard some rustling and felt himself being pulled from his wrecked car. If he wasn't so relaxed, damned near unconscious, he might have tried to fight.

"We gotta hurry. If he wakes up and this guy isn't there, he's gonna kill us."

Jude had no idea who "he" was or why these guys were bringing him to whoever it was they worked for. Nor did he have any more time to wonder about it. The drug he had been shot with was powerful stuff. He went out cold a second later.

When he opened his eyes some time later he was in a large room. The windows had cardboard over them. The only light came from a few candles on a cracked dish set on the floor. The room stank of stale air, sweat, blood, and vomit.

Sick to his stomach and disoriented, he started to move and realized he was bound on a mattress. The thing was filthy, stained, and stank. Something moved in the corner of the room. His eyes tried to cut through the dim glow to see what it was. Barely focusing, he saw it was a young man.

"Who are you? Why am I here?"

Tall and lean, with long brown hair, the man moved stealthily out of the shadows. His eyes glowed silver. They were not human eyes.

"Shut up, Jude," Though his tone was soft, it was thick with irritation.

Terror gripped Jude as he tried to break free of the binds. "How do you know who I am?"

The man approached the bed and Jude saw twin fangs peeking out from behind his parted lips. "I make it my business to know anyone who might aid me in my endeavor."

Fangs. The man had fangs. The chilling realization that Allie was right had icy fingers of fear working their way up his spine. Everything Allie told him came back at him in a rush of words in his spinning mind.

Vampires were real, she affirmed over and over again. Each time she spewed that bullshit, Jude called her crazy, threatened to break things off with her if she didn't stop with her foolishness.

But it hadn't been bullshit. Vampires were real and now Jude was caught in some deadly game he wanted no part of.

Goddamn you, Allie...

"I'll give you whatever you want. Just let me go."

The man sat on the edge of the mattress. Jude tried to scurry away but the man stilled his frantic movements by placing a hand on his leg. "You shouldn't make such an offer, Jude."

"Is it money? I'll give you any amount you want." There was a desperate edge to his voice as he pleaded with the creature.

Shaking his head, the man patted Jude's leg. Jude wanted to yank his leg away but he was too afraid of making the vampire mad. "Now what would I want with money when I have plenty of my own?"

"Then what?" Jude's voice rose with fear, taking on a shrill note that cut through the abandoned house like a knife. "What do you want from me?"

Taking his hand from Jude's leg, the man stroked his chin. "What I need is help from you."

Jude shook his head. His mind was a riot of thoughts as terror nearly rendered him as insane as he always accused Allie of being. "I don't understand."

The vampire's eyes shone with malevolence. "I'm looking for something,

Jude. With your help, I think I found an easier way to get to it."

Jude saw a way to get himself out of this alive. "Anything. Whatever you want."

The man tsked and wagged a finger at him. "There you go again, offering anything. I warned you, Jude."

Before Jude could do anything to save himself, the man bared his fangs and leapt at him. His teeth came down hard and deep into Jude's throat. Jude gasped and thrashed wildly when he felt his vein give as those razor-sharp fangs punctured it. He tried to scream but couldn't, helpless to stop the monster pulling his blood from his body.

He couldn't fight tied as he was, though Jude doubted his meager strength would be any match for this creature. The vampire used his body weight to push him back down. Pinned to the bed, Jude gave up the fight as he felt himself growing weaker and colder by the second. He felt his own death coming fast, though something told him this wasn't going to be the end.

He knew he was going to die tonight, even worse, he knew he wasn't going to stay dead.

He prayed for God to save him, but it was too late. His heart beat for the last time.

Falling into the black peace of death, he was yanked out of the abyss by the vampire, who gave Jude back the blood he took from him. Unable to resist, he latched onto the vampire's wrist, drinking from the gaping wound. The blood filled his mouth, slipped down his throat and worked its way through his body.

When human death claimed his body, Jude's scream echoed through the night.

Yet it was the roar that was torn from Jude when he was reborn that brought a smile to the bloodied lips of Stephan. He watched as his newest child woke and took in the night with the burning silver eyes of immortality.

Chapter Eighteen

"What a massive waste of time,"

Allie and Lex were loading the Passport with all the hand-held equipment they brought with them to the Millers.

"You knew it would be," Lex reminded her.

Allie slammed closed the back door of the truck, wincing when she did the same to the tailgate and it nearly rattled off its hinges. It was only a matter of time before the whole truck fell apart.

"It would have been nice to be proved wrong."

"How much did he offer you anyway?"

Shrugging, Allie wondered if maybe she should have put her ethics aside and accepted the payoff Michael Miller offered. She needed the money, and besides, who would be hurt by the lie? All she had to do was do a piece on the B&B in *The Specter* and say she believed the place was haunted. Miller would get his publicity and Allie would get a nice stack of money. Easy. Fast. No harm done.

No harm done except to her conscience.

Lying wasn't her style. That's not how she rolled, not for any reason, especially not money.

"Obviously not enough."

Lex smiled at her, beaming with pride. "I'm glad you didn't take it."

"Me too. I can't believe they tried to bribe me. I may be a weirdo by a normal person's standards, but I do have morals."

About to get into the truck, Lex snorted at that. "You're not a weirdo or crazy. People can be stupid, that's all. If they got to know you they'd see how great you are."

Older sister hero worship was a hell of a thing, never failing to knock Allie for a loop. A lump, feeling suspiciously like a wad of emotion, settled in her throat. She swallowed it down before she started bawling her eyes out.

She loved being an older sister, even with all the responsibility that came with the job. Though she failed miserably in the whole "role-model" thing. Now more than ever she needed to rethink some of the more reckless risks she took with her safety. She couldn't go blindly leaping into a dangerous situation. Not when Lex would be right behind her, ready to jump in too. Nor could she go pulling a stunt like she did last night, where she didn't call to check in when staying out all night.

"Yeah, well, not everyone loves me like you do, sweetheart." Allie climbed up to stand on the side step. She looked over the roof at her sister. "And in case you haven't realized by now, ghost hunting isn't exactly a normal career. Besides, I don't sweat it that people think I'm nuts. I don't want you to either."

Lex tilted her head and regarded her curiously. "Can I ask you something?"

"Anything, sweetheart."

"How come you don't go get a normal full-time job and do the ghost hunting on the side?"

Allie wondered the same thing after she lost her job as a receptionist in the pediatric office four years ago. She'd loved that job, liked the two doctors she worked for. Surprisingly, even got along with the other assistants, though they made no secret of the fact they thought she was weird. Most of all, she loved being around the kids. The newborns were her favorite. She fawned over every new and wrinkled tiny person brought in by their worn out, but adoring parents.

The doctors weren't too fond of the fact she spent her nights ghost hunting and fired her. They felt her working for them brought their credibility down a few notches so they let her go. Depressed, she stayed out of work for three months. When she finally pulled herself together and went to find another job, every door was slammed in her face.

By that time, her reputation as Crazy Allie was well known. After all, word spread fast in a small town. No self-respecting business would "lower" themselves to hire her once people started talking about her being crazy. Ghost hunting and reporting her investigations to *The Specter* became her full-time job.

"Because I *am* considered Crazy Allie, not many people around want me working for them," Allie explained with an indifferent shrug.

"Oh," Lex said softly. "I'm sorry, Allie."

Allie got into the Passport. "For what?"

"For people's stupidity."

God, Lexine had such a good heart. Allie was afraid, since they lived smack in the center of vampire central, that heart was one day going to get Lex in some serious trouble.

"Don't let it bother you, Lex. Besides, I have all the friends I need."

Of course, Allie was referring to the Templars. Having those guys at her back was more than enough friend any woman could ask for.

The Templars were at Seacrest by now. They went to the castle every night to check in with Tristan before going out to hunt. Why they didn't go and live there while they were in Damascus, Allie didn't know. It made no sense to her that they stayed at Randall Manor, where they were far less protected than at Seacrest.

Some things about them she didn't know. Their reluctance to reside at Seacrest seemed to fall into that "unknown" category.

Thinking about the Templars, Allie's mind zeroed in on one in particular. She was definitely suffering from a bad case of the warm and fuzzies, and much to her surprise she found it was nice since he seemed to return the sentiment.

"You seriously like Sebastian, don't you?" Lex asked, obviously seeing the direction Allie's thoughts wandered to.

"You could say that," she laughed. "Sebastian is remarkable in the truest sense of that word. He is a man who should be remarked upon. Everything about him is incredible."

Lex glanced at the time displayed on the radio. "So why don't you go see him? It's still early by a vampire's standards."

At only eleven o'clock, it *was* still early.

Allie held back her laughter when she saw the hopeful gleam in Lex's eyes. Her sister was busting to meet the Templars. Lex made it very obvious she wanted into the shadowy world Allie was a part of. Try as she might to keep her sister out of it, Allie had to concede that maybe—just maybe—it was time she let Lex in.

* * *

As soon as they drove through Seacrest's gatehouse, Allie and Lex felt as if the wind was knocked right out of them. If Allie didn't know better she would swear they crossed time, going back to the days when the original Seacrest Castle was new and teeming with life.

Parking behind the Templar's impressive collection of cars, they got out and stood staring slack-jawed at the lists for a good long while. After all, it wasn't every day a woman got a glimpse into the past at what genuine medieval warriors looked like clashing swords under the pale light of the moon.

Four gorgeous Templars—minus Lucian, unfortunately—assembled on the lists as they would have done centuries past in all their medieval glory.

Sebastian and Raphael went at each other savagely, Tristan and Constantine cheering on the ruthless battle as only true knights would.

The clash of blades echoed loudly throughout the courtyard. Muscles worked under pale skin as two vampire-knights battled each other with a brutality that came from knowing death was no longer a possibility. The way they moved, sidestepping each other's swords, looked like a carefully choreographed dance. Each movement fluid as they faced off with a strength and agility no human could match.

Sebastian possessed such grace, fighting with the ease of a man who was bred for battle. The savagery in the way he fought would have destroyed a lesser man than Raphael.

Fascinated by the way they moved and the passion for the fight gleaming in their eyes, it was easy to see why the Knights Templar were considered the elite in their day. They fought with the belief that if they fell in battle, they would ascend straight to God. That belief gave them an advantage over their enemies. After all, how do you win against men who fought with nothing to lose and all to gain?

If Allie looked hard enough, she could see past the modern world and glimpse back to the days when Sebastian was alive. When his flesh was tanned from a life spent outdoors. She could almost see the true color of his eyes—not the glowing sliver they turned when he was reborn—but the warm brown she knew they were in life.

But the watery image faded quickly and Allie was once again reminded of exactly what the Templars were. As if she could ever forget.

Neither showed a hint of exhaustion as they battled each other with inhuman strength and stamina. Though their wounds bled, neither man seemed to notice their injuries.

"Wow," Lex breathed. "They're amazing."

Allie could only nod in agreement, lost for words as she watched her man in battle.

What a glorious sight he made.

Being only two tiny drops of estrogen in a huge bucket of testosterone, it was enough to give Allie and Lex sensory overload.

Tearing his gaze from the fight, Tristan turned and stared curiously at Lex for only a heartbeat. Allie knew that was all it took for him to sense who her sister was.

Lex pressed herself against Allie's side, blushing clear to the roots of her hair. Allie couldn't blame her for her reaction. If she were thrust into the

Templar's world under different circumstances, she would have reacted exactly the same way. Having her throat bitten, her body beaten, and her mind a mess, she didn't have the luxury of getting all hot and bothered when she first encountered them.

"They're huge!" Lex was gawking at Tristan, who was staring back at Lex in obvious amusement.

Allie had to laugh at that. "I warned you they were fierce boys. C'mon." Allie gave Lex a gentle tug on her arm. "Wipe the drool off your chin and I'll introduce you."

Dragging Lex across the courtyard, Allie caught Sebastian throwing glances at her. She winked at him and then cringed when Raphael stabbed him in the leg.

"Bloody hell," Sebastian swore.

He stumbled under the impact of the blow before coming back with a sharp thrust of his sword. Raphael blocked the attack, not giving Sage a second to recover before nearly catching Sebastian in the other leg.

Lex gasped at the sight of the blood that spurted out of Sebastian's leg.

"Trust me, he's fine," Allie assured her, though she felt sick inside to see her man wounded. "Vampire, remember? They can't die."

"Can they feel pain?" Lex asked in a whisper.

Allie nodded. "Sure they can. Isn't that right, Sebastian?"

Sebastian slapped away Raphael's attack with a growl. "It burns like bloody hell."

"Stop being such a girl. It's only a flesh wound," Raphael shot back.

Sebastian charged. He caught Raphael in the shoulder, the sword sinking deep. Rogue jumped back and the blade pulled free. "Son of a bitch. You got me!"

"You'll live."

"Fuck you, asshole," Raphael gritted out.

They continued their brutal dance of blades as Allie introduced Lex to Tristan. Guardian, God bless his medieval heart, brought Lex's hand to his lips. Her sister got flustered when he placed a feathery kiss upon her knuckles.

"It's a pleasure to finally meet you, Lexine."

"He's cold," she whispered to Allie, believing only her sister could hear her.

Tristan shared a small smile with Allie over Lex's head. What Lex didn't realize was how exceptional a vampire's hearing was. "He's dead, Lex. Hence, the cold skin."

Lex's mouth formed a perfect "O". Much to her credit, she recovered quickly. Still, she looked overwhelmed by the barrage to her senses. Allie should have better prepared Lex for this meeting. Sure, she gave her sister the basic run-down about vampires, but she didn't get into the dirty details of what they were or what a shock to the system it would be to come face to face with them.

Besides, being told was one thing. Actually being in the presence of the Templars was another thing entirely. It wasn't something anyone could truly be prepared for.

"Where's Lucian?" Allie asked Tristan.

"He went to the supermarket."

Lex's brows shot up in surprise. "Vampires shop at the supermarket?"

Tristan gave her a small smile. Constantine, who was pointedly ignoring both Allie and Lexine, grunted but refused to turn around. The surly bastard didn't even bother to glance in their direction which Allie found weird since it was the first time Constantine ever ignored her.

He might be bad-tempered but he was never rude, at least not to her. He adored her, which was why he was always nice to her. That, and the fact that she was the only female who didn't take his shit. He knew full well she'd plant her foot up his ass if he pulled attitude with her.

"The supermarket is what the Templars call The Gate." she explained to Lex.

Lex looked confused. "Why?"

"It's where we go to hunt," Tristan replied gently.

Again, Lex's lips formed an "O".

Allie didn't want to get into the whole feeding thing right then. It was bad enough to finally have her sister and the Templars together. That discussion could wait for another day.

"Did Sebastian tell you about Grandma Buckman and that scroll?"

"He did. Unfortunately that's a dead end."

Tristan's frustration was clear. It mirrored the frustration they all felt.

"Don't worry, Tris. We'll find the Daystar."

He nodded gravely. Allie could see he wanted to believe that. So did she, though she had to wonder how many more women had to die before they finally found the relic.

"What's the Daystar?"

"I'll tell you later," Allie said to Lex. When Constantine refused to turn and acknowledge her sister, Allie went over and gave him a good shove. Of course, the brick wall that he was, he didn't budge. "Stop being rude to my sister, C."

Constantine reluctantly turned around. Allie only had a second to appreciate his shirt, which read *I even scare my own family,* before Lex sucked in a sharp breath and stabbed a finger at Constantine. "Oh my God!" she exclaimed breathlessly. She looked him over from head to foot, her wide eyes missing nothing. "You're a Templar!"

"Obviously," he drawled.

Allie put her hands on her waist and shot both Constantine and Lex a suspicious look. "Let me guess, this isn't the first time you've met?"

Lex had the good grace to look contrite. Constantine cocked a brow at Allie arrogantly. She was *not* about to be intimidated by him. Not now. Not ever.

"We met once before. The last time I came to visit," Lexine explained in a rush.

Lex failed to realize she was a horrible liar. Allie pinned Constantine with a hard glare. "Are you going to back her bullshit up?" He nodded curtly.

"Seriously? Then why didn't you tell me you knew my sister?"

"I didn't know she was your sister."

Allie was impressed Constantine managed to keep a straight face when he fed her that nonsense.

Three Templars froze and shot him incredulous looks. Raphael—and how Allie adored him for his humor—coughed out the word "bullshit". The promise of genuine pain in the look Constantine threw him had her holding back a laugh.

"Could you at least try to lie with a bit more finesse?" Allie said to Lex and Constantine with a disgusted roll of her eyes and shake of her head.

Constantine had the audacity to raise his chin in indignation. "I never lie."

Allie snorted. "Oh please."

"Are you mad?" Lex whispered.

How in the world could Allie be mad at Lex when her sister was giving her that wounded puppy-dog look? "Not if you keep looking at me like that," she grouched. Leave it to those big eyes of Lex's to knock the heat right out her temper.

Constantine had the nerve—the sheer nerve—to throw a supportive and protective arm around Lex's shoulders. And damn it all if Lex didn't inch closer to him. Who the hell did he think he needed to protect Lexine from? Her? Oh Lord, this was too much. Imagine, the meanest Templar of the bunch taking a shine to Lexine.

Somehow, it just figured.

Sebastian, leg already healed, strode up behind Allie and threw his arms around her. He smelled incredible. Like spice and fresh night air. She leaned into him and smiled. She could spend the rest of her life right where she was.

"Why don't we ditch this crowd for a while?" he whispered seductively in her ear.

Wonderful chills ran traveled over her skin. "I don't want to leave my sister alone with these dogs." She gave Constantine a dirty look.

Of course, Allie was teasing and they all knew it. If she didn't trust the Templars she would have never brought Lex here in the first place.

"I promise it will be worth your while."

Allie's knees went weak.

She turned to Lex. "Are you going to be okay on your own?"

Tristan and Raphael held back their amusement at how quick Allie gave in to Sebastian.

Lex rolled her eyes. "Of course I'll be okay," she said with a note of frustration. "I'm not ten years old anymore, Allie. Go." She actually shooed Allie away, much to the amusement, and admiration, of the Templars.

It seemed that though Lex looked as delicate as the petal of a flower, her backbone was forged of pure steel.

Oh yeah, she was going to fit right in to this macabre little family of outcasts.

As Allie followed Sebastian to the keep, they heard Lexine remark to Constantine that Raphael was cute. Constantine, in turn, dragged Raphael right back onto the lists.

"Go ahead and bloody me up, you grumpy bastard. I'll have Lexine nurse me back to health. Won't you, love?"

Before Lex could answer, Constantine's ferocious battle cry was heard a second before the clash of swords rang out. It was followed by Lex's husky laughter.

Yep—Lex was going to be just fine.

Chapter Nineteen

Much like he did the night before, Sebastian led Allie to the room. This chamber, which Tristan kept for him, wasn't nearly as modern as his bedroom at Randall Manor.

If Allie ever envisioned what a "chamber" looked like, this was it. Spacious. Sparsely decorated, it was exactly the sort of room she imagined for him when she thought about Rydon Castle.

Though she knew Sebastian never used this room, she thought it was considerate Tristan kept chambers here for all the Templars. The promise of always having a sanctuary had to be extremely comforting to them all since their existence was plagued with so much threat.

Sinking down on the enormous bed, Allie watched Sebastian as he closed and locked the door. This time, she didn't feel the same apprehension as the other night. Tonight she had the confidence of a woman who knew her lover's touch and wanted more. Her gaze followed him as he went to the hearth and crouched before it. With his back to her, he lit a fire, stoking the flames to life for a few silent minutes. She took the chance to enjoy the sight of the man who, literally, crossed time to reach her.

Only once he got a roaring fire going and took a moment to steal some warmth from it, did he rise to his full and imposing height. Allie felt breathless as he strode over to her, his intent evident in his eyes.

For such a large man he moved with surprising grace. His body was that of a warrior, muscular, tight, perfectly honed for battle. His hands, calloused and scared, were huge, large enough that a hilt of a sword nestled comfortably in them, yet when he touched her he did so with infinite care. To see him was to see a man who knew war and death, who'd faced archangel and devil alike and still stood proud, a force to be reckoned with.

He stood before her and ran his hand through her unbound hair. "I like your hair like this,"

She craned her neck to look at him, smiling as he let her hair run through his fingers. "I like your hair too."

He looked at peculiarly. "I don't have any hair."

"I hadn't noticed," she teased. She let her fingers dance down his bare chest. "How come the others have long hair and you don't have any?"

"I hated the lice." A shiver of disgust passed through him. "After three years of begging for my head to be shaved to stave off the vermin, the sadistic bastards at Chinon found it amusing to do so only days before my execution."

What an awful way to be tormented,

She wrapped her arms around his waist and laid her cheek against his chest. "I'm so sorry, Sebastian."

He tangled his hands in her hair, pressing her even closer to him. "Don't be, sunshine. I deserved it."

"No you didn't."

He grasped her chin, forcing her to look at him. "Yes. I did, and if I ever forget that, the centuries I've spent atoning for my sins will have been for nothing."

As much as she didn't want to bring back his painful memories, Allie couldn't stop herself from asking, "What made you go off on Crusade?"

He gave an indifferent shrug, though Allie knew he was anything but apathetic. "Tristan."

That answer surprised her. She expected to hear he went out of devotion to God, out of faith. Maybe even for glory and the promise of riches. A million reasons why a man would give his life to go off and fight a war in God's name ran through her mind, none of which involved him following Tristan off to war.

From what Allie read of the Templars, they were the elite in a time when men were bred for battle. Feared, respected, and loved, they rose to the level of being more legend than real. They grew so powerful and wealthy that they created the first banking system. Feeling the threat of their might, the King of France charged them with heresy and had the entire Order in France arrested to rid the world of them.

Given the legends that only continued to grow about the Knight Templars, Philip of France hadn't done too good a job.

It spoke volumes of the men, and fighters the Templars were, to have been allowed in the sacred Order of the Knights Templar. True, they'd lost their faith, but who knew the horrors they'd witnessed. Allie couldn't begin to imagine the atrocities they'd committed in the name of God fighting a war against the Muslims.

That they held onto their faith as long as they had was a wonder to her. Most people danced on the fine line of belief and doubt, stepping away from God with an ease that attested to how fragile their faith was to begin with.

But not the Templars. She knew it took a long while for them to leave their faith on the battlefield.

Even Allie had doubts, suffering a crisis of faith after Christian died. It lasted until she fell into the Templar's world and was confronted with the fact God did, indeed, exist.

"I didn't know you knew Tristan before you joined the Templar Order."

"Seacrest bordered Rydon. We grew up together." Moving away from her, he went to the hearth. He gripped the mantle and stared into the flames. "When we were sixteen, Guy Sinclair came looking for able bodies to join him on Crusade. Tristan wanted to go for the glory. I wanted to go to get as far away from my family as possible."

Allie stroked his chest, fully aware of how his body tightened at her touch. "You had real winners in the parent department too, huh?"

"They were products of their time." He glanced at her. "We all were."

"No, I don't believe that," she countered, her own anger at her parents coming through. "A shitty parent is a shitty parent. Period. I don't care what time in history they were born in."

"I'll give you that. Anyway," he continued, "after four years fighting for Sinclair, Tristan decided to join the Knights Templar. The rest of us, who grew as close as brothers, went along with him. We all heard of the Warrior Monks and we wanted in."

They were all young and proud warriors. Of course they would want to strive to be the best, to rise above the ranks to etch their names in history.

"You must have all must have been extremely religious to have given up everything when you joined the Order."

He shook his head, his hand idly running through her hair, every now and then his fingers tickling the nape of her neck, her shoulders, sending wonderful chills throughout her body. "Not at all. Lucian was the devout one. He had enough religious conviction for the rest of us. It'd been bred right into him from birth. The rest of us went along solely for the glory."

"No wonder you lost your faith," she remarked softly. "You didn't have much to begin with."

He shook his head. "No. It didn't take much for me to lose what small amount I had, especially not after what we were all forced to do in His name."

"I can't even imagine."

Everything in him changed in the flash of an instant. He grabbed her wrists and held them tightly. His fangs were bared in a vicious snarl, which held all the pain and anger burning him in as he recalled his bloody past. "How could you? The things I've done were unspeakable."

"Sebastian…"

"I wasn't damned the day I died," he gritted roughly. "I was damned long before that. I sealed my fate the day we took a village filled with nothing but women and children. The men went off to fight, leaving behind only a handful of bodies to protect their families. They were no match for us when we charged in. We took them easily, cutting them down like grass. We burned every home, slaughtered every animal. We were told to leave no one alive. So you know what I did, Allie?" He gave her a hard shake, tears glistening in her eyes. His pain flowed into her in crashing waves of torment. "I murdered children while they were in their mama's arms, and then I killed the mothers too."

Though she knew his every rasping breath had to be hurting him, she doubted he cared about the pain. Even realized it. He wasn't here with her now. He stared out into nothing. Allie could almost see what he did, not where he was now, but where he'd once been.

Blood accumulated in the corners of his eyes. With a terrible growl, he dropped her wrists and went to stalk from the room. Allie wasn't about to let him go. She chased after him, catching his arm. He spun around, pinning her with a ferocious glare.

"Don't touch me."

She didn't let go. "What you did wasn't your fault. It was war and war is brutal and it's ugly. There's no shame in what you were forced to do."

"What the fuck do you know about war and death? How do you know I didn't like what I did? That I didn't relish the kill like the demon I was damned to be."

Allie dropped her arm, yet made no motion to move away from him. She knew this was Sebastian showing her the ugly he believed festered in him, asking her to accept him. "I may not have been to war, Sebastian, but I watched the battle Christian fought against heroin. I can swear to you it was as ugly as any fight you'd ever fought. And as for death, I know it all too well. It took one of the only people I've ever loved and I hated God for it. I hated Him with the same passion you did when you were forced to kill. I wanted to hunt down the old lady who hit him with her car. I wanted to hurt her for taking my brother. So you see, Sebastian? You can't make me hate you, no matter what you did. I love you too much to judge you."

"Jesus Christ, how can you say that when God judged me and found me sinful enough to damn me?"

Allie shrugged and offered him a small smile. "Yeah, well, I'm not God, am I?"

Feeling as if his heart kicked to life, pumping with the force of Allie's love, Sebastian pushed her back on the bed, coming to lie over her, careful not to crush her with his weight. Her warmth and life seeped into him as he claimed her lips with his mouth and her body with his hands.

Sebastian pulled his mouth from hers, needing to taste her flesh. He trailed his tongue along her neck, pulling a breathless whimper from her as he licked his way down to her collarbone, teasing her with his fangs. He loved the way she gasped each time he nipped her, her fingers digging into his back and her legs squeezing him tight.

Nestled between her thighs, he felt her heat through her clothes, her scent filling him as he lingered over her jugular, pressing his lips to the pulsating vein, taking in the delicious aroma of her blood.

Licking his way back to her mouth, he dragged his tongue over her bottom lip before taking it between his teeth and giving it a gentle bite. She rasped out a breath and thrust her hips up, grinding into his groin. His groan mixed with her whimper when she opened her mouth to him. He took what she offered, kissing her hard and deep.

Her hands settled at the small of his back. The gentle pressure she applied drove him mad with desire.

"Ready for a ride, sunshine?"

His woman, tiny but tough, grinned wickedly at him. "Always, baby."

That was all Sebastian needed to hear.

Baring his fangs, he let out a rumbling growl a second before he reclaimed her mouth. The kiss was hard, as he let loose the animal in him, taking her in ways she only dreamed two bodies could come together.

By the time he was done with her, Allie knew what it meant to be a well-sated woman. She also realized one very distinct advantage to having a lover who happened to be a medieval vampire.

Stamina.

* * *

Constantine leaned against the keep watching Tristan and Raphael out on the lists. Even after almost seven hundred years, he still hadn't tired of the remarkable sound of steel against steel.

A man born to wield a sword, his entire being was designed for it. His fate was to travel down a road paved in blood and lined with death. Such a path was forced upon him even before his bitch of a mother shit him out into this world.

From the time he took his first breath, he was being trained to become a warrior. To become a man who shed blood without care or conscience. Each blow delivered from the fists of his sire made him stronger. Harder. Henry Draegon battered him until he made certain he beat the humanity right out of his son. Until all that remained was an angry, bitter boy who grew into a savage man with a gift for killing.

His mother's voice echoed in his mind, her voice dripping with ice when she declared she would not abide a weak son. If Aislin Draegon saw him now, he was sure the bloodthirsty bitch would be proud of what she, Henry, and that cocksucker Ulric Chambers created.

Over the course of his life the man was beat out of him and replaced with a cold-hearted creature who faced an archangel defiantly and dared him to take his soul.

The mere thought of Ulric, the man he was given to for the price of a bag of gold, was enough to have Constantine wanting to hurt someone. He needed to take the pain out of himself by beating it into another.

Yet when Lex's husky laugher drifted to him, it chased away memories better left forgotten. They were memories that made him dangerous when allowed to poison his mind.

He looked over at Allie's sister and felt a stab right through his dead heart. Her beauty made his eyes hurt. Small and delicate and so damn clean he was afraid if he touched her with his filth he'd soil one of God's most glorious creations.

Yet he sensed there was more to her than met the eye. He felt what others couldn't, not even the other Templars. There was trouble all over what he felt brewing in her. He felt a power in her, a strength he doubted she even knew she possessed.

She must have felt his hot gaze on her since she turned to him and pierced him with her intense stare. Her eyes cut him clean to the place his soul should have been.

If she knew half the things he wanted to do to her, he wondered if she would still look upon him as if she could see past the monster everyone else saw to the man he might have been if given the chance.

Their fight finished, Tristan and Raphael walked off the lists. Rogue went over to Lex and draped his arm around her shoulders. When Raphael said something to her that made her laugh, he wanted to seriously hurt him.

Fuck it all. Constantine pushed himself away from the wall with a grunt. He had to get away from Lexine Parker. She made him dare to imagine things he had no goddamn business thinking about.

Like having her open herself to him so he could taste the clean of her.

Constantine moved to go back inside the keep but Lex's husky voice stopped him dead. "Constantine?" She came over to him, her tiny hand lightly resting on his arm. Her touch felt like fire on his flesh. "Where are you going?"

His eyes devoured her, taking in every nuance of her, committing it to memory to get him through the coming nights when he needed a bit of peace to calm his rage. "Inside."

"Oh."

Now why in the hell did she look so disappointed? She should be glad he was going away. No one liked being around him, he doubted even his fellow Templars could stomach him for too long.

"Dragon," Tristan shouted to him. "Are you ready for a go?"

His eyes stayed on Lex, her hopeful expression a dagger to his heart.

Never one to turn down a fight, Constantine shook her hand from him. With effort, he managed to take his eyes from her. He looked over her head at Tristan. "You haven't been able to beat me in over seven hundred years. What makes tonight any different?"

Tristan cocked a brow. "I have Lexine to cheer me on." He winked at Lex. She turned bright red.

Constantine stalked to the lists, pissed off at Tristan's easy manner with her. He'd never have that, it wasn't in him to be playful, to color a woman's cheeks with an adorable blush. They might like his dark looks, want to have a go at him for the thrill of danger surrounding him, but that's where it began and ended. He was too scarred, inside and out to provoke anything other than disgust in a woman, which was why he made damn sure he never got close to any one, merely used them for a quick fuck and feed and was done with them.

Yet here was Lex, beautiful, innocent, struggling to keep pace with him as if she actually *liked* being around him. Didn't she know she should be running to get as far away from him as possible?

Obviously Allie failed to inform her sister the threat Constantine posed to her.

By the time he got to the lists, he was tightly wound with frustration and primed to do harm, ready to beat Tristan into the ground. He peeled off his shirt and threw it aside. He heard Lex's small intake of breath at the sight of his bare chest.

He felt branded by the heat of her gaze taking in his tattoos and his scars. Whip marks cut across his back, his legs as well, though his pants covered those. As for his tattoos, he bore an angel on each pectoral; one with white wings, the other with black. On his upper left arm was a blood-red heart with a sword of the Order cutting down it, the flames engulfing the heart creeping up the side of his neck.

He attacked Tristan with a brute force that had Raphael stepping in to end the fight even before it started. No one stopped him when he threw down his sword and walked away without a word.

Instead of heading toward the keep, he strode out of the bailey. He needed to get away. He needed to think. Or maybe he already thought too much. At this point, he didn't know which. Nor did he give a shit. All he knew was he had to get away from Lex before he lost his control and did something stupid.

Like forget he was a monster and dare to take what he saw offered in the depths of her captivating eyes.

Confused by Constantine's fury, Lex looked to Tristan, who stood watching him go with a brother's worry lighting his eyes. "Is he going to be okay?"

Tristan glanced down at her, his burning silver eyes striking in an incredibly handsome face. "He'll be fine. He needs time to cool down."

As Lex's gaze followed Constantine, she felt a stab of pain in her heart as he was swallowed by the night.

Chapter Twenty

Lucian was coming out of The Gate when he felt the familiar prickling sensation at the nape of his neck.

He hated that bloody feeling since it meant only one thing and right now he wasn't in the mood for a fight. Dawn was coming and all he wanted to do was get back to Randal Manor to sleep the long day away.

Still warm with the blood of the woman he'd fed from, he stopped in mid-step. Tearing his yearning stare off his car, he pulled free his sword. He felt the sensation of being watched and looked across the road and into the trees. Though he knew something was out there watching him he couldn't see it.

Still, he sensed it waiting for him.

Call it instinct but he knew whoever was watching him was the same son of a bitch who killed those girls and left them for him to find.

Good. Come out from hiding you sadistic prick.

Listening to the night, Lucian reached out with all of his senses to locate exactly where the renegades were lying in wait for him.

He sensed an ancient death all around him. It made the air heavy as he searched the darkness for the renegade he believed to be stalking him.

Frustratingly, there was nothing to see. Nor could he hear anything besides the quiet sounds of the country summer night. That is, until a faint whispering of his name reached him.

He knew that voice, one he hadn't heard in seven hundred years.

"*Lucian...*"

Lucian's hand came off his sword. Suddenly weak, he went down to his knees, as his past came back to him in a myriad of sights and sounds. He shook his head as if trying to shake the voice out of his head. It couldn't be. That voice didn't belong here. His mind must playing tricks on him.

Suddenly, and completely unbidden, a tear of blood slipped from his eye to travel down his cheek. This was the first time he wept since so long ago when the monster overtook the man and everything he'd ever known was lost in a single moment of madness.

Slapping the tear away, all he did was smear it across his cheek. Lucian forced the memory from his mind. He couldn't allow himself to remember that night when he dragged his starving and mindless self back to Penwick. The memories were too painful.

He'd spent the last centuries begging God to forgive him for the sins committed that night. Yet with every plea he knew it was a forgiveness he'd never get nor deserved.

Lucian finally caught sight of the renegade who hid in the shadows. He pushed himself up and stepped out onto the road. There it was—the faint and shadowy silhouette of a man.

He came meandering out from between the two trees. Dressed all in black, he reminded Lucian of moving night. His burning silver eyes cut through the darkness. The renegade pierced him with such stark hatred that Lucian felt as if he was going to shatter under its weight.

A face he knew well slowly came into sight as the vampire walked closer. A face so like his own, yet so different. He couldn't be seeing this. Not now and not here.

Yet the man came closer. Close enough now to see every nuance of the renegade's face...

Renegade.

Jesus Christ, it couldn't be. "Stephan."

Lucian's mouth formed a name he hadn't spoken in six hundred and ninety-five years.

The vampire came right over to him. Arrogantly. Daring him without words to strike.

Normally, Lucian would have attacked already, taking the renegade's head with little effort. But not this time. He could no more fight this vampire than he could fight one of his fellow Templars. Instead, all he could do was take in the sight of the man standing before him. Face to face with his past.

Face to face with his sins.

They were the same height, their hair the same color brown. Though now Lucian's was longer, at one time it was as neatly cut.

The differences of the two were as striking as their similarities. Where Lucian's face held the edge of a man who knew too much war and death, Stephan's possessed a softer, more youthful look to it, bearing the look of a man who was never touched by the ugliness of life.

At least not until Lucian returned to Penwick, bringing Hell with him.

Oh sweet God, what have I done?

"No," Lucian's mind rebelled at the sight of Stephan, at what he'd become.

Stephan's lips drew back, revealing fangs. Lucian hissed out a sharp breath and staggered backward. "Surprised to see me, Lucian?"

"You're not Stephan." His hand shot to his sword. "Stephan is dead."

He pulled the blade free and raised it to strike as the events of the last weeks rushed him and all the pieces fell neatly into place. It all made sense now. Why it was his name written in blood and why he couldn't place the scent he detected.

He couldn't place it because he couldn't accept it.

His arm dropped, the tip of his sword scratching across the concrete of the road. Stephan laughed, evil delight gleaming in his eyes. Four other vampires came out from the trees. One of them Lucian recognized as Jude.

Oh God, when the others found out Allie's ex-boyfriend had joined the ranks of the renegades they were going to tear him apart. Especially if they ever found out Jude's part in whatever it was Stephan had planned.

"Easy, dog," Stephan said nastily. "I *am* Stephan and I *am* dead."

He stepped even closer to Lucian, almost daring him to attack.

Lucian didn't strike. He couldn't. The Knight, who faced down entire armies with a pride that earned him the respect of kings, took a step back. The four renegades came to stand by Stephan. Lucian knew he could take them all. He was that good of a fighter. He had to be in order to be worthy of the Knights Templar. Yet, no matter how he tried, he couldn't bring himself to take them out. For the first time since it was placed in his hands, Lucian's sword slipped from his fingers and clamored on the ground. One of the renegades rushed to grab it. Lucian did nothing, just watched as his weapon was dragged away.

"Look at him." Stephan motioned to Lucian arrogantly. "Look at the Templar. He's nothing but a coward."

"Don't do this, Stephan," Lucian warned between gritted teeth.

Stephan tilted his head and regarded Lucian coldly. "Oh, but I have to. I have to make you suffer as you've made me suffer."

Suffer.

Yes. Lucian had brought so much pain to Stephan. More than he could ever imagine. He did to him, the one thing that would break a man as religious as Stephan had been. He removed him from God's grace.

As he'd done a millions times before, Lucian wished he'd never gone back to Penwick. He wished with everything he was that he could take it all back. Undo the evil he had done. But it was far too late now, his sins finally caught up with him.

His gaze devouring Stephan, he died again at the hatred etched all over his face. It radiated from him, a tangible force between them. The fury blazing in his silver eyes burned him where he stood. Lucian never meant for this to happen. He'd never meant to hurt them. He'd only wanted to go home.

He should have stayed away. So goddamned far away…

"You were the one who kidnapped and murdered those women."

An arrogant grin spread across Stephan's face. "I left them as gifts to you. I wonder if you would have relished their sweet pleas and anguished cries as much as I did. After all, you proved you do love to prey on the innocent and the defenseless."

"Stephan…" Lucian went to reach out to him, but the vampire slapped his hand away.

"You don't touch me," he snarled viciously. "I'm going to make you hurt so bad you're going to beg me to kill you."

Lucian shook his head sadly. "This was never about finding the Daystar was it? It was about me."

Stephan laughed nastily and shook his head. "Of course. The Daystar means nothing to me. What need have I with such power? I never even wanted *this*, but I had no choice in the matter did I? You took that from me. You took it from all from us." He turned to his companions. "Through Allison Parker you can find the Daystar."

Hearing that spurred Lucian into action.

With the roar of a wild animal, Lucian attacked Stephan, grabbing him by the throat and lifting him clear off the ground. When the others came at him, one brandishing Lucian's own sword, he easily knocked them away one by one with no effort at all. Even though the tip of the sword opened a deep wound down his cheek, he held fast to Stephan.

He squeezed the throat of the renegade. "Your fight is with *me*. Hurt her and I'll destroy you."

"Do it," Stephan taunted. He didn't fight Lucian's hold on him. "You killed me once, Lucian. Think you can do it again?"

Lucian felt as if the archangel Michael tore out his heart all over again.

Lucian wasn't going to play this game. He sinned once. He'd not do so again.

With a disgusted grunt, Lucian tossed Stephan back.

He couldn't do it. He couldn't kill his brother twice.

Chapter Twenty~One

"When are you going to start investigating the kidnappings and murders of those girls?"

Allie cringed inwardly even though she expected the question. After all, she knew it was only a matter of time before Josh or Nick brought up the subject of the missing and murdered women.

Not surprisingly, there was a stack of old newspapers compiled in the corner of the stiflingly small room. Josh Bartlett was a packrat, his specialty old newspapers and magazines. Which was why, when she stabbed a finger at the papers, Allie wasn't shocked by the smiling face of Jordan Brewster staring back at her from the front page of the top newspaper on the pile.

Glancing down the table, a rickety metal thing with eight extremely uncomfortable folding chairs surrounding it, she felt the heat of seven pairs of inquisitive eyes staring back at her. Suppressing the urge to squirm uncomfortably at the curious--and suspicious—stares directed at her, she did her best to ignore them.

She hated these monthly staff meetings, when she was reminded of the people she was forced to call colleagues. With every intention of bailing on tonight's meeting, she rethought the idea when Josh threatened to hold her pay unless she attended it.

Sweating to death in the back room of the run-down building in Mount Pleasant was the last place Allie wanted to spend the better part of the evening. Josh and Nick, the two brothers who owned *The Specter*, turned this building in the magazine's headquarters. This was where Nick liked to say they made the magic. Allie hated his flare for the dramatic.

"I'd be wasting my time to investigate those murders." Allie gave Josh her best "I-won't-budge-on-the-matter" voice.

She was impressed at how easily the lie slipped past her teeth.

Nick raised a brow at her in the imperious way that never failed to make her want to grit her teeth in indignation. He held up the article she submitted to him. Not her best work, merely something she slapped together to hand in to make her deadline. Obviously, by the look on Nick's face, he thought it was a flying turd.

"So, let me get this straight. You honestly expect us to believe this article on UFO sightings in some nowhere town of Twin Falls *has* a supernatural element to it?"

"No. Not at all," she retorted smoothly. She didn't like Nick. He was a sneaky bastard who'd sell off his own mother for a dollar. "It has an *extraterrestrial* element to it."

Kelly Fitzpatrick, *The Specter's* resident medium, snickered into her hand. She tried to cover it with a cough, though it was obviously a laugh, clear as day.

Kelly was no more clairvoyant than Allie was, and Allie wasn't at all. She was soft-spoken and sweet, put on a good act, and believed her own bullshit, which put her in high demand when it came to the medium market. That added up for big revenue for the Bartlett brothers and their growing magazine.

"Allie," Davis Mack said slowly, as if addressing one of his five children, who had the manners of a pack of wild dogs. "We all know those girls were killed by vampires. I'm sure you realize your close relationship to those men is clouding your judgment."

"And I'm sure you realize how silly you sound implying those *men* are vampires," Allie shot back, addressing the unspoken accusation he threw at her.

"You expect us to believe they aren't?" Madam Morgana exclaimed in her high pitched, and vastly annoying, voice.

Madam Morgana, or rather Rachel Meyer, was a purple nightmare. A tight purple belly shirt made her flat chest flatter. Purple flip-flops brought the whole mess together. Jesus, she even had a big purple bow holding back her messy yellow hair. Garish makeup, complete with a fake beauty mark above her top lip, made for one ridiculous sight.

Rachel/Morgana was the psychic of the group. She honestly believed she could see into the future.

Whenever she was in a room with these people, Allie was reminded why people thought her crazy. Look at the nutballs she was forced to be in league with. Embarrassed wasn't even a word profound enough to describe how she felt sitting among this motley crew. Where were the normal paranormal experts like she saw on television? Certainly not at this table!

The only halfway normal one among the bunch was Walter Prescott, a polite elderly gentleman, who also happened to be a demonologist.

"I'm not going to have this discussion again," Allie announced with exasperation. "We've done this at every staff meeting for the past five months. It's gotten old."

"C'mon, Allie, admit they're vampires and we'll leave you alone."

Sure you will, Allie thought as she eyed Evan, the muscle who hefted around Davis' equipment. "I have nothing to admit. Those girls were murdered by transients. The police said so."

"Fine," Josh huffed, slapping her article down on the table. The entire table shook. "So we'll print this bullshit and let a real story pass us by."

"I could do it," Davis piped in. His gravely voice grated on what was left of Allie's last nerve. "I could go and investigate these vampire murders."

Nick rolled his eyes and shook his head. "Sure, with your kids in tow. That'll work."

For once, Nick was right, it'd be a bad idea to drag five unruly kids along on a murder investigation. Vampire or otherwise.

Because Davis's wife couldn't stand to be alone with the bunch of animals she called children, whenever he went on a hunt his kids went with him.

With no one else to do it, the subject was blessedly dropped. Allie settled back in her uncomfortable chair and tuned out as the bunch of them tossed around ideas for September's cover. Like she cared. All she wanted was her check so she could get to the Manor where Sebastian was waiting for her.

She got breathless imagining all the wonderfully wicked things Sebastian promised to do to her body tonight. Now, if only Josh and Nick, who loved to hear their own voices, would shut up and wrap this stupid meeting, she'd be able to leave and have Sebastian put his money where his mouth was.

* * *

Shit.

Allie realized, too late, she was being watched.

She figured the renegades would at least be subtle about it. Obviously they hadn't taken Stalking 101. If they did, they would have known hiding out in the open in a shiny silver Lexus wasn't exactly incognito.

Allie had just come out of the meeting, which went on far longer than necessary, when she spotted the car sitting across the road as bold as you please.

Two renegades watched her from the car, not trying to be stealthy about it.

Even from the short distance, she saw the threat gleaming in their glowing silver eyes. With the staff of *The Specter* only a few feet away, a run-in with renegades was the last thing she needed.

Right about now she wished she hadn't cut out of the meeting so fast as the old saying, *safety in numbers*, screamed through her mind. Quickly glancing to the right, she eyed her truck parked in the lot only a few feet away. It might as well have been miles away. She'd never get to it in time. Not even at a dead run. Vampires moved too fast for a human. They'd have her before she even got to the truck, much less by the time she unlocked it, started it, and drove away.

She could always go back into the building, but given the menacing gleam in their eyes, she knew they'd follow her. She wasn't going to have a mass slaughter on her conscience Not even her asshole co-workers deserved to go out as the main course on a vamp's menu.

Wiping the sweat from her brow with the back of her hand, Allie made sure she didn't take her eyes off the vampires as she calmly began to make her way to her truck. It wouldn't do for her to panic or try to run. At this point, if she tried it would probably just piss them off.

The passenger, who was leaning forward in his seat to see around the driver, had the gall to blow a kiss at her. Then the driver winked at her. She went cold with dread, yet wasn't about to let the bastards get away with trying to intimidate her. She may be scared shitless, but she'd be damned if she'd show it.

Tristan had a great saying, one she took to heart. "Better to die on your feet than live on your knees". Every Templar had lived, and died by it. Twice now, Allie faced the possibility of dying like a coward or with bravery.

With the motto running through her mind, she threw them a smirk and flipped them the bird.

The renegades got out of the car, their anger evident. Obviously they hadn't appreciated the universal sign of "fuck you". Allie's mouth ran dry with fear when the passenger came around to the driver's side and gave her a sarcastic look. They were daring her without words to make a move. Well shit, she may be fearless, but she wasn't stupid. She knew damn well this was a game. One she knew she was going to lose.

Every breath hurt as she remembered what it had felt like to have a renegade bite her.

God, she didn't want to go out like that, like those women Lucian found.

Sebastian and the Templars were going to demand blood for her death. Lex was going to be left alone. She hoped her sister would stay with the Templars and not go back to Florida and wilt under the oppressive negligence of their parents.

Staring the driver right in the eyes, she knew this was it. They were going to get her and it was best if she played along for now and tried not to get too hurt in the process.

Goddamn it. Why now? Allie felt a desperate misery. Why did this shit have to go down now, when she had so much to live for?

Trying to stop herself from panicking, especially since she knew they could feel her fear and were most likely thriving on it, she changed direction and walked toward them. "Are you going to stand there all night, or are we going to get this done?"

Despite her brave words, Allie's voice shook with her fear. The driver smiled, his fangs long and white. He stepped toward her and she had to resist the futile urge to try to make a run for it. The bad part about hanging with vampires was that she knew full well what they were capable of and exactly what they were going to do to her.

The passenger, who was tall, lithe, and blond, stepped away from the car. Pure evil charged the air all around him. "Are you gonna fight us?"

"Not tonight. But thanks for asking," Allie called out, positioning her keys in her fist so they were sticking out from between her fingers. If it came down to a fight, at least the keys would provide her with a makeshift weapon.

"Too bad." The driver pouted almost prettily. Shorter than his companion, everything about him was extremely dark and menacing. "I like to hear a woman scream."

I bet you do, you sadistic prick.

"Sorry to disappoint you but I'm not a screamer."

"C'mon girl, fight us to make it fun."

"I'll tell you what," she said smoothly. "Why don't you both go fuck yourselves instead?"

"That was a dumb thing to say, girlie."

Yeah, she knew it was, but she couldn't have stopped herself from that one. She was screwed no matter how she did this. Whether she went nice and quiet or if she kicked and screamed, they were going to do what they would with her. The least she could do was match their arrogant sarcasm with some of her own.

The blond one came forward. Allie didn't fight, but she was prepared to get in at least one good punch with her makeshift brass knuckles if she had to. She fought back her fear when he grabbed her by the arm. Up close, she was stunned to see how young he was. He couldn't even have seen his twentieth birthday before he was turned.

When he fingered her hair she suppressed a disgusted shudder. "You're a pretty thing with all that red hair of yours. I always liked me a redhead."

"I knew I should have dyed my hair black."

"You got a smart mouth on you, girl," he hissed. "That's gonna get you in trouble."

He got her moving with a hard jerk to her arm. The keys dropped from her hand. She stared at them helplessly as she was dragged away from her only weapon.

"Oh, God, don't let my death go on for days like those other girls," she prayed desperately. *"Please make it quick."*

Before she was thrown into the backseat the vampire hauled her against him. She tried to turn her face away but he managed to slam his mouth down on hers. She gagged at the blood she tasted in his mouth.

His arms were a steel band around her, making it impossible to push away from him. She slapped and clawed at him as he assaulted her mouth. She heard the other vampire grumble to her attacker that it wasn't fair he was *"keeping her all to himself"*. The thought of being raped by the two gave her a strength that came from deep within her.

Bringing her knee up, she met the vampire's groin in a hard hit that had him falling against the car, He howled with pain as the driver snickered. "She's got some spirit to her."

The blond pinned her with a fierce glare that had Allie going numb with terror. "That was a real stupid thing to do." He grabbed her wrists, spun her around, and shoved her hard against the car. She grunted when he came up behind her, pressing his body to hers. Her stomach rolled and vomit rose in her throat. "You got no idea what's waiting for you. You're gonna need a friend where you're going and I was your only bet."

He let her go. Allie turned back to him. She looked right into his handsome young face and spit.

"Honey," she purred, "I have all the friends I need, and if you knew anything about the Templars, then you'd know you're already dust."

The punch to her face was the last thing she knew before her whole world exploded into white-hot pain.

The bliss of oblivion followed it.

Chapter Twenty~Two

Lex sat cross-legged on the couch, totally engrossed in Brad Pitt wielding a sword in *Troy*. The ringing phone, which lay all but forgotten on the couch next to her, was a harsh interruption of the movie. She answered the cordless, expecting it to be Allie again warning her she'd better stay in or else. Lex wasn't brave enough to ask what the "or else" was.

"For the thousandth time, I promise not to go anywhere."

"Lexine?"

Obviously it wasn't her sister on the other end. "Who's this?" She didn't immediately recognize the deep male voice on the other end.

"It's Sebastian."

"Oh, hey!" she said excitedly. "What's up?" She paused the movie. God forbid she missed a second of gorgeous guys running around in mini skirts and brandishing swords.

"Is Allie home?"

"No, why? She told me she was going to see you after she got out of her meeting."

"I know." His tone had a sick feeling building in Lex's stomach. "Have you spoken to her at all since she left?"

Lex glanced at the clock on the DVD player. Eleven already, the meeting wouldn't have gone on for six hours. Not even Josh and Nick could run on at the mouth for that long. And man, did those two *love* to talk.

Lex jumped off the couch, grabbed the universal remote from the coffee table and turned off the TV and DVD player. Panic tightened like a fist around her heart. "No. She hasn't called here. What's going on, Sebastian?"

"I need you to listen to me very closely, Lex." Though his tone was steady and clam, Lex felt his unease as if it was a living thing that came through the phone to grab at her soul. "I need you to lock every door and window in the house and wait for Constantine. Do *not* open the door to anyone but him. Do you understand?"

She nodded, even though she knew he couldn't see her. "I understand. Sebastian?"

"What is it?"

Lex swallowed the lump that lodged in her throat. "Is my sister okay?"

She expected a quick reassurance, what she got was a dose of brutal truth instead. "I don't know."

She admired his honesty even though she hated his answer. "Find her, Sebastian. Please."

He didn't even hesitate in the slightest. "I will. Don't you doubt that for a moment."

For now, his assurance would have to be enough.

Lex hung up the phone before running around the house locking the windows and doors. She even shut off all the lights except for the small lamp on the table beside the couch. Her mouth ran dry and her gut twisted painfully at the thought of anything happening to her sister.

Allie was all she had left, she couldn't lose her sister too.

She couldn't go through that again. Couldn't bury another person she loved.

With shaking hands, she grabbed the cordless phone and crouched on the floor, pressing her back against the couch. She drew up her knees and folded her arms across them. Resting her chin on her arms, Lex closed her eyes and did the only thing she could. She prayed.

In the name of the father

And of the son

And of the Holy Ghost

Please God, protect my sister. Please don't take her from me too. Amen.

Lex chanted her short prayer over and over in her head as she wept silent tears of worry, waiting for Constantine to come for her.

* * *

At Randall Manor, Constantine stood in the doorway of the kitchen. Arms folding over his chest, feet braced apart, he already knew what Sage had to say.

Sebastian cursed as he slammed the phone down on the table. "She's not home."

Raphael ended the call to Tristan. "Luc isn't at Seacrest."

"Bloody hell." Sebastian's frustration was evident in his tone.

Allie and Lucian were gone and no matter how hard he tried, Constantine couldn't sense who took them or where they were. His goddamn brain hurt from the effort of reaching out with his mind to locate them. All that came back to him was nothingness—never a good thing.

As soon as Constantine woke for the night, the overwhelming absence of Lucian hit him like a physical blow to the mind. He felt the loss of his brother as keenly as if a piece of his own body had been torn away.

He immediately woke Sebastian and Raphael. The moment they gained consciousness they too felt Lucian's absence.

None of them ever spent a night away from the safety of their sanctuary. Not in seven centuries. For Luc to have done so now didn't bode well for what might have gone down last night.

This was the first time since Constantine became a vampire that he couldn't feel the presence of one of his fellow Templars. Needless to say the feeling was on par with what it felt like for him to have his soul ripped out of his body. He may be a miserable son of a bitch on his best day, but after hundreds years of having those bastards in his head, it was a hell of a thing now to have one of his blood-brothers gone.

At first they assumed Lucian's sudden disappearance was the work of the Obyri, fellow cursed Templars who couldn't give a shit less about redemption. They rejected that idea almost as soon as they thought it. If those fuckers managed to get to Luc, Constantine would have known it immediately. He would have felt their presence the second they passed into the area.

That left them to assume it was renegades who took Lucian and Allie. It forced their hand, pushing them to declare open war on the inferior vampires. Once it was done, such an order couldn't—nor wouldn't—be undone. Shit was going to go down badly and would bring too much attention to their existence. Tristan might even be forced to leave Damascus, something damned dangerous for all the Templars, since this was where the relic the Guardian protected needed to be.

"I want blood for this." Raphael's incensed declaration vibrated through Constantine. Rogue's fury caused his own to rise to a seriously dangerous level.

"You'll get your blood," Sebastian promised with ominous intent.

The only time Constantine ever saw the promise of death light Sebastian's eyes was right before they charged into battle, when Sage, always the logical one, transformed. The cool facade of civility was stripped away and in its place was the fierce warrior who lay beneath it.

Constantine also felt his fear.

The others might believe Sebastian had loved Selena, but Constantine knew the truth. Sebastian couldn't have loved her. How could he, when the woman was nothing more than shadows? Sage stayed by her, watching over her, protecting her, out of obligation. Not out of love. That he reserved solely for Allie.

She had his heart—what was left of it after Michael destroyed it.

Constantine stepped forward and, in a rare show of affection, put his hand on Sebastian's shoulder. "We'll find them, Sage."

Sebastian gave him a nod, beyond words as his emotions ran so hot Constantine had to step away from him lest Sebastian's rage burn him. "Of that I have no doubt."

Sebastian had every intention of hunting down the bastards who took Allie and Lucian. He would bring a reckoning to them that would rock Hell itself.

He turned to Constantine. "Go to Allie's and get Lexine. I want her at Seacrest where she'll be safe." Then to Raphael, "I need you to go to The Gate and see if you can find anything that might tell us what happened with Lucian,"

"I'm already there, Sage." Raphael had his keys in hand and his body loaded with weapons. He tied his blond hair back in a queue before tugging on the long black trench coat that concealed the various blades strapped to his person. "I'll meet you both at Seacrest."

Sebastian nodded curtly. Even though vampires didn't age, right then he felt every one of his years pressing down on him. The weight was oppressive, nearly crushing him as his worry for Allie and Lucian shook him to his core.

He felt so goddamn helpless.

He should have forced her not to go to that bloody meeting, should have gone with her if he couldn't talk her out of going. Lucian shouldn't have gone to The Gate alone...

"At least they're still alive, Sebastian," Constantine said to him. "Remember that and try to hold it together. We can't have you losing your shit and going off."

Sebastian ran a hand over his shorn head. "I know." His tone held all the pent up emotions he was fighting back. "I can't loose her, C."

Even he heard the note of desperation in his voice. "Fuck all, what if they have Luc in a cage..."

He couldn't go on, couldn't even entertain the idea of Allie and Lucian being held like animals. If his thoughts went there, his mind would snap and he'd be no better than a mindless beast out for blood.

Constantine gave him a curt nod to acknowledge the unspoken

understanding.

The worst thing you could do to a Templar was to cage them. After three years in that French prison, the last place any of them wanted to be was at the mercy of a captor. Not even an eternity in Hell was as much of a threat to their sanity as one moment of captivity was.

They'd all been through that and had the scars to prove it—both inside and out.

The need for blood raged in Sebastian as he went to his room and grabbed his baldric. The weapon felt good in his hands, calming him somewhat and taking the edge off his fury. As long as he had his sword he'd never be helpless.

At least she's alive.

He ran his hand over the cross pattee in the pommel of his sword as Constantine's words came back to him.

Alive.

Yes. Allie was life, and so much a part of him he no longer knew where he ended and she began.

When he was a boy he never knew love, never knew it to miss it. As a man he gave his life to the sword and to God, having no desire to know a love other than for the thrill of battle. Once dead, he believed himself beyond something to be loved or who could love in return. Yet Allie burst into his existence and became the soul he lost.

Allie's love for him held the power to chase away lifetimes of loneliness and cold. For that alone he would make damn sure the ground ran red with the blood of those who dared to take her from him.

He pulled on his baldric and his duster before grabbing his keys off the dresser. He stomped down the stairs, past Constantine who was strapping an arsenal of weapons to his body, and out to his car.

His only thought was of finding Allie and Lucian. He fully intended on bringing Hell down upon the renegades who had them. The need to spill their blood consumed him as he slammed the Charger into drive and hauled ass to *The Specter's* office.

The renegades, who dared to take from them, were going to learn exactly why the Templars were the most feared creatures this side of Hell.

Chapter Twenty~Three

Slapping the palms of his hands to his temples, Constantine doubled over as a blinding pain pierced his skull. Robbing him of sight and reason, all he could do was drag air into his dead lungs as blades picked away at his brain.

And the screaming—*Jesus Christ*, the screaming of his name over and over inside his mind…

Too much for his senses to take, he felt like his goddamn head was going to explode.

"Fuck it all," he hissed out between gritted teeth. He dropped to his knees with a tortured groan, wished for the millionth time Fate hadn't forced these visions on him.

The agony of the visions nearly unbearable, he wondered if he was ever going to know an existence free of pain.

Having gone to Allie's to get Lex, they were only now returning to Seacrest.

As soon as the vision hit him, bringing with it the pain, Lex fell to her knees beside him. Sebastian, already back from *The Specter's* office, came running over when she reached out her hand to touch him.

"No!" he yelled, causing her to pull back her arm and jump away. "If you touch him you'll only make it worse."

Constantine, infinitely grateful Sage stopped her, knew if he felt her gentle touch on him he'd shatter into a thousand pieces.

Grinding out a groan between clenched teeth, Constantine held his head in his hands and rocked back and forth as agony stabbed at his brain.

"What's happening to him?"

Constantine heard the fear in Lex's tone. Fear *for* him, not *of* him. Out of the corner of his eye he saw she still knelt beside him, her hands hovering over him.

"He has telepathy," Tristan explained to her. "If the connection is too strong, thoughts, images, sounds, all come at him in furious assault to him senses."

Her fingers brushed through his hair and he nearly died. Again.

"But he'll be okay, right?" Her concerned whisper pushed him over the edge.

Seeing a scene playing out in his head through Allie's eyes, he saw two renegades take her, though what he saw was blurry at best. Allie's riotous thoughts came at him too fast and loud to distinguish one from another. The one clear vision was of Allie being hit. The punch to her face turned her world black.

Too much of an assault to his senses, Constantine's body began to shake violently as agony tore through him with the force of a freight train. He opened his mouth to speak but words were lost to him. All he could do was grab at Sebastian and pull him down to his level. He brought Sage's face a mere inch from his and growled. His fangs were bared in a vicious snarl as struggled against the waves of pain washing through him.

Sebastian nodded his understanding. Constantine let him go and sagged with relief. "Help me, Tris." He heard Sebastian say. "He's a heavy fucker."

Next thing he knew, Sebastian and Tristan lifted him off the floor and carried him to the sofa. Lex came racing around, keeping herself as close to him as possible without getting in the way. Why she gave a shit, he didn't know, but he was damn glad she did. Her being near seemed to make the pain ease a bit. When her hand went to her mouth and her eyes filled with tears, he wanted to tell her not to cry, to save her tears for someone who was worthy of them. But again, words were beyond him.

"Is it Lucian?" Sebastian asked him.

"No,"

That came out in a harsh hiss laced with all the pain that wracked his body.

"Allie?" The note of desperation in Sage's voice pushed through the fog of pain.

Gritting his teeth, he nodded. "Renegades," he rasped out as voices and visions invaded his brain at a lighting speed. So fast they made his eyes feel as if they were going to pop right out of their sockets. "She's alive."

Though it damn near killed him to push those words out, he had to give Sebastian that one small assurance. Sage was good to him and he loved Allie. Constantine had to give him hope his mate was alive.

At least for now.

* * *

Alive.

Allie was alive. He hadn't lost her. Somewhere behind him, Sebastian heard Lex whisper, "Thank God." She said what he was thinking.

"Thank you, God. Thank you…"

Still, knowing Allie was alive did nothing to quiet the violent fury shooting through him. It demanded vengeance. It called for renegade blood. He knew the rage wouldn't quiet until that need was meet.

Until Allie was back with him where she belonged.

His hand went to the pocket of his jeans, resting over Allie's keys. He found them in front of *The Specter's* office. As soon as he touched them he felt Allie's fear. It lingered on the air, choking him with its intensity.

He wanted to go off half-cocked and hunt down the bastards who put that fear into his woman. But his reason overcame his emotions and he returned to Seacrest to wait for Constantine and Raphael. A life spent in battle taught him not to charge blindly in without the Templars at his back. Especially not with Allie and Lucian's lives on the line.

Why renegades would target Allie and Lucian made no sense. It was also suicide. Renegades, knowing they were inferior vampires, liked their immortality too much to give it up in a losing battle with Templars.

The only equals the Templars had in the nocturnal hierarchy were the Order of the Rose, a sisterhood of vampires who were the daughters of a Druid priestess. And you did *not* fuck with them. Ever.

Since four members of the Order made their home here in Damascus, Templars would occasionally brush past one of them. That's where their contact began and ended. Seemed only Raphael was able to cozy up with the Order, and even he gave those women wide berth.

If Lucian was right, and renegades were gunning for him, it still wouldn't explain why they would take Allie too. She didn't know anything about the Daystar. If she did, the Templars would have the thing in their possession by now.

Shit wasn't adding up. A piece of the puzzle was missing and Sebastian was determined to find it.

Tristan came to stand behind the sofa as Lex dropped to her knees before Constantine, who looked as he had back in Chinon the night they broke him.

Lex was silently weeping with worry for Dragon.

"Don't worry, Constantine, I won't touch you," she said softly, wringing her hands.

A long while passed, the only sounds in the hall the hissing of the fire dancing in the hearth and Constantine's ragged breathing. One of his hands gripped the edge of the cushions. The other held tight to the back of the sofa. Every muscle in his body strained under his pallid flesh. His mouth was set in a hard line as he fought back his pain.

"How are you doing?" Tristan asked when Constantine finally looked as if his body was starting to relax.

"Great. You?" Dragon ground out sarcastically. He slammed his eyes shut. Sebastian knew he was assailed with another barrage of visions.

He wanted to demand Constantine tell him what he saw. He needed to know what Allie was showing him. But he held his tongue. He wouldn't add to his suffering by making Constantine tell him the things he ached to know.

Constantine opened his eyes and ran a hand through his mess of hair. A muscle ticked in his jaw. "Dark," he ground out roughly. His upper lip drew back in a nasty snarl. He continued to gasp for air. "Tied up."

That information hit Sebastian hard.

Hard enough to cause him to stumble backwards and collapse into one of the chairs. He dragged a hand over his head as everything in him rebelled at the idea of Allie bound in the dark.

His fury too great for him to control, he needed to put his fist through something. Anything. But most especially, he needed to hurt the renegades hurting his Allie.

"Dead. Every last bloody one of them." The declaration was pulled from the dark place within Sebastian he rarely set free.

"I can see the house she's in," Constantine gritted out hoarsely. "Old farm house. Boarded windows."

Rage, pure and hot, surged through Sebastian as Constantine's words took shape in his mind.

Constantine began shaking furiously. "Just relax now, C. Go easy," Tristan said soothingly. "Raphael's not even back, so we're not going anywhere yet."

Sebastian stood and went over to the sofa. Standing next to Lex, he was surprised when Allie's sister rested her hand on his leg. Such a simple touch, yet in it was a wealth of emotion. The poor girl was terrified she was going to lose her sister.

He put a hand on her shoulder and felt she was shaking with fear. "We'll find her and bring her home," he said to her. She sniffled and nodded before wiping the tears from her face.

"Sorry."

Gaping, Sebastian looked to Constantine when he whispered that hoarsely. This was the first time he'd had ever heard the word "sorry" pass

Constantine's lips. "Rest now, you miserable bastard," he said lightly. "We're going to need you battle-ready come tomorrow night."

Constantine nodded before his head sagged to the side. His eyes slid closed. "Put your hands on me."

She complied without hesitation. She ran one hand through his hair. The other, she rested lightly on his chest. "I'll be here as long as you need me."

Constantine gave him a barely perceivable nod before slipping into unconsciousness. As soon as he was out, Tristan sank down on the one of the high-backed chairs to keep vigil over Constantine along with Lexine.

Tonight was going to be a long night.

* * *

Sebastian used the time to do something he hadn't dared in centuries.

He went to the chapel to pray.

Knowing they wouldn't be able to go out tonight and hunt the renegades, he stalked out of the hall, his destination the chapel. He knew if he stayed, watching Constantine suffer, the walls would close in on him, adding to his already dangerous level of fury.

He didn't know why he came here since he knew God didn't want him near His house. Nor did he know why he was torturing himself with being so close to holy ground. Though he stood a good distance away already the bottoms of his feet began to heat, a promise of the burns to come. Not even the thick soles of his boots could protect him from God's wrath for daring to put his damned feet on His hallowed ground.

He looked at the chapel, his eyes aching as he looked upon the holy building. Such a simple structure, small and unremarkable, no one would ever imagine the power housed within. He felt the pull of it throughout his body, whispering promises that filled his head and body with need. This was the temptation Tristan faced every moment of his existence and which forced the Templars to avoid Seacrest to the point of making their home at Randall

Manor instead of the castle.

His gaze lingered over the stained glass windows, which depicted the Templars journey from living Knights to the damned creatures they became. It brought back so many memories. Painful memories best left forgotten.

Sebastian didn't dare enter the chapel. He tried that nonsense once when he felt he needed to feel God's warmth on him. Once was more than enough. He wasn't up for that party again. As the chosen Guardian, only Tristan could enter the chapel. Only he could touch the ancient relic it housed. The rest of them were here to protect Tristan. It was what God demanded of them in order to earn redemption.

Remembering the day he died, the feel of the flames licking at him, Sebastian couldn't stop the shiver of revulsion that ran through him. Even after all this time he couldn't forget the stink of his melting flesh, or the agony of slowly burning to death. Nor could he ever forget what it had felt like to have Michael tear his soul from him.

He wished he could say he was wrongly arrested. Wrongly imprisoned. He wanted to be able to say he didn't deserve that awful death or his damnation. But that would all be lies. He did deserve it. All of it. They all did. They were the guilty among the innocent.

Genuflecting, Sebastian bowed his head. He made the sign of the cross. A horrific burn cut a path across him in the wake of his hands.

"In the name of the Father."

"And of the Son."

His flesh was scorched from head to heart.

"And of the Holy Ghost…"

A trail of a fire ran shoulder to shoulder.

Sebastian prayed to God to watch over and protect Allie. He asked the Lord to keep her safe and whisper in her ear that he was coming for her and to not be afraid of the dark she was in, for He was with her. He prayed for God to look past Lucian's sins and watch over the Knight as well.

As he prayed he felt his knees burning at the prolonged contact with the consecrated ground. Not that he cared. To pray for Allie and Lucian, he would risk his entire body bursting into flames.

Besides, he'd been burned worse.

Burned until he died.

He'd stay here praying until the skin damn near melted clean off the bone if that was what it took for God to hear his prayers.

Chapter Twenty-Four

When Allie blinked open her eyes, she was met with complete darkness. Forcing down her panic, for a fleeting moment she actually believed she might be dead.

Or undead—since she still felt very much alive.

As quickly as the possibility came was as fast as it went. Aside from feeling like warmed over shit, she quickly regained all of her functions and realized she felt her heart not merely beating, but hammering against her ribcage painfully as terror ripped through her.

Once her head cleared of the haze after being knocked unconscious, Allie felt too weak to sit. Instead, she turned her head from side to side in an attempt to see where she was. She saw nothing but black. She felt as if she were in a tomb. And for all she knew she was, since her eyes saw nothing but the dark.

Robbed of sight, Allie's other senses flared to life, making her aware of the stench that rose around her like a living, breathing thing. The stink of filth sat on the still, stale air, making each breath torturous. She heard faint sounds coming from beyond the room, muffled voices she couldn't make out clearly.

Facedown, when she went to move to push herself up she became all-too aware her hands were bound behind her back. "Oh Christ," she swore, pulling at the ropes binding her wrists.

Like a wild-woman, Allie fought against the rope, twisting and turning until she was grunting with exhaustion from the futile effort to free herself. Her only thoughts were of those other women. They'd been tortured, used as food, raped, and slaughtered before being left to rot like garbage. She didn't want to go out like that, her soul stolen, trapping her between life and death like the very ghosts she devoted the last years of her life to hunting.

When she was done with this world, Allie didn't want her eternity spent as a ghost. Caught between realms. Haunting life. Dear God, the thought was enough to have her growing physically sick. Gagging, she fought down her vomit and tried not to think about what might be waiting for her in the dark.

Fighting for calm, Allie used her face as leverage to somehow manage to sit up. Once she was on her knees, her gaze darted wildly around the room, trying to see through the darkness. She couldn't make out a damn thing. Though Allie never had a fear of the dark, she found this complete blackness terrifying. If she was the type to give in to terror, she might have wept from fear. Thankfully she was the type who fought, not about to waste her energy on tears.

With no idea how long she'd been knocked out, she didn't know how much time went by since the two renegades brought her here. For all she knew it could have been hours or days. All she did know was that by now, everyone had to know she was gone.

Hopefully that meant they'd find her and come charging in to rescue her from whoever it was who wanted her brought here.

You have no idea what's waiting for you...

The renegade's words came back to her. Sick dread rose in the form of bile in her throat as she searched through the darkness. Something nagged at her, whispering to her. Telling her she wasn't alone in here. Violent tremors wracked her when she could feel eyes on her.

Oh God, help me.

Terrified or not, she wasn't about to sit there and do nothing, waiting for whoever—*whatever*—was in here with her to leap at her through the dark. "You might as well say something since I know I'm not alone."

When a match flared to life her entire body went numb with fear. The light of it barely illuminated the man holding it. Still, she could vaguely make out long, thick brown hair that fell around a gorgeous and deathly pale, face.

Twin burning silver eyes cut through the dark to pin her with a savage stare.

The vampire brought the match down to a taper set in a wrought iron holder. Its light broke the complete dark, giving Allie an idea of the man who lit it and room she was in.

She saw the vampire sat with his back against the wall. His long legs stretched out before him and crossed at the ankle, he looked extremely relaxed.

Young, though not as young as the renegades who abducted her, what he lacked in years he made up for in the evil reflected in his chilling eyes.

Taking advantage of the faint light, Allie gave the tiny room a quick once over. Stripped bare, the only furniture was the mattress she was kneeling on. The window was boarded up to keep out the sun.

These creatures were faster and stronger than her, leaving her no hope of being able to either fight or sneak her way out if their guard happened to be down. They'd smell her wherever she went and drag her right back.

The vampire pushed himself off the floor. Long and lean, he came at her in four long strides. He took up all the space around her. Allie fought down her fear, staying perfectly still, watching him as he set the candle down. When he sat on the edge of the mattress, she felt her heart slam against her ribcage as terror washed over her like an icy wave.

"I was afraid you were going to sleep the entire night away." His English accent added to his air of aristocracy.

"Next time I'm knocked cold by one of your dogs, I'll try not to stay unconscious so long."

His smile was unnerving. Even though she was used to seeing fangs, his caused fingers of dread to inch up her spine. "Brandon said you had spirit."

She imaged Brandon had to be the vamp with the good right hook. She hoped he was the first one Sebastian sent to Hell—if the Templars ever found her.

The vampire took her chin in his hand. Allie's skin crawled at the contact. He examined her swollen and bruised left cheek with an almost feminine pout. Allie knew he wasn't as apologetic about it as he tried to appear. He was a vampire, and though that wasn't always a bad thing—look at the Templars—he *was* a renegade. That made all the difference in the world. It made him a cold killer.

"He shouldn't have damaged your face." How dare he have the nerve to look sincere? "A face as beautiful as yours was made to be cherished."

Oh, he was good. He had the whole charming Dracula thing going for him. Shame Allie wasn't buying his bullshit. "So, is this what you did to Sarah, Jordan, and Amanda before you murdered them? Did the whole 'nice-guy' thing?"

He released her jaw and fingered a lock of her hair. He inhaled softly, taking in the scent of her. She shivered with disgust, not wanting any part of her person to give this monster any pleasure.

"I had nothing to do with their deaths."

Sure he didn't. "Am I supposed to believe that?" she shot back.

Scared to death, Allie couldn't stop her shaking no matter how hard she tried. She knew the vampire could feel that fear and she hated that fact.

"Stephan killed them, though I won't lie and say I didn't enjoy those women before he did." He ran his knuckles down her cheek. He grunted when she pulled away from him. "Once he had what he wanted, he made good on his word and gave us what was promised."

She didn't know who Stephan was, having never heard the name before. "Why me?"

The candlelight played off of his rich brown hair and the sharp planes of his face when he stood. He turned and stared down at her. It was unnerving to have him towering over her like that. "Ah, right to the point. I like that." He moved around the room with astounding grace. "You have something I want."

Something he wanted? What in the hell was he talking about? "What could I possibly have that you would want?"

What Allie didn't add, but thought, was, *What is so important that you would risk the Templar's wrath for it?*

"The Daystar."

Well now, that surely was enough for any renegade to put their existence on the line for. To kill for.

Allie's blood ran cold. "I don't know what you're talking about."

In a swift and seamless motion, he yanked her up by her arms. She held in her cry when the rope bit into her wrists. He set her roughly on her feet and pulled her to him. Only an inch or two away from his face, she was close enough to see that his eyes weren't nearly as cold as she first thought.

No, they weren't cold at all. This close, she saw the fires of Hell blazed beneath that icy surface.

And it scared her. She went to move away from him but his hand closed around her upper arm, his fingers squeezing her until she thought the bone might snap.

"Don't play stupid with me, Allison. You know exactly what I'm talking about. You have the Daystar and I want it."

The determination she heard in his tone was reflected in the depths of eyes. It chilled her to her bones.

"Constantine, you'd better be listening. Get me the hell out of here. This crazy bastard thinks I have the Daystar."

Allie shook her head frantically. "I don't have it. If I did, don't you think I would have given it to the Templars by now?"

He gave her such a hard shake her head snapped back and forth. "Stephan said you have it."

"I swear to God I don't." She tried to keep her terror out of her tone, but failed horribly.

He brought her *very* close to his face. His growl actually had the power to pull a whimper of fear from her. "Mention that name again and I'll cut your tongue out."

Allie shook with such violent force her teeth clashed together. "I'm telling you I don't have the Daystar."

His eyes narrowed on her. He sniffed at her like an animal took in the scent of its prey. She heard a deep rumble coming from him that only added to her terror. "Then it's you. You're the Daystar."

For a second Allie thought she heard him wrong. When what he said finally registered, Allie choked out a sick sound and tried to pull away from him. "Are you crazy? Do you hear yourself? The Daystar isn't a person."

With her hands tied behind her back, Allie couldn't fight him when his other hand came around her throat like a vice. He squeezed hard enough to restrict her air without completely cutting it off. "No one knows what the Daystar is, do they? The legend was lost over the ages. So you see, Allison? The Daystar could very well be a person. It could even be you."

Blinking back tears, the same tears she swore not to waste her energy on, she fought for air. "You're wrong. I'm just an ordinary human."

He tilted his head, his lips playing over the skin on her throat. Allie shivered with disgust. "Ordinary? No, I don't think so."

His hold on her throat lessened even as his hand on her arm grew firmer. He sniffed at her again before glancing around her to look down at her bloody wrists. He spun her around, his hands hovering at the rope. "I would hate to have to end our fun before it begins." The warning in his tone damn near scared the life out of her. "If you fight me, I'll make it hurt."

Allie went cold even as she began to sweat, fear lumping in her throat. "I won't fight."

Her survival depended on her staying calm and rational. The Templars were going to find her. *Sebastian* was going to find her. That was a chant in her mind as she forced herself to hold onto hope. She couldn't let herself believe this was where her life was going to end. Not here. Not at this creature's hands.

The Templars wouldn't allow it.

He broke the rope and turned her back around. Allie watched in complete horror when he lifted her arm and licked her bloody wrists. She wanted to tell him he would know if she was the Daystar by taking in her blood, but she knew she was standing on a dangerous edge. He'd do exactly as he threatened if she pushed him.

Her death would be bad.

He brought her close to him and leaned down to whisper in her ear. Allie wanted to slap him away from her, but instead stayed stock still as her stomach turned with revulsion. "I want to hear my name on your lips. Say it. Say 'Daniel'."

She would rather eat broken glass. Nevertheless, her need for survival was strong. She didn't want to give this sick bastard the satisfaction of killing her. That meant, if he wanted her to call him by name, then that's what she was going to do. Even if it killed her pride to relent.

Better her pride destroyed than her life.

"Daniel." His name was poison on her tongue.

He let out a satisfied purr and ran his fangs over her neck. Her teeth bit down hard on her bottom lip to keep in her groan of disgust. She needed to keep her hands fisted at her sides so as not to attempt to try to fight him off.

"By the time I'm done with you, I'm going to know you body *and* soul."

Without warning, his teeth sank deep into her neck. Allie hissed, unable to let loose the scream of pain caught in her throat.

Instinct won over as she clawed at him wildly in her mad fight for life. When that didn't work to get him off her, she slapped at him, fighting like hell to do everything she could to get free of him. His arms came around her like two steel bands. He held her so tight she was unable to move or even barely breathe, so crushing was his hold.

The feel of his fangs in her, of him pulling at her blood revolted her. With tears spilling down her cheeks, all Allie could do was accept what was happening and hold on to the vision of Sebastian that filled her mind when she closed her eyes.

As she felt her blood being stolen from her body she grew weaker and weaker until she was nothing more than a rag-doll in the vampire's arms. When he finally pulled his teeth from her, he released her. Limp, drained, and repulsed, Allie dropped to the mattress. She felt as if this monster took a piece of her along with her blood.

A tear slipped down her face as cold tore through her. Too weak to wipe it away, all she could think was how this monster robbed a small part of her soul.

* * *

The next time Allie woke, she was again engulfed in absolute darkness. This time, however, she knew she was alone. *Thank God.* She didn't want to have another face to face with that renegade again. Not after what he did to her. Her skin crawled and she bit back a disgusted cry at the thought of his fangs at her neck.

Her entire body hurt and she was so weak she could barely move. Shivering, she struggled to ignore the stench of the mattress, curling into herself in a vain attempt to keep warm.

"I think she's awake," she heard someone say beyond the door. She jumped at least a foot at the loud bang on the door. "You up in there?" The voice belonged to the driver who kidnapped her. He didn't wait for her to answer. "Yeah. She's awake." He yelled.

Only a few seconds later she heard someone fiddling with the lock. Dread ran though her, turning her body numb and causing her mouth to run dry, her heart thundering painfully as she curled tighter. When the door swung open her breath caught and she threw her arm over her face at the sudden flood of light hitting her eyes.

Assuming it was Daniel again, Allie didn't even bother to look at him. She kept her arm over her closed eyes, refusing to acknowledge him.

"Well, well, well," the vampire said from directly above her. "Seems you got yourself into a bit of trouble, didn't you, Allie?"

Allie lowered her arm and forced herself to stop shaking. She went even colder when she saw the icy hatred in Jude's silvery eyes.

Holy shit...

They'd turned Jude.

He stood staring down at her with his usual smug expression. She slowly pushed herself into a sitting position, even as every bone in her body protested the movement.

All she could think as she stared at him was, he had absolutely no reason to look so smug. If anyone looked wrong as a vampire, Jude did. He was stuffed with too much false bravado and overblown arrogance to make what he now was a good fit on him.

"Not nearly as much trouble as you seem to be in." Her voice sounded weak and thin, even to her own ears.

He smirked at her in the way that never failed to make her want to slap the taste right out of his mouth. "I don't think so, Allie. I'm immortal and you, well, you're pretty much fucked."

Allie wished she could stand, might have even attempted to if she thought her legs would support her. It galled her how Jude hovered over her.

"Immortal?" she asked casually. "Is that what they told you? I have news for you, Jude, vampires can die. Why do you think every renegade this side of Hell wants the Daystar? Besides, you're more fucked than me at this point."

"Now how do you figure that?" The sarcasm in his tone left no room for doubt that he believed he was unstoppable now that he was a vampire.

Allie slapped on a smirk that could rival Jude's on his best day. "I don't have the Templars gunning for me. You do. And when they get you, it's going to get real ugly for you."

If Jude were smart he would have realized the threat. Obviously a few brain cells short of smart, he backhanded her hard enough to split her lip.

"You stupid bitch!" he roared. "I was bitten because of you. They know you have the Daystar. They thought to use me to get it from you."

Allie touched a finger to her lip and came away with blood. Jude's eyes narrowed on her mouth. She quickly licked the blood away and threw her hands up to protect her face when Jude went to hit her again. Much to Allie's surprise, Daniel grabbed his arm, preventing that second blow from coming.

"They'll be none of that, Jude." Though Daniel said it calmly, it was an order meant to be obeyed. "I'll not have her face ruined until I'm done with her."

Daniel's hot gaze raked over her, making her wish she was draped head to foot in baggy black wool instead of the low-rise jeans and white half-shirt that revealed way too much of her.

Jude yanked his arm away from Daniel and stepped back, obviously affronted but wisely keep his mouth shut about it. Her ex might be ballsy when it came to beating on a woman, but he was smart enough to know that against a vampire with some years behind him, he didn't stand a chance.

"She's not yours," Jude muttered pathetically.

"You don't think so?" He tilted his head and regarded Jude for a pregnant moment, a cool grin lifting his lips. "Take yourself out of my sight, Jude, before I'm forced to end you."

Jude took another step back when he saw a fire ignite in Daniel's eyes. She knew he wasn't used to being second fiddle. Not in a town where he was the prized son of Grant and Michelle Summers. It had to sting his pride something awful to have to bow down to someone.

Allie prayed the two of them would fight it out. Just tear each other apart in their ridiculous testosterone driven battle.

Much to her disappointment, Jude spun on his heel and strode from the room. His anger and indignation lingered after he was gone.

When Daniel turned his attention back to her, Allie wished he'd kill her. Fast and painless, over and done before she even realized what happened. She didn't want his hands on her again, erasing Sebastian's touch.

When he sat down next to her she instinctively moved to put more distance between them. Daniel wasn't too pleased by that. He took hold of her arm and pulled her back to him. "You don't *ever* move away from me. I own you."

To prove his point, he shoved her down on her back and climbed on top of her. At that moment, Allie didn't care one bit about consequence. All she wanted was for him to get off of her. His threat of a painful death went right out of her head as she fought him for her very life.

Even if she weren't so weak, she still wouldn't have been any match for his vampire's strength. He overpowered her easily, taking hold of her wrists and pinning them over her head.

"I like your fight, but I'm afraid I'm going to have to break it out of you."

"Get the fuck off me," she gritted out between clenched teeth.

He smiled, his fangs reminding her of sleek ivory daggers. Cold fear gripped her, disgust riding close on its heels as he ground his body against hers

"The getting off part isn't going to happen." He licked her neck. "As for the fucking part, that, I can assure you, definitely will."

He took hold of both her wrists in one hand. With his other, he shoved her shirt up. Everything in Allie went cold, her mind rejecting what was happening.

His hands on her, running over her stomach, inching toward her breasts, his mouth above hers, saliva dripping from his fangs, her mind snapped and she did something so utterly ridiculous it had Daniel laughing down at her.

She screamed.

Chapter Twenty-Five

At the exact moment the sun set behind the mountains, Sebastian, Constantine, and Raphael headed out to find Allie and Lucian and bring them home.

With some "gentle persuasion" they convinced Tristan he had to stay behind with Lexine. The last thing they needed was for the Guardian to be caught in this fight. Like Constantine liked to remind him, his fight was coming soon enough.

Before leaving Seacrest, the Templars made sure they were strapped with enough weaponry to take out a small village. Along with their swords and daggers, they added some firepower to their arsenal. The guns might not be able to end a vampire, but bullets would hurt like hell. Hurt enough to stun should they find themselves in need of a few seconds to gain an upper hand.

None of them were so arrogant as to believe they were indestructible. The things that could take out an ordinary vampire could take them out as easily. The sun had the power to burn them to dust. A blade could take their head as quickly as it could a renegade's. And anything holy would cause as much damage to them, as Sebastian's knee, which was burnt to the bone proved.

Much to Sebastian's frustration it took the better part of three hours of driving down roads no more than dirt trails before they finally found the house Constantine saw in his mind. Driving up the narrow road, Sebastian peered through the black of the night, broken only by the pale glow of the half moon. His gaze lit on the large white house standing in the distance. Old and dilapidated, set in the middle of a huge barren field, it stood out against the desolate backdrop.

They passed under a leaning wooden archway that read *Double D Ranch*. The barn long since collapsed into a heap of rotting wood. The tremendous stable looked like it wasn't going to make it through even one more harsh mountain winter. But what caught, and held, his attention was the sleek silver Lexus and white Lincoln Navigator.

Leaving the Charger behind the truck, Sebastian got out, the stink of death crept around him, mingling with Allie's fear. Good God, it was everywhere. Death, fear, and pain thickened the air. They filled his senses until he thought he'd be dragged down by the weight of the them.

Constantine followed him, and took a deep breath. He grunted with frustration and voiced what they all already knew. "Lucian's not here."

Raphael, usually so blithe, had the look of the warrior he was. Gone was the easy smile and seductive gleam in his eyes. Replacing it was the hard edge of the Templar Knight he had been in life. Everything about him proclaimed his intent to cut down those renegades who dared to harm those closest to him.

These renegades made a detrimental mistake thinking they could strike against the Templars and not bring down their wrath, complete and without remorse.

"At least we found Allie." Raphael's tone was tight. "We'll get our girl out of here and then we'll find Luc."

Constantine's muttered curse gained Sebastian's attention. A second later he went sick with dread when a scream broke through the night.

There was no mistaking it was Allie. That knowledge slammed into Sebastian like a hammer to his gut.

Everything feral in him came to the forefront. All he fought to suppress over the centuries rose like a violent storm. It broke his thin hold on humanity, flaring to life the feral instinct in him to protect his mate. The need to spill the blood of his enemies was an all-consuming hunger needing to be fed.

With a vicious snarl and a bellow of rage, he shrugged his shoulders and loosened his duster only enough so he could pull free his sword. Grasping the hilt, he welcomed the weight of the weapon, which was more of an extension of his own arm than a separate entity.

"He's mine," he declared just before he broke into a dead run toward the house.

Who "he" was didn't need to be clarified. It didn't matter who he was specifically. He was the bastard hurting Allie.

As far as Sebastian was concerned, taking out the prick who pulled that scream from Allie was non-negotiable.

Over the ages he bled and killed for God. He killed to protect the lives of his brothers-in-arms. He fought for so many reasons, but never for love. That was the one thing he never believed in enough to shed blood for. Until Allie. For her he was willing to bleed himself dry. For her he was willing to walk through the fires of hell.

Leaping onto the porch, Sebastian slammed his shoulder into the door. The old, dried wood splintered off the frame and crashed to the floor in pieces as two renegades met them with katanas. Sebastian ended one with nothing more than a single cut of his sword, severing the vampire's head. He exploded into dust before he even hit the floor.

Constantine took on the second renegade. This one was more experienced with his sword, giving the Dragon, if not a good fight, at least one that wasn't ended in less than ten seconds. Constantine was able to make quick work of him, ending the vampire in a few strokes of his blades. When the renegade was reduced to dust, Constantine broke through the cloud bodily to follow Sebastian up the stairs.

Raphael turned his back to the fight and guarded the entrance. Here was where he would stay, primed to prevent any other vampires from entering while Sebastian and Constantine searched for Allie.

As Sebastian climbed the steps to the second level two at a time, he saw Allie's ex-boyfriend at the top of the stairs. He and two other renegades stood before a closed door. Sebastian sensed Allie inside. She wasn't alone. A renegade was with her and she was terrified.

He narrowed his eyes on Jude, drawing back his sword to strike him down. He stood in front of a closed door. "Get the fuck out of my way."

Jude, too stupid for his own good, gave Sebastian that same arrogant smirk he gave to everyone. The other two renegades, knowing the threat Templars were to their immortality, wisely took a step back.

"He's not going to let you have her," Jude announced arrogantly.

Sebastian cocked a brow at that. He leveled his blade at Jude's neck. Allie's ex looked like he was going to shit himself. "He doesn't have a choice."

With a violent shove, Sebastian sent the blade clean through Jude's throat. The tip of it embedded in the plaster with a solid thud. Pinned to the wall, Jude's eyes went wide with shock as he grabbed at the blade. He lost two fingers in his frantic bid to pull the sword free.

The digits burst into dust before they even hit the floor.

Sebastian hissed with pain when he was stabbed from behind. He felt the blade being pulled free just as he gave his own sword a vicious jerk to the right. Jude tried to scream as blood pooled in his throat. The gash was enough to end him.

The moment Jude turned to ash Sebastian pulled his sword from the wall and turned to his attacker. He deflected the young renegade's blows, though he couldn't get in a quick killing blow. The renegade proved a good fighter and had surprising agility. Unfortunately for the renegade, what he lacked that Sebastian possessed was the determination to get to Allie. He wasn't about to let anyone stand in his way while she was being hurt.

Able to call on that determination, Sebastian drove the renegade back with one hard shove and kept him there as he showered down a rapid succession of blows. Unable to match skill with a Templar, the vampire quickly tired and got sloppy. He dropped his sword and it was all the advantage Sebastian needed to get in the killing blow.

Swinging his sword around, he severed the vampire's head in a brutal, but clean, blow.

Ash exploded around him as the vampire disintegrated. Bleeding from his stomach wound, Sebastian lunged for the door. Another renegade thought to stop him by throwing a dagger at him. It caught him in the left shoulder. He pulled the dagger free and spun on the renegade and hurled the dagger back at him. His aim was true. The dagger landed in the renegade's throat. Choking on blood, the vampire stumbled back. Sebastian lunged, stabbing the renegade in the chest. With a fierce growl he took hold of the dagger and used it to take the bastard's head.

Sebastian caught sight of Constantine, just as he impaled the youngblood he was fighting with his daggers. Pinned to the wall, the vampire snarled and tried to pull himself free.

"You're fucked now, aren't you, boy?" Constantine taunted.

"Screw you," the renegade spat out.

Pulling the dagger from the renegade's right shoulder, Constantine held it against the vampire's throat. "See you in Hell."

In one swift motion, Constantine cut deep enough to sever the head. He stepped back carelessly when the vampire went to dust.

Time came to a crashing halt when Sebastian charged the door, splintering it off the frame.

Frozen, Sebastian saw Allie being held roughly against the chest of a renegade. Sebastian knew the bastard. His name was Daniel Parsons. A particularly brutal vampire, he cut a bloody path through Europe, beginning shortly after he was turned sometime around the time of Queen Victoria.

Daniel held a knife to Allie's throat as tears slipped down her face. Each one of those tears cut though Sebastian like a knife. He heard the thundering of her heart, the roar of her blood pushing through her veins, felt her fear like a punch to his gut.

Sebastian let his gaze travel over her and take in her pale color, her dry and cracked lips, the two bruises on her face the size of men's fists, and the blood on her neck. Rage, hot and swift, shot through him when he noticed the puncture wounds left behind by a vampire's bite.

Snarling, Sebastian moved forward. Only when Daniel pressed the blade harder against her neck did he realize he'd advanced on them. He came to a dead halt, though Daniel kept the knife pressed hard on her.

A thin line of blood formed under the blade. Sebastian's nostrils flared at the scent of her blood. Allie's gaze, wide with terror, locked on him as she bit back a whimper.

"Take one more step and I'll slit her throat."

Allie went to say something but the renegade gave her a hard squeeze. The movement caused the blade to cut deeper into her flesh. A thin line of blood appeared on her throat. Any words she might have uttered stilled on her tongue.

"This fight has nothing to do with her." Sebastian struggled to remain as calm as possible despite the fact that he wanted to hack him to pieces and leave Daniel for the sun. "Let her go."

Daniel's lips curled in a lazy smile. "That's where you're wrong, Templar. This has everything to do with her." He jerked Allie. This time she cried out as the blade scraped her neck. Blood trickled from the shallow slice. "Stay back, Dragon, or I'll bleed the bitch."

Sebastian motioned to Constantine to cease his slow advance. Constantine froze, though Sebastian could hear his furious thoughts in his head.

"We're not moving. We're staying right where we are. Right, C?" Sebastian asked calmly. Constantine nodded and grunted an affirmation. There wasn't any doubt if given the chance, Constantine would have torn the vampire to pieces.

Daniel smirked and pulled Allie even closer. She looked like nothing more than a rag doll in the bastard's arms. "You truly have no idea what she is, do you?"

"No, so why don't you tell me?" Sebastian figured as long as the situation remained calm, and he kept the bastard talking, that knife wouldn't cut any deeper into Allie's throat.

If he lost her…

He couldn't allow himself to dwell on that thought. If he did, he'd snap and do something stupid, something that couldn't be undone.

He eyed the scabbard at the vampire's hip. He knew if he lost focus, things could turn ugly fast. Which was why he was trying to keep the situation as calm as possible, even as everything feral in him wanted to tear out the renegade's spinal cord.

When Daniel rubbed his cheek over her hair, Sebastian saw Allie squeeze her eyes shut and bite down on her bottom lip to keep from crying out. Her bravery astounded him, even as he saw her body convulse with revulsion.

Helpless to move without putting Allie in further jeopardy, all Sebastian could do was let out an ominous growl as he watched the vampire's hand play over the flesh of her stomach.

Behind him he heard a sound ripped right out of Hell come from deep within Constantine.

Sebastian wanted to strike. Now. Take out the bastard and send him to the devil. Reason held him back. As long as the blade bit into Allie's throat, neither Templar dared to make a move.

They'd never get to him in time to prevent him from slitting her throat.

Daniel's eyes narrowed on him. An almost maniacal light gleamed in the depths of them, making it all too clear he was half crazed. A slow, sinister grin pulled at his lips. His words, when he spoke them, blew colder than the bitter breath of Death.

"She's the Daystar."

Sebastian's gut twisted sickly when Daniel dropped that announcement. He saw Allie's eyes fly open and lock on him. The desperation he saw reflected in them caused a physical pain in his chest.

If this maniac believed that, it was safe to assume he'd do anything to take the power he believed she possessed. One wrong move on his part, and Allie was going to die.

Behind him, he felt the tension in Constantine, as the Dragon strained to hold himself back. *"Go easy, C."*

"I can feel her in me. She's screaming in my fucking head."

The tortured way Constantine said that was a kick to his heart. *"Tell her it's going to be alright. Tell her I love her."*

Constantine let out a grunt and took a step back. *"She can't hear me."*

What Constantine didn't say, but what Sebastian knew, was that Allie couldn't hear him past her own screams.

Sebastian's hand tightened around the hilt of his sword and his entire being hurt to take this vampire's blood. Still, he remained outwardly calm as a war of emotion raged within in.

"Whoever told you she's the Daystar was wrong."

Daniel shifted his hold on Allie. Sebastian stood still, afraid to move as the renegade took hold of Allie's chin. She choked on a sob when he lifted her head. The knife was still at her throat, slowly cutting into her. The vampire brought his mouth down to the side of her neck. His fangs hovered over her furiously throbbing vein.

"Care to put that to the test, Templar?"

This time it was Constantine who had to control Sebastian.

Sebastian needed to be physically restrained by Constantine to keep him from lunging toward Daniel. The vampire laughed, his fangs nipping at Allie's neck. Her terrified whimper cut right through his brain, robbing him of reason. Like a man possessed, he tried to fight off Constantine's hold, going so far as to try to cut at Dragon's arms with his sword.

"No, Sage," Constantine hissed in his ear. "That's what he wants."

He knew Constantine was right, but God help him all he wanted to do was tear the bastard away from Allie and send him to Lucifer where he belonged.

"Get the fuck off of me," Sebastian demanded. *"The prick is bluffing. He won't kill her as long as he thinks she's the Daystar."*

"And if he's not bluffing?" Constantine growled back. *"You want to take that chance, Sage? You want to risk him killing her?"*

Sebastian knew Constantine was right. He needed to get control over himself and not have his emotions rule his mind. If he allowed that to happen he'd get sloppy and sloppy would get Allie killed.

Calling on all the lessons he'd learned over the centuries, he wasn't going to let Daniel to goad him any more than the renegade already had.

Narrowing his eyes on Daniel, in his stare was the promise of Hell, which the renegade was smart enough to shrink from. Stepping back, he dragged Allie with him. From the smug expression on his face, Sebastian knew.

He *knew* he had them, that they were his fucking puppets in this twisted game.

* * *

Feeling Daniel's hold on her ease a bit, Allie took advantage of her captor's distraction to make a move to try to free herself from his deadly hold. Twisting in his arms, she brought her knee up hard, catching him directly between the legs. Though dead, he could still feel pain and he howled and doubled over. The sword fell to the floor. She lunged for it, grabbing it before Daniel could. She tried to get away from him, but Daniel's arm came down on hers.

With a roar that shook the very foundation of the house, Sebastian charged. He grabbed Daniel by the throat and slammed him against the wall. Unfortunately, Daniel's hold on Allie brought her back with him. She hit the wall with a grunt. Dazed, she slid to the floor, the weapon falling from her hand. It skidded to a halt near her feet. She kicked it away, preventing Daniel from grabbing it and using it against Sebastian.

Yanking her arm away from Daniel, she tried for the knife again, but the fight going on above her forced her to crawl away before she was caught in the middle of it.

Constantine rushed toward her. For a second she thought he was going to join the fray and help Sebastian end Daniel. Instead, he came for her.

One second she was trying to crawl away from the fight and the next she was scooped up in Constantine's arms and carried across the room. When they got to the doorway renegades blocked their exit.

"Fuck all," Constantine swore, and unceremoniously dropped her.

Allie went to the floor with a thud and rolled out of the way. Constantine fought off the attack as she scurried over to the far corner of the room and crouched down low. Her energy spent, she was so weak she couldn't see straight. Sebastian and Daniel looked like a blur, locked in battle. Giving Daniel a good punch that sent him flying, Sebastian turned to her and warned her to stay where she was. Out of the corner of her eye she saw Daniel grab at the dropped sword and screamed out a warning.

A few years ago she would have thought a gun was mightier than a sword. She'd since learned that wasn't the case since a bullet didn't do shit to a vampire.

Especially if the sword happened to be in the hands of a Templar.

Constantine palmed the sword that hung at his hip. He swung the thing with an expertise that rivaled Sebastian's. The sound was deafening as blades crossed and clashed. Allie put her hands over her ears and kept her focus on Sebastian as he battled Daniel. After what the renegade did to her, she didn't want to miss her Sebastian ending the bastard who had every intention of killing her.

The sudden explosion of dust pulled her attention away from Sebastian's fight, however. Constantine took out one of the vampires. The other was proving harder to finish off. The bastard was a damn good opponent. He also fought with that same hacking, brutal style as the Templars.

Turning her attention back to Sebastian, her head spun from the fog of weakness. Still, she saw Daniel keeping pace with him. For every hammering blow of Sebastian's sword, Daniel managed to dance out of the way. He swiped at Sebastian, who easily knocked the blade away, countering with blow of his own.

At the second explosion of ash, Allie didn't need to look to know Constantine ended the second vampire.

Dragon came at her, was reaching for her, when Sebastian's foot hit the corner of the mattress. He stumbled and that was all the advantage Daniel needed.

Or so Allie thought.

In her unfocused and confused state, all she could think was that Daniel was going to kill Sebastian. When Constantine's arms came at her, she found the strength to throw herself in front of Sebastian. Coming between him and Daniel's sword, she saw Constantine dive for her, heard Sebastian's grunt when she hit into him. Spinning around, she saw Daniel's smirking face as his blade came down.

She heard Sebastian roar only a heartbeat before she felt something cold pass across her neck.

Cold as ice.

Chapter Twenty-Six

As if in slow motion, Allie watched Daniel jump back. She saw blood on the blade of his sword.

She turned back to Sebastian, an odd sensation of biting cold across her neck. He wore a look of stark horror. Her hands went to her throat. She felt no pain, only an odd sensation she couldn't readily identify.

When she took her hands away they were covered with blood.

Swaying, Allie almost fell over. Sebastian made a move to get to her but Daniel's sword stopped him, slicing across his chest, keeping them separated as Sebastian was forced to continue the battle.

Her arms outstretched, all Allie wanted to do was go to Sebastian, but someone came from behind her and wrapped their arms around her. She was snatched away from Sebastian and out of the room.

Constantine was hauling ass down the stairs when the pain came.

The agony was intense, bringing with it the realization of what happened. When she threw herself in front of Sebastian, Daniel's blade caught her instead of him. Her throat had been slit and that was why Sebastian let out that God-awful battle cry.

Thank God.

If one of them had to die she was glad it was going to be her. At least she was going to Heaven. If it had been Sebastian... Allie couldn't even bear the thought of where he'd be if Daniel ended him instead if her.

This was as it should be. This was right. Her life to save his soul was a sacrifice that had been worth making.

As Constantine sprinted down the steps, all Allie could think was that when she died, she'd get to see the angels. True, she wouldn't see Sebastian again, but she was okay with that as long as knew she died saving him from Hell. That knowledge alone would sustain her as her life bled out and she was delivered to wherever it was she was headed once it was done and she was gone.

"Don't you leave us, Allie."

Constantine put that in her mind as her body went numb. She liked numb. Numb meant no more pain. She didn't even feel Constantine holding her anymore, like she was no longer part of anything happening around her.

Wanting to answer him but unable to, Allie gave up and relaxed in Constantine's arms as he carried her out of the house. She didn't want to leave Sebastian, but she knew there was nothing more she could do for him. She'd already done all she could.

She gave her life for him.

She wanted Sebastian with her in these last moments. She wanted to take the sight of him with her when she looked last at life. But that wasn't going to happen. Not with Constantine rushing her out of the house, pushing past Raphael, who stood sentinel in the doorway.

Allie saw Rogue's eyes go wide with horror. "Oh my God…"

He sheathed his sword and ran after them, asking after Sebastian. Constantine came to stop in the middle of the front yard and answered that Sebastian was still upstairs fighting Daniel Parsons. Allie thought she heard Raphael mutter out a curse, but she couldn't be sure. Her vision was dimming and her body getting so cold she felt as if her hands and feet were nothing more than blocks of ice.

And the wetness—it was everywhere, sticky and warm. She knew it was her blood.

Constantine crouched down and carefully laid her on the grass. It afforded Allie the chance to see his face and it broke her heart. This was the first time she ever saw him show real emotion.

God, he looked so sad.

She brought her hand to his cheek, wishing she could take the grief from him. He curled his hand around hers, giving it a hard squeeze. He looked away, that mysterious silver gaze lighting on Raphael. They were talking to each other through telepathy. If she could have, she would have demanded they stop and say whatever it was aloud. After all, whatever was being said between them, she had every right to hear.

And then Constantine and Raphael simply went away. They were there one second, talking amongst themselves, and then they were simply gone.

She turned her head to where Raphael should have been but all she saw was dark. Everywhere, surrounding her, overtaking the vast mountain range, the dark blocked out everything, including the clear night sky.

Yet the dark didn't conceal everything.

In it came her brother.

At first Christian was out of focus. Gradually however, the image of him sharpened, until she saw him standing beside her, as real as he'd been in life.

"Christian—my God…"

The broken whimper was torn, not from her throat, but from her heart, still aching with grief.

Her gaze greedily devoured every nuance of him, from the top of his dark brown hair right down to the faded blue denim of his jeans. He looked exactly as he did the night he died.

And then he smiled and Allie shattered into a million pieces.

All traces of his heroin addiction were stripped away. Even after being clean for a year, that hadn't been enough time to fully flesh him out. But now, he didn't carry that erosion. His body was no longer gaunt. He glowed with life. He looked so handsome. Peaceful.

If she had more energy in her, she might have wept at the beautiful sight of him.

Her brother. He came for her, her angel to take her home to God.

"No, Allie. This is your home. You have to fight now."

She didn't want to fight. Tired of fighting and of being strong, she wanted to sleep now.

"Please, Allie. Fight for him."

Thoughts of Sebastian drifted in and out of her mind as that sweet oblivion pulled at her. Promising her peace and love waiting for her in the dark all around her.

"No," Christian said to her. *"Not yet. Lex needs you here.* He *needs you here. Hold on for them."*

"I miss you so much. I should have told you I love you more, but I was so angry with you, and I'm sorry. I'm sorry I couldn't save you."

His smile made her cry inside her mind. *"You did save me."* He knelt down and touched her, so warm and comforting. *"You were with me when I left, you and Lex both. I felt your love all around me and I wasn't scared."*

Allie had so much to tell him, much that needed to be said, but words were beyond her as the pain slowly began to come back to her.

"I know, Allie. I can hear you." He squeezed her hand. *"You don't belong where I am. You have to love him enough to fight for him."*

Sebastian. The "he" Christian was referring to was Sebastian. He needed her and the truth was, Allie needed him just as much. She couldn't give up on him. What good was Heaven if he wasn't there to share it with her? She might as well be condemned to Hell.

Christian nodded, knowing her thoughts. *"Don't be scared and never forget that I love you and Lex. God may have my soul, but my sisters will always have my heart."*

He began to fade, leaving her, and this time Allie knew she wouldn't see him again for lifetimes.

She let her brother go and began to fight for life.

Or was it her death?

When did the planes of existence get so complicated? When did the lines of what constituted life and what was death become so blurred?

The dark became the night again. The moon hung in the sky. Raphael and Constantine were back.

Constantine had her hand, staring down at her in a way that made her know he was waiting for something from her.

The pain was getting worse. Her bones felt like ice. She could actually feel death's breath blowing over her and it scared her. Christian was right. Now wasn't the time for her to go, she still had too much here. She couldn't give in to the warmth that waited beyond the cold.

Violent tremors wracked her. She tried to tell Constantine to turn her. That she wasn't ready to die. That she wasn't ready to leave Sebastian. When she couldn't form words, she screamed it over and over in her mind. He heard her and held fast to her hand. He pulled his gaze from her and looked to Raphael, giving him a slight nod.

Raphael was saying something to Constantine. She could vaguely hear them over the roar of her blood as it raced to her throat, spilling out of her too quickly for her to last much longer. Her slowing heartbeat was a sickening feeling. Her vision was going black. She didn't know how much longer she could hold on to the life she had left.

Oh God, she thought frantically, Sebastian's face flashing in her mind. *Please don't let me die.*

* * *

"I can't do it." Constantine felt the life spilling from Allie, staining the ground red.

They were losing her. With every passing moment she was slipping further away from life, inching toward what lay beyond. Still, he couldn't do it. He couldn't bring himself to turn her, not even to save her.

"You have to hurry, C. She's fading fast." Raphael urged him desperately. "Don't let her go."

"Don't let me die…" Allie's voice echoed in his mind. *"Please…"*

Constantine pinned Raphael with a powerful stare. "Fuck," he ground out roughly. "I can't. I can't do this to her."

Raphael went to push him away. "Then get the hell out of the way and I will."

Constantine roared out a violent warning. Raphael backed off. "Stay away from her."

"She can't hold on much longer. She's lost too much blood. We don't have time for this. Do it now or she's going to die on us."

"Please, Constantine, don't let me die. I'm not ready to go. I can't leave Sebastian."

Agonized over what he was about to do, Constantine grabbed Allie and lifted her cold, limp body off the grass. He held her gently against him, praying for the fortitude to do what needed to be done.

When her head fell back, he saw the deep gash running across her throat. It spanned ear to ear, her blood now pouring out of it, onto him, as the bloodlust rose in him like a phoenix rising from the flames, a monster overtaking him.

She was so close to death even he felt its cold breath at his neck. He had to close his eyes, to block out who it was he was doing this do, who he was damning to an eternity of darkness.

The sounds of Allie's rasping breaths, the furious clash of Sebastian and Daniel's blades, Raphael's tormented thoughts, they all filled Constantine's head. But above all those sounds, he could hear her heartbeat ebbing, slowing near to a dead stop.

"Now, Constantine. Please…"

Allie was trying desperately to hold onto her last bit of life, but it was fading fast. He knew not one more moment could be lost or else she'd be too far for him to bring back.

"This is it, Red."

Constantine lowered his head to her throat. All he had to do was open his mouth. Her blood immediately flowed into him. It slipped down his throat, the sweet metallic warmth of it empowering him. Even dying, Allie's lifeforce was strong enough to send a violent shock to his system.

As he took in her blood, Constantine felt like he was stealing from her.

He had no right to do this, to take her life and give her immortality. Sebastian should be the one. He should be the one to share this bond with Allie.

When he pulled out enough of Allie's blood, her body went completely limp. Her silent cries were a thousand blades in him. Stabbing at him as he took her life, listening to her heartbeat slowing. It was gently thundering down to a stop as she wept with fear.

Raphael put a hand on her head, smoothing her bloodied hair away from her face before taking her hand in his. "You aren't alone, Red. We're here with you."

She whimpered, unable to cry out, as her body began to convulse. Constantine held onto her, taking in the last flow of blood. Her heart was barely beating when he finally pulled away. Raphael sat back on his heels but wouldn't let go of her hand. Nor did he stop whispering words of comfort to her as the last moments of her life were upon her.

Constantine bit his wrist and pressed the wound to Allie's mouth. Her eyes slid closed as her lips parted. His blood spilled into her mouth. She choked it down as her heart beat for the last time.

This being the first time blood was ever taken from him, the only time he ever dared to turn a human; Constantine wasn't prepared for the barrage of Allie's memories invading his mind. Like lightening strikes he saw flashes of her life play out. From her birth right to this moment of her death, he saw it all.

More than that, he felt her being push inside of his mind. They were becoming one, until he couldn't distinguish one of his own thoughts from one of hers.

The visions went as quickly as they came, her life now a part of his death. Her pain hit him like a sword to his throat and he knew Allie's death was dragging him down into the abyss of blackness. He wrested his wrist away from her mouth, praying to God she took enough of his blood into herself.

Allie's head slumped to the side and her heart beat one last time. She was dead. Now, all they could do was wait.

* * *

Constantine dragged his sleeve across his mouth, wiping away Allie's blood. Her spirit was strong, lending him life as it warmed him from the inside out.

It seemed an eternity passed as he and Raphael waited and watched, their gazes locked on Allie. They searched for any signs of life and were about to give up hope when her body jerked violently. Her back arched and her head fell back as a guttural scream was pulled from deep within her.

Raphael fell backwards when she pulled her hand from his grasp. He sat watching her transformation, eyes wide and filled with awe.

Constantine knelt beside her, as close to her as possible as she writhed on the floor, her body dying a mortal death. He felt it then, a bonding between them which came from him turning her, a bond no time or space could break. They were now one person divided into two separate bodies.

He didn't feel alone for the first time since he took his first breath of life.

She may be Sebastian's mate, but she was his Blood-Kin. Neither would ever feel alone again.

* * *

Allie felt as if her body was literally being torn apart. Lightning strikes of pain blinded her, deafening her. Robbing her of the ability to think or move. The agony seemed to slice her to shreds, tearing her insides apart. Ripping her soul from her.

Visions flashed in her head in furious succession, too quick to distinguish one from another. As she caught fragmented images of her parents, her and Lex laughing as little girls, and Christian full of life and promise, she realized she was seeing her life play out.

Yet of these myriad visions, the one that stood out clearly was of Sebastian.

She saw her proud warrior astride a giant black destrier, he and his horse both draped in the white Templar mantle, the blood red cross standing out sharply against the pristine white. Sword in hand, he held it high, thundering across a desert, sand kicked up in his wake, the brutal sun blazing overhead in a cloudless sky.

Buried beneath layers of civility, hidden behind the mask of a modern man, *this* was who Sebastian was. This was the man he was born and bred to be.

A Knight Templar in all his glory, he was an amazing sight to behold.

She saw other things. Terrible things, all happening to a beautiful boy with bright blue eyes—a boy too young to have to endure such suffering.

Constantine. She was seeing Constantine. Somehow, his life was playing out behind her eyes in all its brutal vivacity and she wanted it to stop. She didn't want to have to see the things she was forced to watch.

Oh God, no wonder he grew to become a dragon.

That Constantine survived at all was a miracle.

Then it was all gone and she was left with pain—intense enough to pierce her soul.

She jerked upward so forcefully her spine should have snapped, yet didn't. She tried to scream but her ruined throat prevented it. She tried to see but saw only black. She tried to hear, but the only sound she heard was of her own silent cries that echoed in her mind past the beats of her heart.

And then it was over.

A strange peace came over her and she went limp.

She died.

Chapter Twenty~Seven

"Jesus Christ. We waited too long, C. She's gone."

Constantine ignored the note of panic in Raphael's voice. Constantine shook his head. "No she's not."

"How do you know?"

Constantine never took his eyes from Allie when he answered. "I just do."

Raphael looked horrified "Holy shit, Dragon, tell me you didn't take her soul."

Constantine ripped his gaze from Allie and leveled Raphael with a hard glare. "Fuck you."

Raphael leaned over Allie and grabbed Constantine by the front of his bloody shirt. "Then how do you know she's not dead? What if it didn't work?"

Lifting a single brow, Constantine shot Raphael a cold look. "We're bonded, that's how I know she's still in there."

Raphael's jaw went slack. "Does this mean…"

Constantine shook his head curtly. "I told you, I left her soul."

"But…"

"Leave it alone, Rogue."

Thankfully Raphael knew better than to press the matter right then. Constantine, always a powder keg waiting for the flame to ignite him, was dancing close to the fire as Allie's pain and death still coursed through him. To push him now would be suicide, even for a fellow Templar.

Constantine bent over Allie and touched a hand to her chest. Oh yeah, she was in there all right. Her body was adjusting to this new form of existence. He felt her soul still strong in her, keeping her warm and chasing away the cold of death.

Her soul had been a hell of a thing to resist. It took all his strength to fight the lure of it as he drew her life from her with every drop of blood he drank. And when he gave her the life back...

That was as close to ecstasy as he'd ever come.

Though she was covered with blood, he saw her throat already mended. The gash was now a scar, faded as if from time, death taking the newness of it. The flush was gone from her, leaving her pale. With her lips parted, he saw the tips of two razor-sharp fangs.

And then her eyes slowly opened. Gone was the vivid green they'd been. They glowed with the eerie silver radiance of her immortality.

No longer alive. Not dead. Caught between both realms of existence. She would walk the night outside of God's grace. As much as he felt like a monster to have done this to her, Constantine couldn't have stood by and watched her die. Not when he heard her in his mind begging for life.

He gave her the only life he could, even though it was one of death.

* * *

Allie came out of a hard sleep sharply. Dizzy and disoriented, she sat up slowly, her body free of pain, and ran her hands through her hair to get the bloody mass away from her face. Her mind was jumbled and her body felt different. Too different.

She wasn't breathing nor was her heart beating, and she could *see*. Her gaze cut right through the darkness, saw too far for a mere human. She possessed the sight of a predator.

Still trying to focus, make sense of what she was feeling, she listened to the sounds of the night all around her. The rustling of the leaves on the trees, the gentle sway of the blades of grass, and the beating hearts of the animals scurrying in the woods—all of it she heard as if it were as loud as thunder in her ears

Slowly gaining her orientation, she looked over at Constantine, who was watching her intently. More than merely seeing him, she *felt* him like they were one being. His thoughts and emotions wrapped around hers, blurring the line that separated them. His life played out in her head in a flash of sights and sounds and pain.

Over almost as quickly as it began, she stared at him in wonder, a catch in her throat when she realized what happened to him in his past to make him into who he was tonight.

He nodded his head curtly; acknowledging what took place in her. In his eyes she saw her own life played out for him as well.

She opened her mouth and touched her teeth. She fingered the fangs that took the place of her human incisors and looked to Constantine in amazement.

"I'm dead," she whispered.

Constantine nodded and she whimpered with dread.

Raphael went to move toward her but Allie jumped up with a quickness and agility that surprised her, used to only the limitations of human immortality.

Her mind cleared, the events of the night playing out on a sudden flood of images behind her eyes. She shook her head to dispel the flashing visions. That's when she heard the clash of steel that overrode all other sounds.

"Sebastian…" His name was torn from her as she worked her dead vocal cords.

"Still in the house," Constantine told her.

Not needing to hear more, Allie looked to the house, sensing Sebastian's anguish.

When she went to make a move toward the house, Constantine clamped a hand on her arm. She shook it off with a strength that surprised them both. She retrieved Constantine's dagger and turned the blade on them.

"He killed me," she spat. "I'll not leave Sebastian to fight this alone."

Without waiting for them, she raced toward the house, feeling they weren't far behind. Bursting through the door, Allie raced up the stairs and skidded to a halt in the doorway where Sebastian and Daniel were still locked in battle, awestruck at the scene playing out within the room. Her brave and beautiful warrior needed no help from her.

Her senses filled with him, she knew he fought to avenge her. He believed her dead, and nothing was going to keep him from ending Daniel and sending him straight to Lucifer where he belonged.

* * *

Daniel was a good fighter—better than good actually. His determination lent him the strength and skill to go toe to toe with a Templar. Still, he was no match for Sebastian, who fought with vengeance of his side.

When Daniel swung his sword high, Sebastian jumped back. "You're getting sloppy, Daniel." Sebastian smiled coolly, jabbing his blade into the renegade's left thigh. "Can you feel him? Can you feel Lucifer standing at your back, ready to drag you down to Hell?"

Daniel grabbed at his bleeding thigh. "Fuck you, Templar. I'm going to put you down like a dog."

In answer, Sebastian stabbed him in his right thigh. "Give it a go then."

Daniel charged, their blades clashing as Sebastian parried his expert attack. Nearly matched in skill, albeit not in strength, they danced around the room, as their swords met again and again. The sound of steel against steel rattled the very foundation of the house.

Unfortunately for Daniel, Sebastian fought with fires of vengeance fueling him. It woke the savagery in Sebastian that lay dormant since the days when he fought on the sands of the Holy Land with God at his back as he ran the ground red with blood in His name.

Daniel swung his blade up, thinking to catch Sebastian across the middle to render him incapacitated, which would give him the upper hand to go in for the kill. Sebastian however, was faster, able to grab his hand and twist it until the bone in his arm snapped. The sword clattered to the floor and Sebastian kicked it away. He used the hilt of his own sword to deliver a hard blow to the renegade's face. Blood burst from his nose when it broke. As Daniel fought his hold on him, Sebastian pulled on the broken arm. Holding it out, he hacked at it with his sword. Daniel's agonized howl as his arm was severed echoed throughout the house.

The arm evaporated into dust as Daniel stumbled back. Sebastian prevented him from getting far by grabbing him by the front of his shirt. The renegade's eyes were wide with horror, seeing his own death reflected in Sebastian's crazed eyes.

"I'm going to take you apart piece by miserable piece and leave you for the fucking sun."

Daniel swallowed down his terror, his eyes narrowing on Sebastian as a slow smile split his bloody face. "Do your worst, Templar."

Sebastian, mad with grief, grabbed the renegade's other arm with the intent to make good on his promise to hack him to pieces.

Daniel, the slippery bastard, proved agile. He yanked his arm free with a force that pulled the shoulder clean from the socket. He ducked the blow and dropped to the floor to retrieve his sword. Sebastian sidestepped the swipe of Daniel's blade. He brought his sword down with such brute force he sliced Daniel's right thigh almost completely off. If Daniel hadn't jumped away he'd be less another appendage. Of course, Sebastian wasn't finished with him yet.

Blood was everywhere, most Daniel's, some her own, Allie realized as the scent came at her in a rush, filling her, calling her, whispering the promise of life. With his leg nearly severed through, useless, Daniel had no balance when he swung his blade at Sebastian.

Sebastian stepped back, easily countering the sloppy attack. He swung around, the cross pattee glinting blood-red. He drew the sword around hard, catching Daniel across the left leg. The sword cut clean, taking the leg, which exploded into dust.

Daniel fell to the floor, his screams of agony a horrible sound that cut right through Allie's brain Sebastian's sword still poised in the air, ready to come down and take Daniel apart piece by miserable piece. Yet he refrained, unable to extract such revenge. Such were the ways of the renegades or the Obyri, not a Templar.

Allie was gone, lost to him. She was with God now, home, and that knowledge was what brought Sebastian back to his oath. If he lowered himself to a renegade's level, or worse, an Obyri's, there'd be no going back. If he allowed himself to be consumed by grief, to start down that road, it would lead him right to Hell.

The road would take him further and further away from Allie, until the possibility of ever seeing her again became a brutal reality he couldn't bear.

"You took from me. Now I take from you."

Sebastian pressed the blade of his sword against Daniel's neck. The renegade choked out an unintelligible sound that sounded more like a cry than an actual word. In one clean swipe, he opened the vampire's neck enough that his head nearly came clean off. Daniel's hands went to his throat and he fell back. Before he hit the floor, the renegade ended in an explosion of dust.

Sebastian killed him clean and quick, the way a Templar ended his enemies. His empty, victorious battle cry was filled with enough pain to make the angels weep.

The sword slipped from his grip and he dropped down to his knees, bloody tears running in rivulets down his face. Dropping his head in his bloody hands, Sebastian felt an emptiness that ran through him colder than death.

She was gone. His Allie. His beautiful, funny, brave girl. His sunshine. Gone.

He clawed at his chest as a terrible agony tore through him over the place where his heart sat still behind his ribs. He wanted to rip the dead thing out and make the hurt stop.

Nothing had ever caused him such agony as the loss of Allie. Not the three years of imprisonment in Chinon. Not being burned to death, not even having Michael tear his soul from him. Only the loss of his sunshine hurt with the force of a million blades slicing through him.

Then he heard her voice, reaching him through his anguish. Already he was losing his mind. *Jesus Christ*, was he to suffer an eternity of madness to go along with his grief?

"Sebastian?"

Her voice came from right behind him. He didn't dare turn around. He didn't want to face the truth that it was his own mind talking to him. Still, he pushed himself from the floor and slowly turned. She stood behind him, bloody, pale, alive, her beautiful brown eyes silver with immortality.

"Oh God..."

Not alive.

Pallid, death having robbed her of the glow of life. Silver eyes watched him intently. Fangs peeked out from behind parted lips. Constantine's dagger was gripped in her hand. She was covered in blood, soaking her clothes, her hair.

A scar ran ear to ear, the mark of her death.

When he went to take a step toward her, his legs threatened to drop him back down to his knees. His body was numb with disbelief as he raked his hungry gaze over her from head to feet.

"My God, Allie, what have you done?"

She reached out to him, moving with fluidity. He came close enough to touch her but he didn't, afraid if he put his hand on her she would fade away. But when her tiny hand came to rest on his cheek, he knew she was real. She was still warm. Her soul thrived within her, giving her a warmth Sebastian would never know.

"I died."

Finally, he dared to touch her. Sebastian wiped at the blood on her neck. Putting his hand on her chin, he turned her head to the side, hissing when he saw the two small puckered scars where she was bitten and drained, literally, to death.

"Oh God, Allie, I failed you."

She placed her hands on his cheeks, her thumbs smearing away his tears of blood. "No, Sebastian, you did everything to protect me. This was Fate."

His fingers trailed over her mouth. He lifted her top lip, taking in the sight of her fangs. "Why did you do it, sunshine?"

She smiled sadly. "I wasn't ready to leave you."

They'd come so far so fast yet it seemed like only yesterday he was doing everything he could to avoid her. Now, he couldn't imagine one moment without her.

"I wasn't ready to have you leave."

Sebastian didn't need to ask who turned her. He felt the strength of the Dragon inside her. They were bonded now, their blood mixed. He was glad it was Constantine who turned her. He was strong, strong enough to have resisted the temptation of her soul. If it had been anyone else, even Raphael—the thought wasn't even one he could entertain.

If her soul would have been taken and she turned, she'd be enslaved to her Blood-Sire. Much the same way the Templars were to God. She'd be no more his than if he'd never known her at all—or rather if she never knew *him*. He'd go on suffering with love and she would travel through eternity with what they'd shared nothing more than a pleasant dream slowly fading with every passing night.

Needing to feel her in his arms, he grabbed her roughly and gathered her in a fierce embrace. He never wanted to let her go.

Her heartbeat was gone. He felt no life left in her. Yet her soul thrived. The force of it radiated from her, too strong to be extinguished.

When she laid her cheek against his chest, he ran his hand down her hair. "I couldn't bear the thought of this world without you in it."

Her hand came to rest on his chest, right over the scar where Michael killed his heart. "I saw Christian as I was dying. He told me it wasn't my time. He made me fight for you when I was ready to give in to death."

He doubted she realized she'd stood on the very edge of life, peered right into the eyes of death and came back for him. *Him.* If he ever needed to be reminded that she was a gift from God, a true miracle, all he had to do was remember what she gave up to come back to him.

"I'm sorry you lost Heaven, Allie."

She shook her head. "No, baby, I didn't lose Heaven. Without you, it would have been Hell."

A knot of emotion tightened in his chest, nearly made his heart feel as if it was kick-started back to life. "I love you, Allie. I'll love you until the stars burn out." He gave her a long, hard kiss. "And then I'll love you more."

Her arms came around his waist. She looked at him, her eyes glowing with immortality. "Then show me the night, Sebastian."

The night.

It's where he was cursed to dwell, yet with Allie at his side, it wasn't as dark as it had been before she came bursting into his existence. Her spirit and her love was a midnight sun that led him out of the darkness and brought him back into the light. Showed him what it was to love.

He would show her the night and she would give him Heaven.

Epilogue

Allie found being a vampire in the Templar's world was definitely a hell of a thing. She figured it would take her lifetimes to get used to.

Hopefully she had plenty of those stretching before her to share with Sebastian.

A month passed since the night she died and Sebastian set aside time each night to whisper to her the secrets of the ages. Stories unfolded in vivid detail as he described his life as a man and the centuries as a vampire. He told her of Michael and what it was like to face an archangel. He'd met many prominent historical figures; his life—and death—played out like one long history lesson.

He'd led an incredible life, even after he died.

With patience she was sure only he would show her, he answered her every question about the world, history, and most of all, the Templar Order. Not a night went by when she didn't tease him and the Templars that she was going to call the History Channel and spill the beans on all those mysteries the scholars of the world were dying to know.

The hardest part of her new existence was getting over her reluctance to feed, but once the hunger hit for the first time she got over that reservation right quick.

It hurt. *Bad*. If she had to imagine what it felt like to have her insides torn out, that was exactly it. Not to mention with it came a thirst that turned her mouth into sand. Never up for that party again, she made sure to feed as soon as the bloodlust hit her, surprised she wasn't repulsed by biting a human and drinking from them. As a matter of fact, it felt completely natural.

When the dust settled after the fight Allie was terrified she was a renegade now. Sebastian assured her she was far from one of them. The blood of a Templar flowed through her, which shot her to the top of the nocturnal food chain.

With Sebastian to guide her through the night, she was adjusting to her new life—or rather, her death—surprisingly well. She still found it strange to have no heartbeat and breath, but slowly, she was coming to terms with it all.

They all resided at Seacrest Castle now, even Lex, who was the sole drop of life among the dead. Here they would stay until the Daystar was found.

Not only was Seacrest a massive stone fortress, Tristan had a state of the art security system installed years ago. Every year he had it upgraded with the latest technology. Basically, nothing, alive or dead, was getting past the gatehouse unless Tristan wanted them to.

The only missing piece to their odd family was Lucian.

As long as he was lost somewhere out there, the Templars wouldn't rest until they found him.

Meet Rene Lyons

Devouring books since the age of fifteen, Rene Lyons always knew that writing was something she just had to do. With her great love of history and all things dark and mysterious (especially vampires), she couldn't resist the call of the Templars. They pounded on her brain, leaving her no choice but to write them (they haven't shut up yet!). Then came the hard part: Sending it out to a publisher. The rest, as they say, is history.

Rene lives in New York with her incredible and supportive husband, her adorable daughter (who she calls her miracle), and two crazy cats.

Rene loves to hear from her readers. You can drop her a line at:

rene@renelyons.net

Rene's website and Yahoo Group:

http://www.renelyons.net

http://renelyons.blogspot.com/

Samhain Publishing, Ltd.

It's all about the story...

Action/Adventure
Fantasy
Historical
Horror
Mainstream
Mystery/Suspense
Non-Fiction
Paranormal
Red Hots!
Romance
Science Fiction
Western
Young Adult

http://www.samhainpublishing.com